BOXCAR CHRISTMAS

BY LINDSAY MCKENNA

Blue Turtle Publishing

Praise for Lindsay McKenna

"A treasure of a book . . . highly recommended reading that everyone will enjoy and learn from."

—Chief Michael Jaco, US Navy SEAL, retired, on Breaking Point

"Readers will root for this complex heroine, scarred both inside and out, and hope she finds peace with her steadfast and loving hero. Rife with realistic conflict and spiced with danger, this is a worthy page-turner."

—BookPage.com on Taking Fire
March 2015 Top Pick in Romance

". . . is fast-paced romantic suspense that renders a beautiful love story, start to finish. McKenna's writing is flawless, and her story line fully absorbing. More, please."

—Annalisa Pesek, Library Journal on Taking Fire

"Ms. McKenna masterfully blends the two different paces to convey a beautiful saga about love, trust, patience and having faith in each other."

—Fresh Fiction on Never Surrender

"Genuine and moving, this romantic story set in the complex world of military ops grabs at the heart."

—RT Book Reviews on Risk Taker

"McKenna does a beautiful job of illustrating difficult topics through the development of well-formed, sympathetic characters."

—Publisher's Weekly (starred review) on Wolf Haven
One of the Best Books of 2014, Publisher's Weekly

"McKenna delivers a story that is raw and heartfelt. The relationship between Kell and Leah is both passionate and tender. Kell is the hero every woman wants, and McKenna employs skill and empathy to craft a physically and emotionally abused character in Leah. Using tension and steady pacing, McKenna is adept at expressing growing, tender love in the midst of high stakes danger."

—RT Book Reviews on Taking Fire

"Her military background lends authenticity to this outstanding tale, and readers will fall in love with the upstanding hero and his fierce determination to save the woman he loves.

—Publishers Weekly (starred review) on Never Surrender
One of the Best Books of 2014, Publisher's Weekly

"Readers will find this addition to the Shadow Warriors series full of intensity and action-packed romance. There is great chemistry between the characters and tremendous realism, making Breaking Point a great read."

—RT Book Reviews

"This sequel to Risk Taker is an action-packed, compelling story, and the sizzling chemistry between Ethan and Sarah makes this a good read."

—RT Book Reviews on Degree of Risk

"McKenna elicits tears, laughter, fist-pumping triumph, and most all, a desire for the next tale in this powerful series."

—Publishers Weekly (starred review) on Running Fire

"McKenna's military experience shines through in this moving tale . . . McKenna (High Country Rebel) skillfully takes readers on an emotional journey into modern warfare and two people's hearts."

—Publisher's Weekly on Down Range

"Lindsay McKenna has proven that she knows what she's doing when it comes to these military action/romance books."

—Terry Lynn, Amazon on Zone of Fire.

"At no time do you want to put your book down and come back to it later! Last Chance is a well written, fast paced, short (remember that) story that will please any military romance reader!"

—LBDDiaries, Amazon on Last Chance.

Available from
Lindsay McKenna

Blue Turtle Publishing

DELOS

Last Chance, prologue novella to Nowhere to Hide
Nowhere to Hide, Book 1
Tangled Pursuit, Book 2
Forged in Fire, Book 3

2016

Broken Dreams, Book 4
Blind Sided, BN2
Secret Dream, B1B novella, epilogue to Nowhere to Hide
Hold On, Book 5
Hold Me, 5B1, sequel to Hold On
Unbound Pursuit, 2B1 novella, epilogue to Tangled Pursuit
Secrets, 2B2 novella, sequel to Unbound Pursuit, 2B1

2017

Snowflake's Gift, Book 6
Never Enough, 3B1, novella, sequel to Forged in Fire
Dream of Me, 4B1, novella, sequel to Broken Dreams
Trapped, Book 7
Taking a Chance 7B1, novella, sequel to Trapped
The Hidden Heart, 7B2, novella, sequel to Taking A Chance

2018

Boxcar Christmas, Book 8

Harlequin/HQN/Harlequin Romantic Suspense

SHADOW WARRIORS
Danger Close
Down Range
Risk Taker
Degree of Risk
Breaking Point
Never Surrender
Zone of Fire
Taking Fire
On Fire
Running Fire

THE WYOMING SERIES
Shadows From The Past
Deadly Identity
Deadly Silence
The Last Cowboy
The Wrangler
The Defender
The Loner
High Country Rebel
Wolf Haven
Night Hawk
Out Rider

WIND RIVER VALLEY SERIES, Kensington

2016
Wind River Wrangler
Wind River Rancher

2017
Wind River Cowboy
Christmas with my Cowboy
Wrangler's Challenge

Boxcar Christmas

Dedication

To Blackie, my beloved Border Collie who watched over me when I had to walk across the 3-span train bridge over the Snake River, near Ontario, Oregon.

Dear Reader,

Boxcar Christmas is a very personal book for me to write. When I was six years old, we lived on an island in the middle of the mighty Snake River near Ontario, Oregon. There was a huge 3-span train bridge stretching across the Snake River I had to walk over every day to go meet the school bus. And I had to walk across it two times daily, five days a week during school.

I don't know if you can imagine this but my mother taught me how to walk across it BY MYSELF after she showed me how to do it. There was a big problem: I was dizzied by the brownish/green water far below me if I looked down. And I'd lose my balance. The chances of me falling off the bridge were very real. Consequently, I learned to walk those trestles above the water WITHOUT LOOKING DOWN, which increased exponentially, my miscalculating and stumbling and thereby, pitching off the bridge, falling into the water and drowning. Even at five, I understand all of that! In 1950, there were no safeguards on bridges for anyone, much less a 6-year-old little girl.

My mother worked, so she too had to walk across that bridge twice a day, too. She would park our car on the bank, near the bridge, and walk across to our home on that island. She taught me that if a train came? I was to lay down in the middle of the tracks, flatten out and keep my arms and legs within the rails while the train passed above me. That way, I'd survive.

Now, it's 2017. Can you imagine ANY mother doing that nowadays with a 5-year-old, much less a child of any age under 18? I'm sure you wouldn't. She did NOT accompany me across the bridge after that—I was on my own. She was already at work and couldn't do it even though she wanted too. My step father was too injured from the war to do much walking, so that was out, too. BUT….we had Blackie, an older Border Collie, who we found on the island when we moved into the house. He adopted us.

And he would accompany me to the bridge, stand watch, but not go across it because he was frightened of it. So was I. My greatest fear was not hearing a train coming behind me and then having to do my safety thing to survive it. That scared me more than walking across the bridge. Blackie would then meet me in the afternoon when the school bus dropped me off and I had to walk the bridge to get back home.

I loved that dog with my life. He sensed how frightened I was of that bridge, sensing that if I looked down, I'd get dizzy, lose my balance and fall in and drown in the Snake River. He was my guardian.

I wanted to write a book about a Border Collie based upon my childhood experiences with Blackie. I wanted to honor him and his breed. So, there's lots of wonderful emotions I was able to write into *Boxcar Christmas* and I know my readers will feel it as they read Freya's story of survival. And how she helped her two humans immensely and in important ways after they rescued her.

The Border Collie on the book's cover looks EXACTLY like my beloved Blackie. Every time I see that cover, I smile and my heart expands with love for my guardian angel dog who met me every day for a year when I had to walk that train bridge over the Snake River.

Now, you know the 'rest of the story!'

CHAPTER 1

November 1

IT WASN'T MUCH to look at. The wooden slats that made up the ancient red caboose were weathered, the boxcar sitting on the edge of a flat yellow grass meadow, backed by thousands of evergreens in western Montana. Early-November wind whistled and cut at Jesse Myer's exposed face. She felt the icy morning coldness seep through her rain dampened, olive green Army jacket as she emerged cautiously out of the woods. She had discovered the boxcar while hunting rosehips scattered along the banks of the Bitterroot River. It was a source of protein for her tightened, gnawing stomach in want of food.

The large, oval-shaped meadow bordered the water and the rose hips were a substantial source of food when in the back country. She chewed slowly on another one, knowing it was packed with nutrition. Shivering, she felt hope spike through her as she walked out of the woods that lay west of Hamilton, a small hunting and fishing tourist town. She had followed the river in search of a place to pitch her tent outside the city limits. Standing on the edge of the meadow, she fully surveyed it. It rained at dusk last night and then snowflakes had fallen thick and fast throughout the nighttime hours. Toward dawn the ground was covered with about six inches of the white stuff. As a gray dawn sluggishly crawled upon the eastern horizon, the flakes had turned into a soft, constant rain once more. Most of the snow had melted as the temperature rose, but patches of white still existed here and there—it was an Indian summer event. Jesse sincerely hoped that it meant warmer weather would come into the area and warm it up for a couple of weeks while she hunted for a place to live.

She'd discovered the ancient Union Pacific caboose at the edge of the meadow by accident. There was no telling how old it was, the slats of tongue-and-groove wood that composed its sides were worn, the paint chipped off but still solidly in place despite the harsh winter weather that it had obviously endured over the years. There were no railroad tracks around from what she could see. The under carriage of the caboose had been removed and set upon a rectangular concrete slab, reminding her of the tiny house craze sweeping through her Millennial generation. Her gaze absorbed the forty-foot-long boxcar and she could see that at one time, it had been well cared for. But now, it looked utterly abandoned, the paint dull and peeling off the sturdy oak staves beneath it. Someone had brought this caboose out here. Was it someone who lived in Hamilton? Maybe the owner of this plot of land used it as a cabin to hunt and fish on weekends? Jesse had no idea, but there it was. Maybe it could be a home for her instead of the tent she had strapped to the huge knapsack she carried on her back. She wanted to make sure no one was living in it presently and thought about trespassing to find out. Even though it went against her grain, Jesse couldn't explain the allure to do just that.

She called out several times, her voice echoing around the meadow. There was no response or movement from inside the boxcar. The four windows along the meadow side were dirty, and she longed to clean them. Deciding either no one was home or living in it, she curved her hand around the rusted metal railing at the rear platform of the boxcar and took the first tentative step upward. The ends of the wooden steps were buckled from age and now rested precariously on the metal frame beneath each one, the nails pulled out by rain and snow over the years. The step groaned. Not that she weighed that much. In the Army, she had been a hundred and sixty pounds; but three months ago when she received an honorable medical discharge at the end of eight years of service, she had slowly lost at least twenty-five pounds due to lack of appetite and no money to buy food. Her Army jacket, the only reminder of her life since age eighteen, hung loosely on her frame.

Her gloves were threadbare, her fingertips numb. She hauled herself up the rest of the creaking wooden steps and leaned forward, cupping her hands around her eyes and peering through the dirty glass of the door to see what was inside the caboose. It *was* a possible place to live. She'd just gotten a job at Katie's Koffee Bean in Hamilton as a dish washer. But it was part time and Jesse had no money yet to rent a room in town, much less an apartment. She had lived in her tent since leaving the Army and was prepared to do it now, but maybe her luck was about to change.

Jesse opened the door, feeling guilty about trespassing. It creaked as she pushed it open. Stepping inside, she shut the door and turned, peering around the gloomy interior of the caboose because the sun still hadn't risen above the carpet of evergreens on the slope above where it sat. She spotted a propane gas stove, a table with two simple, carved wooden chairs nearby, and a bed at the other end of it. In the middle of the car was a kitchen sink and opposite the sink was a long leather couch. To her delight, there was also a rocking chair and an overstuffed leather chair that probably housed a lot of field mice, the stuffing looking like popcorn along the thin, separating seams of leather. The couch was long enough to sleep on and was a possibility because the mattress on that bed looked very old and needed to be replaced—but she considered it a far better upgrade to her tent.

It was dusty and dirty, mouse pellets scattered here and there along the dulled oak floor. Some parts of the oriental carpet had been eaten into, probably by mice who took those fibers to make a warm nest somewhere else in the car. Walking to the other end of the caboose, she saw that the bedroom was roomy with a full-sized bed in it. A few blankets that were probably once folded at the bottom, were now open and spread haphazardly across the bed. Some of the drawers were partially opened, and appeared to be empty. This caboose could be a good place to protect her from the coming winter, and she could buy a tank of propane to keep the boxcar warm instead of freezing to death from hypothermia in her tent. The last year of her enlistment in the Army had turned into a nightmare, all her hopes and dreams smashed and shattered. She'd been out of control, unable to fit in and be "normal" in order to perform her duties. Not wanting to think about her downfall, Jesse walked toward the center of the caboose and studied the ivory colored Formica counter that surrounded the double aluminum sink. This was a place that could be cared for once again and brought back to life. Seeing herself in the same condition as this boxcar made her want to stay here and use it as a place to begin to heal from her recent past.

She mentally calculated her weekly salary and compared it to what a tank of propane gas would cost, plus having to buy food, and needing a source of water in order to survive. The numbers churned in her head. Maybe some blankets and a pillow would be a nice addition as well. She'd seen a Goodwill store in Hamilton that would be the perfect place to pick up used bedding. Her parents had wanted to give her money to survive on until she could get a good job and manage her life once more, but she'd refused it. They had worked hard for their savings and Jesse didn't want to steal from their nest egg meant for retirement. Maybe she could call them in a couple of weeks if she could keep this new job and ask for a loan. Jesse had never taken a handout in her life. She'd always worked hard for everything she'd earned, just like her parents had.

The morning light filtered in through the windows of the caboose, illuminating the interior. She could see the electric lights along both walls, sconces that still had a hurricane lamp in each of them—dirty but still looking usable. There were no electric lines out here and she looked around for a generator outside somewhere, but saw nothing. At another time, there must have been one because the sconces would only work if there had been a generator present. Besides, even if there had been one, she couldn't afford to pay for the gasoline needed to run it. And she didn't have any wheels. She had to walk everywhere, no matter what the weather did around her. Still, she felt a trickle of hope because the oak tongue-and-groove ceiling looked solid—there were no leaks along it to indicate water had gotten inside, and that was good news.

Stepping carefully to the meadow-facing side of the car, she grazed one of the windows with her fingertips. The insulation around the frames needed to be replaced so heat wouldn't leak out and make the car drafty. The tatty old red and yellow oriental rug beneath her boots was smudged with dirt and hadn't been swept for a long, long time. She looked around and spotted a long, vertical door near the kitchen table. Going over to it, she opened one side panel of the door. To her delight, there was not only an ancient-looking broom, but dust cloths hanging off hooks, a mop, two small aluminum buckets and several usable sponges. Everything she'd need to clean up this place.

She treaded lightly, her Army boots heavy and clunky, the floor creaking here and there. Jesse closed the closet door, turned and simply absorbed this small, comfy looking place. It could definitely become a temporary home for her. Her eyes adjusted to the low dawn light, and she realized this was more than a fishing and hunting cabin. The small kitchen table against the wall was still covered with a dusty red and white checkered tablecloth. A pair of cut glass salt and pepper shakers stood in the middle of it. On a shelf above the kitchen sink, she saw dust-laden, brightly colored Fiesta dishes. To her right, were more shelves that held a set of bowls, a couple of aluminum pans and some cookbooks. Jesse liked the feeling in this caboose. It truly had been someone's home once. The person probably lived here full time, her intuition told her. Maybe years earlier it had been a warm, cozy house, but now, it had been abandoned for some unknown reason, no longer loved and cared for. She wondered who had made this caboose their home. She liked the small bathroom next to the bedroom. There was a shower stall in there as well as a Formica counter with an aluminum bowl in it.

The caboose was forty feet long and ten feet wide: four-hundred square feet of living space. It felt like a warm nest to Jesse and she couldn't explain why this beaten down train car suddenly meant so much to her. She managed a strangled laugh because symbolically and physically, she was beaten down, too. The inside of her looked like the inside of this car. But even in disrepair, the caboose showed the potential of what it could become if a little care and love was bestowed upon it. Was the same true of her? Could that be her outcome as well?

The right thing to do was to walk back into Hamilton, locate the county recorder's office and find out who owned the caboose on this property. She needed to know because she wasn't going to just move in without permission. Even though this train car was in disrepair, it was owned by someone. Maybe, if she could find the owner, she could ask them to allow her to live in it, hoping that the rent wouldn't be very much and that she could afford it. Jesse adamantly refused to become a squatter. In her world of morals and values, one didn't just take over a house of any kind without permission and without paying some sort of rent. She already felt guilty enough that she'd entered the place without permission. The door wasn't locked, but that wasn't an excuse to trespass. That wasn't like her, but she was invisibly driven to explore the inside of it.

She turned and she left the caboose, shut the door and carefully made her way down to the concrete slab where it sat. She picked up her heavy pack and unstrapped her tent—there was a lot to do today. This was her off day from work and it would take thirty minutes to walk through the woods to the south end of Hamilton. Hope threaded through her, feeling grateful that she'd miraculously stumbled upon this place. She placed her rolled up tent on the metal and wood platform of the caboose. If she couldn't find the owner, she would pitch her tent just inside the evergreen tree line for protection from the elements and stay in it, instead. Jesse took out her phone, a gift from her parents, and located the GPS for the caboose. That information would be instrumental in locating the owner. Hitching the heavy knapsack that carried everything she owned in it, Jesse gave the red caboose a wistful farewell look and then turned away, heading into the woods to walk back into Hamilton. Glancing at her watch, she realized that she would have to locate the county seat office and wait until they opened up at nine a.m.

TRAVIS RAMSEY WAS behind the counter of Ramsey Fishing Guides when the bell above the door tinkled, telling him he had an early morning visitor. His fishing guide business was mostly dormant during this time of the year and he had little to do over the coming winter months. Next April when the snows left the Bitterroot Valley where Hamilton sat, fishermen from around the world would stream in to take advantage of the world-class trout in the creeks and river. Looking up he saw a young woman, her short black hair emphasizing the paleness of her features. Straightening, he saw her look around the large, two-story building. As her blue gaze met his, he frowned. She was wearing an Army jacket. A real one, with patches that he quickly recognized. Had she bought it at an Army-Navy store or was she the real deal? She was tall, her shoulders thrown back, wearing a heavy Army rucksack on her back. His gaze dropped to her long legs wrapped in denim, and then to her boots. Those were Army boots. There was something about her, a sense that she was probably ex-military. So was he.

"Can I help you?" he called, walking toward the end of the maple counter that had been in his family since the late 1800s. He saw her blue eyes narrow, silently evaluating him. There was a glittering intelligence in them, something he rarely saw outside the military. Her fingers tightened around the strap of her rucksack curved across her shoulder. He'd been a Delta Force operator and missed nothing. If she was ex-Army, she wasn't office personnel. No, she was carefully assessing him on every potential level as he was her. There had been women in Delta Force for over a decade. She certainly behaved like an operator and his respect for her was already amping up. He halted at the end of the counter. "I'm Travis Ramsey. How may I help you?"

The woman looked disheveled, but clean, her clothes showing wear and tear. Something pinged his intuition as she headed toward him, her lips set in a line that suggested she was afraid of his response to whatever she wanted or needed from him. Travis couldn't prove it, but he never dismissed an intuitive hit. It had saved his life way too many times.

"I'm Jesse Myers. I was walking in the woods along the Bitterroot River when I saw a red caboose in the nearby meadow. I went to the county record-er's office here in Hamilton to find the owner and they said it belonged to you." She hesitated and then said, "I'm looking for a place to rent. I have a part-time job at Katie's Koffee Bean down the street. I can't afford much, but I would take good care of that boxcar if you're open to renting it to me."

Stunned by her request, he nodded, watching fear and hope alternate in her eyes. "You did your homework."

Jesse managed a weak smile. "It's my nature. I fell in love with the caboose and thought it would be a great place to stay. I'm not making enough money to rent something in town, yet. I could clean it up, maybe paint it and repair some of the things inside and make it livable once more. I'm pretty good with mechanical and electrical stuff."

Travis liked her low, husky voice. She might be fearful that he'd say no, but she stood her ground and kept good eye contact with him. "You have family around here?" Hamilton was a town of four-thousand plus people and he knew all of them because his family was one of the first to settle in this town.

Shaking her head, she said, "No, sir, I don't. I was born and raised in Billings, Montana and that's where my folks live."

Things didn't add up. "And you've come to Hamilton to get a job?" Travis knew there were no jobs after tourist season, which ended in late September and didn't begin again until the first of April. Everyone who worked here was seasonal. What was her story?

"Yes, sir, I have. Growing up, my parents' favorite place to go for a week-end or a vacation was Hamilton. I've always loved this small town, the people, and how it's surrounded by nature." She gave a slight shrug. "I'm not a city person even though I was born in Billings. I need the outdoors, the woods, the water and the quiet."

She appealed to him on so many levels that Travis felt momentarily rocked by this unexpected awareness. Jesse's short hair was mannish in cut and that triggered something in him that he hoped to explore with her. "Listen, I've got an espresso machine at the rear of the store. Why don't we go back there, have a cup of coffee and we can talk?" He gestured toward the front door. "There isn't going to be anyone coming in today. I just bought a half-dozen fresh pastries from the Las Palomas Bakery next door. Let's talk further in my office?" He wasn't looking for a woman, but damned if Jesse Myers didn't call strongly to him, man-to-woman. She was clearly mature for her age, and had morals and values because she went to the county office to find out who owned that caboose and then asked to rent it. He'd seen some vets who passed through the area in the summer who squatted and used the caboose, never asking if they could stay there or not. He liked her honesty.

"Well..."

He gestured toward the other end of the store. "Come on. It's early and I don't know about you, but hot coffee is something we can all use at this time of the morning." Military people were coffee hounds of the first order. He saw her eyes widen momentarily, those thick dark lashes emphasizing them. Pleased, he saw the offer appealed to her.

"Sounds good, Mr. Ramsey."

"Call me Travis and you can put the 'sir' away, too. I'm ex-Army. Are you?" he asked, walking down the length of the counter. He met her at the other end and opened the door to the tourist area of the shop. The waiting room was large, lots of wooden chairs with cushions spaced neatly around the perimeter. At one end was a long table filled with paper coffee cups, boxes of assorted teas, sugar, cream, and spoons, and a very expensive espresso machine. "Put your rucksack on a chair and have a seat," he invited. Partly shutting the door, he went and turned the machine on. "Coffee? Espresso? What's your poison?" He grinned a little, wanting the tension she carried to dissolve. He saw her gently set the fifty-pound pack on the floor next to the chair where she sat down.

"Just plain coffee is fine. Black. Thank you."

Her manners were all military and Travis nodded, getting busy making her that coffee. "Reach over and grab yourself a donut or two," he said, pointing to a box near where she was seated. "Help yourself. Alex Delgado, the daughter of Hector and Maria, now runs the bakery and she's known as the queen of pastries around Hamilton. They all taste great." Jesse was a tall, big boned woman and he noticed how the wrinkled Army jacket hung on her frame. He saw her look wistfully at the pastries and lick her full lower lip. Her hands were taut against the thighs of her jeans. She was hungry. The realization hit him hard. In black ops it was the little things, jigsaw puzzle pieces that alone, didn't tell much. But as an operator in Afghanistan for far too long, it was all these tidbits that came together to paint a fuller picture of a situation. Or in the case of Jesse, that she was definitely an Army vet. There was no question in his mind about that.

Further, she had hesitated momentarily at the door to the coffee room to thoroughly evaluate it. This told him she was clearly an operator, not some office assistant. Maybe she was an intelligence officer or maybe an operator out in the field like himself? When she came into the room after sweeping it thoroughly in a moment with her gaze, she deliberately sat down in one corner, at the end of the table, her back up against a wall, facing the only exit door. An operator always did that. As he put the coffee into the machine, placing a white paper cup beneath the spout, he began to cobble more of her story together in his head. If she'd been in combat, more than likely she had PTSD. The fact that she wasn't at home after leaving the Army told him that. He had many friends, ex-Delta operators, who had their marriages go bust after coming off a deployment because of the years of accumulated PTSD and being unable to adjust to civilian life again. They couldn't go home to their parents, either, because they wouldn't understand the flashbacks, the nightmares, and the ongoing anxiety they carried in them 24/7/365, either.

His mouth flexed in sympathy as he watched her from the corner of his eye. She rose in one fluid motion and picked up a paper napkin, her long, elegant-looking fingers hovering over the mouth-watering array of pastries. When she leaned over, her jacket opened and he saw she was wearing a desert tan shirt he was very familiar with. It was an operator's shirt, with camouflage print on both long sleeves and a tan torso core of one color. Yeah, she was black ops, no question.

"Where were you stationed in Afghanistan?" he asked, turning and placing the steaming brew on the table next to where she'd sat down.

Jesse froze for a second, transfixed by the man's large, slightly narrowed gray eyes as he buttonholed her with that question. His dark brown hair was cut military short, his beard clipped close, showing off his square face and giving him an air of dangerousness. Trying to slough off her shock that he knew what she was in the Army, she replied, "Nangarhar Province." Tensing, she saw several emotions flit across his face. How the hell would he know *that* about her? She hadn't answered his question earlier about being in the Army. The chocolate éclair teased her wide-open senses. Her mouth watered. The scent of the sugar, vanilla pudding and chocolate was too much to resist and she bit slowly into it, savoring it as if her life depended upon it. Closing her eyes, she made a humming sound in the back of her throat. The world stopped in that moment as she tasted the luscious, thick chocolate coating. She finally swallowed, feeling it hit her hungry stomach, the urgent amount of strength that it created within her as the glucose shot into her system.

Slowly, her senses moved outward once more and she heard Travis tinkering with the espresso machine, the fragrance of chocolate surrounding her as the machine hissed and steamed. Opening her eyes, she saw he was making a large mocha latte. He was a tall man, at least six feet and broad shouldered. The blue plaid, flannel cowboy shirt he wore stretched against his powerful chest, a black leather vest worn over the shirt. He was someone who was in top shape, probably in his late twenties, she would guess. There were a lot of crinkles at the corners of his gray eyes, telling her he was outside a lot. She liked his short dark brown hair that sported reddish strands among them.

She decided to take a closer inspection of him because no one was a mind reader. His hands were large, square and calloused. When he made a gesture, she saw that he sported a thick callous on the inside of his right index finger, his trigger finger. Black ops all had that telltale sign. She had it on hers, as well. And he might have spotted it on her hand after she'd removed her gloves. When she'd come into the store, she'd seen him suddenly shift almost invisibly, into a heightened space of alertness aimed at her. It was nothing obvious, but her senses were far too honed not to pick it up and now, she was beginning to put together that this man standing in a cowboy shirt, jeans and scarred, well-worn leather boots, was black ops himself, not regular Army—otherwise he wouldn't have recognized who she was. Questions came, but she sat on them. Right now, she needed a place to rent. Besides, he'd probably find her personal questions rude.

Biting into the éclair once more, Jesse moved inward to appreciate all the wonderful tastes that bloomed in her mouth and wrapped deliciously around her tongue. She wanted to jam the rest of it into her mouth, barely chew it and grab a second and third one to sate her starvation. Hunger was something she dealt with constantly since getting out of the Army. Her manners won over on the purely Neanderthal reflex, and she focused on the fact that Travis Ramsey had been kind enough to offer her something to eat. Not to mention, the delicious hot coffee. Her stomach growled after she'd finished the éclair and she opened her eyes, embarrassed by the loud sound. She looked up, aware Travis had heard it too. He merely pointed to the box.

"Eat all you want."

He hadn't embarrassed her. He sauntered over, grabbed a donut and sat down, his back to the other wall nearby, opposite the partly-opened door. Inwardly, a sheet of relief started to avalanche through Jesse because she now knew without a doubt that Travis had been an operator. He had to be because of the question he'd asked her earlier. She chose a donut with white frosting and colorful sprinkles across it this time.

They ate in silence for the next few minutes. Jesse had the distinct sensation that he was giving her time to get food into her body and allow her to relax before opening up a conversation with her. She felt shame over the condition of her clothes, realizing she looked like a vagrant, not the combat soldier she'd been in her prime. Because Travis was an operator, he would easily have spotted her condition: so many other military vets like herself swam in a sea of confusion, depression and aimlessness after being separated from the military. He probably wondered if she had turned to alcohol or drugs to dull the anxiety that ate constantly at her. That would be a reason for him to not rent that caboose to her. Fear skittered through her over that last thought. How she wished she had done more than use the washcloth and soap she kept in her rucksack at the river before coming into town. She'd scrubbed her face, neck and hands. She had no toothpaste, so she'd taken a twig and gone around each tooth, cleaning it the best she could. Short hair was something that was mandatory for her combat missions. Now, she wished she looked more feminine, not so mannish. Jesse worried that he would see her as a risk, a problem, and might have second thoughts about renting that caboose to her. How badly she wanted that sweet little boxcar. It meant something so important to her she couldn't even give it words. How to convince him she wasn't a risk? That she wasn't going to be a problem in his life? That she would take the very best care of that caboose he owned? The fear built up in her and she decided to confront it head on.

"I just got out of the Army three months ago," she told him, holding his gaze. "I was an interpreter assigned to a Delta Force group out of Jalalabad. I was in from eighteen through age twenty-six. After graduating translation school, I was assigned on every deployment to that province. Most of the time, I was assigned to one of the snatch-and-grab teams and we saw a lot of combat. I was planning on staying in the Army for twenty and then getting out, but my PTSD accumulated and I couldn't function at that high level any more. The Army gave me an honorable medical discharge. I went home to my parents in Billings, but that didn't turn out like I'd hoped. I decided to strike out on my own and try to figure out how to reintegrate back into civilian life." She looked around the room made of glowing cedar planks, the gold and crimson of the wood telling her it was very old because the color was so bold and beautiful. "I came to Hamilton because it was my favorite place when my parents came over here on vacation. I got a part-time job at Katie's Koffee shop as a dish washer. I need to fit back into the world and I don't know how to do it, but I figure dishwashing is a good place to start. It's just me and a machine in the back room of that store. I don't do well with crowds and I don't do well under severe stress. If you could rent me that caboose, I'd take great care of it. I don't smoke, I don't do drugs, and I don't touch alcohol."

It felt as if all her life had flowed out of her in the emotional plea she'd just shared with this stranger. Travis didn't feel like a stranger to her, though. He was a brother—she was sure he'd been in black ops and that was a very small, elite group in the military. Jesse assessed him as he munched on the donut, his gaze never leaving hers. With him she didn't feel like a bug under a microscope. Instead, she felt as if they were kindred spirits because of their shared service experience. Black-ops people were a tight family. Their every move, their attention to detail, either kept those around them safe or opened them up to injury and possible death. Jesse saw a softness filter into his expression as she finished her rushed, almost breathless admittance to him. Ordinarily, she would never share any of these things with anyone, not even her parents. But there was an inner sense that Travis needed to know more about her in order to make his decision.

How badly she wanted that caboose! It was crazy! How could a beaten down old boxcar suddenly become so important to her? And why?

"You've been through a lot," he murmured, voice deep with knowing.

"I think you have too."

He managed a quirked once-sided uptick of his mouth. "Yes, I think we both have. I have a story to tell you about that old red caboose that's sitting on our property. My grandfather, Hiram Ramsey, worked for the Union Pacific railroad for thirty-five years. When he retired, he and his wife Inez, had this old 1940s UP red caboose trucked up there and he sat it on a concrete slab. That meadow was his favorite place as a child growing up and when he retired, he told my father that he wanted to live there, fish, hike and enjoy his pastime, which was photography." He wiped his hands off and dropped the napkin into the wastebasket beneath the table. "Inez, my grandmother, died before I returned home from the Army. And then he passed shortly after that. Since then, the caboose has not been taken care of. I got out of the Army three years ago and took over the business here with my father, Sam, who no longer acts as a fishing guide for the company. I thought he would care for the caboose because it was my grandparents', but he didn't do that. He just let it go. I try to do upkeep on it, but we're busy from April 1 through mid-September. And then the snow usually dumps hard and fast and getting back to the caboose on a dirt road is pretty dicey and sometimes impossible, depending upon when we get blizzards through the area, which is pretty often."

"I took an overland route paralleling the river when I discovered it. I didn't come in via the road."

"Well," he said, amusement in his tone, "you're not the ordinary civilian, either. You probably followed the river and stayed within the tree line so you couldn't be seen. People like us don't need roads to get to where we need to go."

She squelched a grin and gave a slow nod. "You're right. My years in black ops have changed me forever. I'll never look at anything again without assessing its safety or danger to me."

He scratched his head and flashed a dry look in her direction. "Yeah. For sure."

"So? This caboose is a much-loved family heirloom?" she guessed.

"Probably means more to me than to my father. He never got along well with my grandfather. I was more or less raised by Hiram when he was home from his railroad duties. He was the one to teach me tracking, living off the land and how to stay alive. Sometimes, I think he had a premonition that I'd be in black ops someday and would need that kind of life-saving knowledge passed on to me."

She finished the donut and then drained her coffee cup. Wiping her mouth with the napkin, she said, "The feeling I got around the caboose was that there was something special, something good, about it...maybe a lot of happy memories." She shrugged.

"A ton of good things," Travis agreed, his voice thickening for a moment. "He and my grandmother were special in my life. Still are and always will be. Everything they collected over the years in that caboose meant something special to them. Each thing had a story behind it. I wanted to keep it because it was a place where good family memories still dwell."

She pushed her damp palms down her thighs. "Would you consider me renting it on a monthly basis? I could do a lot of work, get it cleaned up, the windows washed, the place swept and the dust removed, as part of my rent?"

"Music to my ears," Travis said. "Off and on, there's been squatters who would use that boxcar as a place to live during the summer season. I try to go out monthly and check up on it because next spring I was planning on putting a new roof on it. Most of the guys who lived in it without permission were vets wandering through the area. They were on drugs or alcohol, doing more damage than anything else to the caboose. I asked them to leave and they would. I felt bad about it, but they were wrecking my grandparents' home, not caring for it." He studied her in the ensuing silence. "You'll take care of it. I know that."

Her heart leaped with hope. "I promise you, I will, Mr. Ramsey." She hated that she suddenly found her voice wobbling with unchecked emotions, showing just how badly she wanted to rent the boxcar.

"Remember? Call me Travis. No more sir and no more Mr. Ramsey. Okay?"

"Yes...thanks...it's just been drilled into me by the Army."

He grinned. "Yeah, I got that. It's okay if you talk in Zulu time to me, though. I've been out three years and I still talk in Zulu, twenty-four-hour clock, not civilian time."

She managed a slight laugh. "I'm glad to know that. I'm having a terrible time with stopping my military lingo, too."

"That's the nice thing about vets working with vets. We know the same foreign language and don't have to translate it to each other like we do our civilian family and friends."

"You're right." Just knowing a little bit of the history of that red caboose endeared it to her even more. *Why?* Why did it have *such* a mesmerizing hold over her? "There's something so calming about your grandparents' home. I can't explain it, Travis," she blurted. She pressed her hand to her heart. "I can't put it into words. It's as if that caboose is filled with magic just waiting to bloom once again. That's the feeling I get."

He wiped his mouth and looked up, pointing to a color photo above the door. "That's my grandfather, Hiram. Red hair, red beard, blue eyes and full of risk taking and adventure. He was always putting something into that caboose from all his journeys across the United States. He was a conductor for UP, and he spent thirty-five years of his life living in a caboose. I think him wanting one to live out the rest of his life in was just a continuation of his dreams, his great memories and the many experiences he had. I always loved sitting at his feet as he rocked in his rocking chair, telling me those stories. So yes, I think their caboose has many, many good, hopeful stories filling it. Maybe you can feel that?"

"Yes, I felt all of that." And more, but Jesse couldn't find the right words to describe what she was picking up on. "I felt hope in their home. I know that sounds silly, but the last three months have been a special kind of hell for me. When I stumbled upon the caboose and approached it, I felt as if this invisible umbrella of hope and safety had descended upon me once more. I'm sure it sounds crazy…"

"No," he interrupted. "Not at all. My grandfather came from Scandinavian Viking blood, and was also half Irish. His side of the family came to America in the 1800s. He was born in New York. Then, his family moved to Montana after that. He met my grandmother, Inez, here in Hamilton. He's told me so many stories of the Irish fairies, the gnomes and elves that lived in Ireland. One time, he said they lived with them in and around the caboose. I never saw them, but he did. He used to tell me about them by name and describe each one of them. He was magical in some ways. When I was having issues with my father as a teenager, I used to go over to his home here in Hamilton and stay with them on weekends. They always liked taking care of me and my younger brother, Kyle." Becoming somber suddenly, he said, "Look, I'll let you stay there rent free if you can help me clean it up and make it fully livable again. I'll pay for the materials to fix it up, the propane, and I'll get a quiet generator out there so you have electricity. I'll pay for the gasoline to run it, too. I believe you when you say you'll take care of it. Black-ops people aren't prone to lying and they understand a woman or man's word has their personal honor and truth backing it up."

Hot tears stung her lids and Jesse swallowed hard to fight them back. "Thanks for giving me a chance, Travis. I won't let you down."

CHAPTER 2

November 1

"LET'S TAKE A drive out to my grandfather's boxcar," Travis said to Jesse. It was ten a.m. and he could see the two pastries that she had consumed made a difference in her energy level. Her cheeks were hallowed out by loss of weight, but there was a tinge of color to them now and for whatever reason, that made him feel good. "I haven't been out there for about six weeks because of the need to be here as a fishing guide to a few our autumn clients."

"I imagine you're pretty busy," she said.

He grunted and shut off the espresso machine. "More than you'll ever know. The Bitterroot Valley and the river here have some of the finest trout fishing in the U.S. Our office assistant quit because my father isn't exactly easy to get along with."

Jesse rose from her chair and pulled the straps of her rucksack over her shoulders, settling the pack on her back. "I'm sorry to hear that."

"Luckily, she quit in late October, so I was able to cover the two jobs and make ends meet."

Jesse waited for Travis to move ahead of her and open the door fully before following him out. He locked the front door and gestured for her to follow him out a side door. The sunlight was bright and she wished she had a pair of dark sunglasses, but instead, placed her hand above her eyes. There were three white pickups with Ramsey Fishing Guides painted on them, a leaping rainbow trout coming out of the water beneath the curved bright red lettering.

Travis halted and turned. "Here, take these keys to the truck next to mine. Follow me out to the caboose?" He placed the keys in her palm. She gave him a shocked look and stared down at the keys and then up at him.

"You're trusting me with one of your company trucks?"

He saw the confusion in her eyes. The sunlight brought out the blue highlights in her slightly curly hair. "Yes. Why shouldn't I?"

"You barely know me."

He studied her briefly, opened the door to his truck and got in. "I know everything I need to know about you, Jesse. Now, let's saddle up?"

She grinned tentatively, fingers flexing over the keys to the other truck. "It feels like I'm back on a black-ops team again." The words came out low, filled with a backlog of feelings. The look he gave her, that sharp eagle-like glance, allowed her to see deeper into who he really was. The discovery wasn't threatening, but rather comforting because the sensation she picked up around him was that he had her back. The weight of that realization gave her real hope for the first time since leaving the Army. This was a man who, if he gave his word, would carry through on it. A part of her heaved a huge sigh of relief. Maybe she had just made a turn in a positive sense toward her new life, the new chapter that she was struggling to come to grips with.

It took her a minute to get used to the truck and where everything was located. Travis was patient, remaining in his truck and waiting for her to give him a thumb's up before he backed out of the parking space. Jesse wondered if he realized just how deep and pervasive her PTSD was. He must, because she saw no anger or impatience in his expression as he calmly sat there until she was ready to follow him out of Hamilton.

As she drove through the small strip mall town her mind reeled. The last year of her life in the Army had been like carrying a thousand pounds of weight on her shoulders. She was relieved of duty when her colonel ordered her to be evaluated at Bagram for PTSD issues. Until then, she'd tried to stuff it all down and operate as usual—and it hadn't worked. She wasn't going to put her team at risk and had gone first to her captain and told him what was going on within her. It shamed her to tell him, but her conscience wouldn't allow her any other choice. That had been the beginning of the end. The darkness that descended upon her as she went through the medical testing and endless psychological evaluations, supported that she was unfit for combat duty. The only good thing was that she had not put her team into a situation to be injured or killed because she could no longer function at that high level.

Very shortly, they were out of town and Travis signaled to turn at an un-named dirt road on their left. She slowed down and followed at a slower pace because the road was rutted, slippery looking and muddy. Evergreens bracketed each side of the road, creating a corridor, as they moved slowly forward, up a slight slope and then down into the huge meadow. She caught sight of the caboose, a dull red against the green of the trees and the yellow of the meadow grass. Ahead, she could see the river not far away. The road led to the other end of the caboose that she'd spotted on her initial walk around the concrete slab. It was roughly half a mile from the main Hamilton highway to the boxcar.

She parked behind Travis's truck and climbed out. She left her pack on the seat, walking up to where he stood waiting for her.

"I'm assuming you went into the boxcar and looked around?" he asked, gesturing toward it.

"Yes. I knew I was trespassing. I shouldn't have done it," she admitted, waiting for some kind of censure from him.

"The door is always unlocked. Don't worry about it." He turned, walking up toward the rear of the caboose. He halted at the bottom of the steps, staring at her rolled up tent laying across the platform.

"Sorry," Jesse said, coming around, grabbing it and getting it out of their way.

"Is that what you've been sleeping in?" he demanded, scowling as she tucked the large roll beneath her left arm.

"Have been since I left the Army."

Travis stared up at the train car. "You can't sleep here tonight. I need to drive to Missoula tomorrow and pick up a new mattress for your bedroom."

She smiled drily. "I've been sleeping in my pup tent, in my sleeping bag, come rain or shine for three months. I'll be fine here."

His scowl deepened. "Not on my watch. I've got a guest bedroom at my cabin. Stay there until we can get this place cleaned up and livable for you. All right?"

Stunned, she blinked once, not expecting such a kind offer. The set of his jaw, the way his mouth thinned, she felt like he had been an officer. "Tell me something," she said, peering up at him, "were you an officer in the Army?"

He tipped the brim of his black Stetson up a little. "Does it show?"

Jesse nodded, trying not to smile. "Just a little."

"Okay," he sighed. "Let me try this again. I'd like you to stay at my cabin because it's warm and dry. It's only temporary until we can get my grandparents' caboose ready for you to live in. Would you prefer to stay under my roof instead of that?" He jabbed an index finger at the tent she held.

"That would be nice to stay at your cabin, but I never expected it. I'm a stranger to you."

"Your black ops, Jesse. I ran a team in Helmand Province in Afghanistan. I never had a woman assigned to it, but that doesn't matter. The caliber and quality of anyone on a Delta Force team is without question. I trust you with my life."

The sincerity burning in his gray glance soothed her in a way that was healing. His words, barely above a growl, spoken with raw honesty, were like a warm wind on the icy coldness that lived within her. Swallowing hard, she gave a jerky nod. "I'll take you up on your offer. Just know I have your back, too."

He rolled his shoulders and looked away for a moment, studying the caboose. Cocking his head, he held her gaze. "Here in Hamilton, I don't think we need to worry about being ambushed." He chuckled and then became serious. "I appreciate you saying that. My father, Sam, is pretty crippled up. In his youth, he rode bulls and nearly won the US championship, but he broke a lot of bones and tore into a lot of joints in the process of getting there. He's in pain a lot of the time and he doesn't go out on our fishing expeditions any more. Usually, he stays at his cabin on the other side of town from where I live, and sometimes, he'll drop into the office. He's a pretty angry guy and easily irritated because the pain meds he's on aren't working. I'm telling you this because sooner or later, he's going to find out about you, and about me bringing my grandparents' caboose back to life instead of letting it fall apart like he did while I was away in the Army."

"I know you said your grandfather didn't have a good relationship with your father. I get it."

"Well," Travis muttered, shaking his head, "Sam is in perpetual pain and he's like an angry grizzly and takes no prisoners, Jesse." Frustration tinged his tone. "I don't want Sam targeting you and taking out his misery and discomfort on you once he finds out I'm renting this to you."

"Right now," Jesse countered, "you're his whipping post. Right?" She watched his expression turn to one of surprise.

"I knew you were smart, not just *how* smart. Did you take psych classes during college when you were in the Army?"

"No. It just comes naturally to me."

"No wonder you were a damn good translator because so much of what humans say is eighty percent nonverbal. You can read that nonverbal really well. I'll bet your team thought you walked on water and you probably did."

Sadness, loss and grief moved through her. "They were my brothers. I love them to this day. We stayed in touch…well, until I left the Army. I've been like a bowling ball rolling all over the place since I was discharged. I haven't had an email account, so I can't get in touch with them. I'll amend that. I did try at a library in Helena one time, but I broke down and started crying because I missed them, missed my old way of life, so much. I was an embarrassment to the patrons around me because I couldn't stop crying no matter how hard I tried. The librarian came over and wanted to know what was wrong and how she could help me. That did it," she said, opening her hand in a helpless gesture, unable to avoid his sharpened look. "I ran out of the place, so ashamed of myself. They didn't know me from Adam, but I felt so beaten down, missing my team so much that I was running away from the pain and grief and losing them. I never tried to go to another library to email them. I was so afraid I'd break down again."

He reached out, briefly touching her slumped shoulder. "If you want, I have Wi-Fi at my cabin, and there's a computer in the guest bedroom. If it feels right, you can get a hold of them there. I'm okay if you want to cry it out. Better out than in."

The pressure in her chest became a tightening sensation, her throat closing up. Oh damn! She was so close to crying again! It took everything Jesse had to fight her reaction and jam it back down into that dark hole where she hid everything bad. Clearing her throat, she said, "Yeah, okay. Thanks. I'll let you know if I want to use it." And then she pivoted the conversation away from her, pointing to the caboose. "What do you need to do inside or outside of this car that I can help you with?" She saw sympathy in Travis's face and then it was gone. Would he let her off this horribly emotional hook or not? She didn't want to keep discussing her past, it was too painful to deal with right now on top of everything else.

Travis pulled out a small notepad from the pocket of his shirt. "I was going to go through the place and write down what needs to be replaced to make this a home for you. I want to take anything out of there if it's broken or worn out. I'll put it in the bed of the truck and haul it out of here. I want your input on everything. So don't be shy. Speak up."

His gruffly spoken words nearly shattered what was left of her strength. *A home for you.* How much she missed being near her parents! Life was so hard. Harder than any combat mission she'd been on in Afghanistan. Afraid to trust her voice, she gave a jerky nod, motioning for him to get up the stairs and she'd follow.

TRAVIS COULD SEE the weariness in Jesse's face as they took the last items out of the caboose and placed them in the back of his truck. They'd roped everything in so nothing would fall out on the way back into town and he finished writing down what he either needed to buy, replace, or fix in the boxcar. For him, it was a quiet joy to bring his grandparents' home, a place where he'd spent his youth on weekends and summer vacation, back to breathing, living life.

They'd gone through every drawer, closet and all of the hidey-holes in the caboose. The mattress and box springs were in the truck bed, along with so many other things, including the overstuffed leather chair that was beyond saving. It was two p.m., and way past time for lunch. "How about we drive into town? There's the Yellow Rose Diner run by Sue Conway, near our office. She's got the best food in town. I'll buy. You've been working hard and it's time to eat." He wasn't going to humiliate her just because he knew she didn't have any money to buy decent food. He'd seen her from time to time, pulling dried rose hips out of her pocket and chewing on them. Like all Delta operators, she had been trained to eat off the land no matter where she was at. There were a lot of wild rose bushes down along the banks of the river and he was sure she had picked all that she could find. It hurt him to realize she was near starvation. Vets deserved better than this, and it burned in his craw. He wouldn't embarrass her by giving her money so she could buy food. No, he'd have to handle this adroitly. Jesse had seen enough humiliation because of her situation. He didn't want to add to it.

"Sounds good, thanks," she said. "I'll take you up on it."

"After lunch, we can get a lot more things done this afternoon if you're game?"

"You bet I am. I'm ready to rock 'n roll."

"Typical military can-do spirit," he teased, shutting his notebook and stuffing it back into his pocket. There was an odd sensation in the center of his chest. How long had it been since he'd become chief caregiver of his father and felt such a wonderful thread of hope? He thought that ability had died when Sam blamed his own father, Hiram, for the fix he physically found himself in. His grandfather had nothing to do with his father's injuries, of course, but Sam had to blame someone. And every year, he got less and less mobile to the point where he had to use his electric wheelchair to get around sometimes. He hated it. He hated the world and he took it out on Travis every chance he got. He couldn't even keep the women he hired to take care of Sam because he rode roughshod over them. They always quit in disgust, not willing to take his cursing abusiveness and anger toward them when they'd done nothing wrong.

Pulling himself out of his own "poor me" moment because he was no stranger to depression—thanks to his PTSD—he glanced at the soft curve of Jesse's lips, instead. She was desirable, there was no question. Travis needed time alone to figure out what his surprising and unexpected reactions to her were all about. Now was not a good time. "Okay," he said, "let's saddle up, pardner." It was easy to consider her as a team buddy. The teams built an unshakable loyalty to one another. It bred a familiarity that only those in that career knew about because they had experienced it firsthand and understood the life-and-death risks undertaken by all of them as a unit. This created an ease with Jesse that he normally would not have with a woman. This was different. *She* was different. And he liked her a helluva lot more than he ever should.

ENTERING THE YELLOW Rose Diner, Jesse deeply inhaled the scents of beef stew, sourdough bread, French fries and strong coffee in the air. It was a place Jesse had been longing to come to but she didn't have the money in her pocket to afford the food. The restaurant was pretty empty at this time of day other than a couple of grizzled elderly fishermen, probably locals, sitting in one of the red vinyl booths having hot coffee and cherry pie with vanilla ice cream on the side. Behind the counter was a blonde woman in her late forties, a white apron tied around her waist. She was dressed in jeans and a long-sleeved red sweater with an embroidered turkey on the front of it.

"Hey," Travis greeted her, lifting his hand. "How are you doing Sue?"

Sue smiled, wiping down the counter with a washcloth. "Fine, Travis. Odd seeing you here this time of day. Your dad doing okay?"

Travis removed his black cowboy hat, hanging it on a nearby peg as he slid into a corner booth seat. "He's still in pain and the meds aren't working. Are you playing waitress today, too?"

She laughed and picked up the coffee pot and two white mugs. "This time of year? Yes. Annie, my waitress, has gone south for the winter to pick up a six-month gig in Phoenix. It's just me and Nick now. Today I'm chief cook, bottle washer and waitress."

"A woman of many talents," Travis said. "Sue, meet Jesse Myers. Nick is her son," he explained to Jesse who sat opposite him at the rectangular table. "He just got married to a really nice lady, Holly McGuire. She runs the Delos Food Charity here in town for the people who are shut ins. Nick does the dishwashing here to help his mother out when they're short staffed during the off season."

"Nice to meet you, Sue." The woman expertly poured them coffee and then set the pot on the edge of the table, along with two menus from beneath her arm.

"Nice to meet you, too, Jesse. I know what Travis wants," Sue told her. "Would you like a minute to decide?"

Jesse shook her head. "I'll take a hamburger, well done, and French fries, please?"

"You got it. Travis? You want the usual? Four French toast, bacon and three eggs over easy?"

"Yes, ma'am," he intoned.

"Got it. I'll get busy on this order."

"Before you go? In case you start to hear gossip around town, I want to let you know that Jesse is going to be renting my grandparents' red caboose out in the meadow. She's not a squatter."

Jesse saw Sue's blonde brows arch. "Good to know, Travis. Because everyone is fishing like mad at the river behind town trying to get the last of the trout before we get snowbound." She shifted to Jesse. "You're new around here, aren't you, Jesse?"

"Yes. I just got a job at Katie's Koffee Bean down the street. I'm going to be her dish washer."

"Gosh, I wish you'd stopped in here first! Nick has his hands full and he pinch hits my dishwashing machine in the back when he can. His wife, Holly, is five months pregnant and they're trying to build a cabin a little ways outside of town before the snows set in."

"If things don't work out there," Jesse said, "I'll come down and see if I'd be a fit for your diner. Fair enough?"

Sue smiled. "Fair enough. Anyway, welcome to Hamilton."

Jesse had her back to the wall and so did Travis. From the booth he'd chosen, she could see both exits, one through the swinging kitchen doors, the other where they'd originally entered the diner and they could easily see who was coming and going. She was pleased he had not placed them near or in front of a window, either. She liked being enclosed by a solid wall, not windows where a sniper could pick them off. As Travis had said, there were no ambushers here in the town. Still, old habits that had kept her alive in-country weren't going to go away anytime soon. She sipped her coffee, absorbing the heat of the mug in her hands as it warmed her cold, numb fingers. It smelled so good, plus she was starving. All the scents were driving her digestion crazy, her stomach growling with hunger.

"One of the things I loved about coming here as a kid was that everyone was so friendly," she told Travis.

"Hamilton is a good place to live. We have our eccentrics, but basically, the people are hardworking, kind and believe in helping one another. My family has lived here since 1875 before the town became a town."

"And your earlier family created the fishing guide company?"

"Yes. I felt like I was born into the family at a very lucky time. My father had a vision to enlarge our company. My grandfather Hiram had said it was fine as is, and didn't want to spend the money or move from the original building because he'd bought it and felt it was large enough."

"Family squabble ensued and you were caught in the middle?"

"Sort of. My father was a real rebellious kid growing up. He didn't want to get saddled running a fishing guide company. He was foot loose and fancy free and loved being on the rodeo circuit here in the west. He was a good bronc rider, but his specialty was bull riding. He came in second at twenty-seven years old to almost becoming the US champion bull rider. On his last ride, he busted his collarbone and the gent who was tied with him for first place, had one more ride at one more rodeo and he picked up the championship, instead. My father never forgave himself. But you can't ride or do anything with a broken collarbone."

"We've both had EMT training, so we understand the anatomy and mechanics of a break like that. He probably didn't?" Jesse guessed.

"No," Travis said, moving the coffee mug slowly a little to the left and to the right of him. "He didn't. My father has a habit of blaming everyone else for his bad luck or his bad decisions and it's fueled by his constant pain. He never forgets the bad things in life, unfortunately, and doesn't remember the good times. He used too. Growing up, he was a very different man, but pain can change you."

"I saw that photo in the glass case in your store," she offered. "That must have been you standing with your grandfather? He had bright red hair and a long red beard. Was it you in the photo with him?"

His mouth quirked. "Yes, that was me at ten. My grandfather had come off the UP-railroad circuit. He and my grandmother had a cabin outside of town. We always spent our summer vacation with them. I loved when he came home because we went everywhere together. I felt like a pretty lucky kid. He always had new, exciting stories to tell me. When I was much younger, my father told me Hiram would put me across his lap and rock me to sleep. I don't remember those times, but I can believe it."

"I love that old rocker in his boxcar," Jesse said wistfully. "It could use a good sanding down and a new coat of varnish. I'd be happy to do that for you, Travis. I thought when I saw the rocker that it meant something special to whoever had lived there."

"It did," Travis said, holding her gaze. "He said that rocking chair reminded him of the constant rocking back and forth motion of his caboose where he lived throughout his career. I grew up loving that old rocker. That would be nice if you had time to take care of it."

"I'd like to do that for you…for him…"

"In the coming week, you can make a list of things you need for the caboose. You can use the company truck to get around in. I'll give you the company credit card to pay for everything. There's no sense you walking to work every day. And you won't be using that much gas, so don't worry about it. We have a gas pump in back of our building where we fuel up all the trucks. So, help yourself."

"You're doing so much to help me, Travis. I truly appreciate it and I swear I'll make your grandparents' caboose glow with life like the old days when they were alive." She wanted to do something for him because he was being incredibly generous toward her. She saw his gray eyes grow warm with memories. It was nice to see a man who wasn't afraid to show his feelings. Travis was comfortable in his own skin, with his masculinity. Many of her team members were so much like him and once more, she felt like she was in a never-ending dream, hoping she would not wake up. She needed this kind of support, having failed in the Army and seeing no way to get up and out of her life-changing dilemma.

"You're one of us," he said. "That's not something that money can buy, Jesse. I know you'll work hard and do your best. That's never been a question I had about you." He smiled a little. "But I have a question that's personal and I don't know if you think I'm butting in where I'm not welcome."

"If I can answer it, I will."

"Can you tell me about your folks?"

That was easy and she drew a sigh of inner relief. For a moment, she thought Travis might ask her about her combat days, and that was simply something she couldn't discuss. At least, not right now. "My family took root in Billings, Montana in 1895. My great-great grandparents started a small hardware store and since then, sort of like your family, we've stayed in that area."

"So that's where you get your mechanical and electrical skills?"

She smiled a little. "Yeah, for sure. My grandparents lived with us in our home and I grew up with them. And like your grandparents, they were wonderful."

"I wonder if you didn't pick up on that energy when you saw the caboose?"

Shrugging, Jesse whispered, "I've got to be honest here. When I walked up to it, I felt like I was coming home. It was the oddest feeling, one I never expected, and I didn't know why then, but I do now."

"We seem to have the same family pattern of sorts. I hope your father isn't like mine?"

"No, my parents are both healthy, thank goodness. I come from good German stock. They are hard-working and low-key. Family and community means everything to them. My mother is our ancestry historian and I learned we have relatives in Germany. She's in touch with them to this day." Giving him a warm look she said, "It's nice to have a good, solid family because I needed it when I got out. I just wasn't expecting that my symptoms would drive me away from them."

"You left to relieve them of your nightmares and flashbacks?"

Grimacing, Jesse nodded. "Yeah, something like that. They wanted to give me money but I refused it because they are in their sixties now and getting old isn't for the faint-of-heart. I wanted them to keep their money in the bank for retirement. I promised them that I'd make it over here in Hamilton."

"That probably made them feel better because they know this town?"

"Yes. I wasn't so sure but I was going to give it a try. I do stay in touch with them. I don't want them worrying about me and I know they are."

"They don't understand the pressures and stresses of combat, that's why," he said.

"My grandfathers were in the Army. I wanted to continue the family tradition, but they weren't in black ops. They did serve in wars but never talked about it."

"No, we don't say much, do we?"

She gave him a wry look. "No."

"Maybe the boxcar will help you mend your soul a little," he said gently.

"I think it's already begun, Travis. Thanks to your generosity."

CHAPTER 3

November 1

JESSE TRIED NOT to look like a kid in awe as she entered Travis's cabin. They had gone from the diner and worked in the caboose until five p.m. The food had fueled her and she felt stronger than ever, but now was hungry once more. The home was more than just a cabin. Although it had cedar logs with white plaster between each, the inside was roomy. It felt like a nurturing nest to her and all the tension in her shoulders disappeared. She stood to one side as Travis entered and shut the door.

"My great-grandparents, Samuel and Hannah, built this cabin," Travis told her, gesturing to the huge, long log beams above them. "My father was born here."

She gazed around the long kitchen that had two large windows over the sink and counter area. "This is beautiful. All made of cedar?"

"Yes. My great grandmother didn't want to deal with pine and bugs getting into the logs, so they had the cedar brought down from Canada." He dropped his Stetson on a wall peg near the door and shrugged out of his denim jacket, hanging it on another one. "Get comfy," he told her. Pointing to a hallway on the other side of the fireplace and living room, he said, "Guest bedroom is the first door on the left. Next to it is the bathroom."

Nodding, Jesse said, "I'd like to get cleaned up." She pointed to the dust on her jeans. They had done a great deal of work that afternoon on the caboose and it was starting to come alive beneath their care.

"Go ahead. I'm going into the kitchen and will rustle us up some elk steaks. Think you'll be ready to eat in about forty or so minutes?"

Her stomach clenched at the thought of a second real meal. "Sure. What can I do to help you?" She saw him shrug.

"Nothing. Go take care of yourself. If you need to have your clothes washed, the laundry room is down at the end of the hall."

"That sounds great. Thanks." She hefted her rucksack over her shoulder and stepped into the large living room, appreciating the flagstone fireplace, the chimney built all the way up to the ceiling. Jesse felt as if she was continuing some wonderful dream as she located the guest bedroom. Inside was a large brass bed, and a very old quilt with colorful patches thrown across the top of it. There was a handmade table carved out of cedar with a computer sitting on it in one corner, along with a wooden chair. This was a very male room, spare and consisting of mostly dark colors. There wasn't much of a woman's touch to it except for that hand-sewn quilt. She wondered if his grandmother had made it. Setting her pack on the bed, she went next door to check out the bathroom. To her joy, there was a claw-foot tub, plus a shower at the other end. She could count on one hand how many times she'd gotten a shower in the last three months. Tubs were her favorite as a child growing up. Running her hand over the white porcelain, she longed for a hot soak.

Dazed by the sudden and unexpected cornucopia of what she saw as gifts, Jesse almost wanted to pinch herself to ensure this was real. The last three months had no shower, no tub, no room or even family household. She felt emotional and overwhelmed by the chance meeting with Travis, his familial connection to the caboose, and being offered a place to stay. It was nearly too much for her to absorb. She had four sets of clothes in her backpack. Usually, she would wash them by hand with a bar of laundry soap, kneeling down at a creek or river bank, scrubbing them and then, hanging them out on tree limbs to dry near her pitched up tent. As the tub filled, she shimmied out of her dirty clothes, ignoring all of the bruises on her legs and arms from too many days spent walking through the forest.

The hot water surrounded her, the heat kneading gently into her tired, exhausted body. All of her worries dissolved in the luxurious, surrounding heat and she closed her eyes. There was a bar of orange-smelling Herbaria soap in a nearby dish. The washcloth, yellow and soft, felt so good later on when she roused herself from near sleep after ten minutes and got cleaned up. The fragrant soap brought back so many memories of her parents, who also believed that handmade soap was the best. Jesse wondered as she scrubbed her skin, if the favored Herbaria soap was a carryover from Travis's past. She liked that he honored the traditional ways because her parents did, too. That was comforting to her and she couldn't explain why, other than that they shared a parallel parental way of living.

Regretfully, she climbed out of the tub, all of the aches and pains gone. Padding on bare feet across the black and white tiles to the shower, Jesse got in and scrubbed her short hair with a bottle of shampoo that was on the shelf. She looked at herself after removing the steam from the mirror and wrinkled her nose. She smelled so fresh after emerging, toweled off and climbed into her last set of clean clothes. It was a pair of wrinkled jeans and a long-sleeved pink tee. How wonderful to have a washer and dryer nearby! It was almost too much for her to take in. It felt so good to be dirt and sweat free!

Her stomach growled and she was familiar with the hunger that was starting up again, a gnawing sensation in her gut. As she opened the bathroom door, the steam escaping, she inhaled the alluring scents of dinner being prepared. Elk steaks had been a family staple because her father, like the men in the family before him, had been hunters. But they killed only what they could eat, never killing for sport. This was something she'd eaten before and her stomach agreed with her. There were other aromas in the air, too, making her mouth water. She glanced down the hall, seeing Travis competently working in the kitchen, his back to her. That relaxed her, too. He was a good human being, respectful of her. Jesse didn't fool herself as she took all of her dirty clothes, including her two towels and wash cloths, and placed them in the washer. Travis was black ops like her. There was no hiding from him how far down she'd fallen. And yet, she knew he was making a real effort not to make her feel even worse about her downfall than she did already. He didn't mention how her clothes looked, or her terribly short hair that she'd cut and hacked at with her Buck knife without a mirror to look into to see what her efforts looked like.

The home was warm and she appreciated the logs snapping and crackling in the fireplace as she wandered through the large living room. There was a very old, but colorful, carpet across the cedar floor and beneath the leather couch and two overstuffed chairs. She felt as if she were back in the 1870s or thereabouts. This home held many generations of the Ramsey family, its past as well as the present. Jesse could feel a contentment embrace her that lived within these walls. She padded across the living room, making sure Travis knew she was nearby so he wouldn't automatically go into defense mode as operators would sometimes do. It was second nature for them to defend themselves out of muscle memory, which could get someone seriously injured or killed.

Halting at the end of the counter, she saw the two huge steaks in a big, old iron skillet. "Those smell wonderful. What can I do to help, Travis?"

Stirring a pan full of brown beans that he'd dropped a tablespoon of brown sugar into earlier, he said, "That cabinet to your left has all the plates. Silverware is in the first drawer below the counter where you're standing. Go ahead and set the table."

Jesse followed his instructions, smiling when she saw the Fiesta plates, cups, saucers and bowls as she opened up the cabinet. "Are these your grandmother's plates?" she wondered, taking down a blue and green one.

"Yes. She loved Fiesta ware. Liked the rainbow colors, as Gram Inez called them. Hiram liked bright colors, too. She had two sets. One is out at the boxcar and I brought the other one in here."

"That explains a lot." She placed the plates on the rectangular dining room table. It was tiger maple; the wood grains a shifting of gold and dark caramel colors beneath the lamps overhead. There was another fragrance filling the kitchen while she set the table. "What's that other smell?" she asked.

"Oh, sourdough biscuits baking," he said, tipping his head a bit toward the oven. "My great-grandmother, Hannah, made sourdough starter nearly a hundred years ago and my Grandmother Inez kept it going, feeding it. She passed the starter on to my mother, but then my mother died of breast cancer when I was a teenager. Before Grams passed, she made me promise that I'd keep the family sourdough fed and keep it alive." He looked sad as he turned off the heat on the pan of beans. "I've done that. I like family traditions and I grew up on sourdough pancakes, biscuits, bread and anything else she could make with that starter."

"I'm sorry your mom passed so early in her life."

"We all were," he admitted. "She was the glue that held our family together. Luckily, Hiram and Inez stepped in and helped me, Kyle and my father through it."

"Still…I'm sorry. That starter is a family heirloom of sorts." She gave him a sympathetic glance, seeing the sadness in his expression. Trying to sound more upbeat, she asked, "Butter or jam for the biscuits?" Every time Travis talked about his family, his voice turned mellow with fondness. It didn't when he mentioned his father, however. Rather, his voice took on a harder edge as if he were defensive or perhaps shielding himself from his father. Jesse noticed the difference, understanding there was a real rift between them.

"Both," he said. "They're in the fridge."

She liked the quiet camaraderie that sprung between them. There were officers in the Army who were a pain in the ass. Her own captain in the Delta Force team, was very much like Travis, however, a good officer, with a calm, quiet voice. Her captain had always remained humble, never setting himself apart from the enlisted people he led. "Okay, butter and jam coming right up."

In no time, Travis placed huge, steaming elk steaks on each plate, a bowl of baked beans with brown sugar and a huge basket of hot sourdough biscuits to go with it. He pulled out a chair for her. "Sorry, but I have military genes in me and we believe in treating a woman like a woman."

Jesse smiled a little and sat down. "Thanks. I won't hold it against you."

"Phew. Good to hear." Travis sat opposite her, handing her the bright red bowl with the beans in it. "Dig in."

"This steak is huge," she protested. "I doubt I can eat half of it."

"No worries. We'll just put the leftovers in the fridge and you can make elk steak sandwiches for lunch tomorrow while we work on the caboose."

"I like your idea. I don't waste any food, either." She spooned the beans onto her plate.

"You look better. There's some color in your cheeks."

"I took a long, hot bath. It was pure heaven."

He grunted and slathered butter over his biscuit. "I've been thinking about how you've dropped into my life. What are the chances that a woman operator who worked in a Delta Force team would suddenly walk into my life here in Hamilton, Montana?"

She buttered her biscuit, taking a bite, letting it melt in her mouth. Swallowing, she gave him a wry look. "I could say the same. When I went into your grandparents' caboose, I felt a kinship with it and I didn't know why. Now I know why. It's because of you, our shared past experience and having families who helped settle Montana."

"You're scary psychic," he muttered, giving her an amused look between bites of steak.

The weight that had been on her for so long was lifting. She could feel it, literally. "No, just observant," she parried. The food was hot, tasty and her shrunken stomach quickly became full. Jesse wanted to eat more, but she knew better. Sliding her plate aside, she allowed herself the dessert of one more sourdough biscuit, this time slathering it thickly with apricot jam. The pastry with the sugar sweetness of the fruit mixed and mingled joyously in her mouth, drawing out a sound of pleasure in her throat. She saw Travis look up, but he said nothing, returning to his own plate of food. Reminding herself that he worked hard today, she was sure she'd probably eat almost as much if she wasn't treading the line of starvation. To eat a lot meant she'd throw it up because her body just wasn't able to handle such a sudden overload. That was not what she wanted to happen.

"You're leaving a lot on your plate, Jesse."

"It will make a great lunch tomorrow. I'm stuffed." She saw him frown, giving her a sharpened look of concern. There was emotional turmoil around him in that glance he gave her. "I'm hoping," she began quietly, "to get some stability in my life. I think between my job as a dish washer at Katie's Koffee Bean and the chance you've given me to live in your grandfather's boxcar, I'll survive."

"I want you to do more than that," he said, his dark brows moving downward. "I want to see you thrive."

Touched, she whispered, "I'll do my best. You've given me more support than I ever dreamed possible, Travis. I won't let you down."

"You shouldn't even be doing dishwashing," he added. "I know how intelligent you really are."

"But I can't handle stress. And doing dishwashing doesn't spike anxiety in me. That's the way it has to be for now. I'm hoping over time, it will lessen, but I don't know if it will or not."

"It will," he promised, mopping up juice left from the steak with half a sourdough biscuit. "My first year home was a rough landing, too, but at least I had a home to come back to. Luckily, my folk's home, this cabin, was mine. My father has his own cabin that he built a while back, down at the other end of Hamilton. I needed to be alone a lot just to grapple with the flashbacks and nightmares. Sam didn't understand what I was going through. He hired several guys each season to handle the fishing guide work. It allowed me to have a softer landing compared to what's happened to you, and to a lot of our other vets."

"I can't tell you how nice it is to have someone like you in my life right now. I think the quiet of the meadow where the boxcar sits and having nature around me, will be a huge support and help." She grimaced. "I'm not fit company for anyone right now."

"I understand. The dishwashing will be easy for you because there's no stress and no crowds of people around you."

"I miss my dog, Tag, that I had as a teenager," she offered. "These last three months I've been so lonely and I've often wished I had a dog at my side."

"I know a number of vets who have a service dog and they tell me all the time what a positive impact it makes on them." He managed a quirked smile. "A dog will love us despite ourselves."

"But you don't have one."

"Sam has our dog, Cyrus, who's real loving mutt. He's fifteen years old. These past three years I've been reclaiming what's left of me and handling the guide business because Sam can't work anymore. His joints were stiffening up to the point where he had to use a cane and on some days, he was relegated to his electric wheelchair, which he hates. He pretty much stays away from the office, but sometimes, when he's really bored, he'll come in and jaw with clients. Cyrus is always with him. There's times when I think if the dog wasn't there, that Sam would turn completely bitter and be miserable to be around all the time."

"I'm glad he has a dog. Everyone should have one."

"If you start stabilizing here," Travis suggested, "you might go down to the no-kill shelter here in Hamilton. And there's some folks you should make friends with, Holly and Nick Conway. Nick was an Army Ranger and has a WMD dog, Snowflake, plus, when he came home, adopted a stray yellow lab named Lady. They're good people. He's a vet like we are."

"That's good to know. You said Holly ran a shut-in charity. I was wondering if she might want or need some part-time help. I believe in giving back. I might not be able to pay you for what you're doing to help me, but I can pass it forward. Do you think they could use some volunteer help from time to time?"

"I'm sure they'd like that. Holly is five months pregnant and she's usually the person who serves the meals to the elders. Nick has a full-time long-distance job with Apple as a software coder. I'm sure as her pregnancy progresses, she's going to need some help. He divides his spare time between being a dish washer for his mother over at the Yellow Rose Diner, and helping feed the shut-ins."

"If I feel more stable, I'd very much like to meet them, but not right now."

He finished cleaning everything up off his plate with the other half of his biscuit. "I was that way the first year. I called it my "hermit" year. Being alone, not being distracted, helped me work through a lot of my adjustments and get square with being a civilian once more. Well, as square as I could. Ever since returning home I've always felt like a square peg in a round hole. But it lessens every year."

She held his self-deprecating gaze. "Do you ever get better?"

"Yes." Travis looked fondly around the cabin. "The vets who get help and support do get better. The first year is always hell because you feel like you're landing in a field of cut glass on an alien planet. No matter what you try to do, or where you go, you're getting cut up and bleeding out. It might not be literal, but it's emotional and mental for all of us. And healing doesn't happen in a straight line, either. I'm sure you're experiencing a lot of ups and downs in those areas?"

"Yes," she sighed. "All the time. It never stops."

"I think if you get a fixed routine living in the caboose and having a low-stress job, it will help you stabilize pretty quickly."

She crossed her fingers. "I hope you're right."

He pushed back from the table, starting to pick up the dishes. "You look pretty tired. You can go to bed whenever you want. I usually stay up until ten or eleven."

It was nearly seven p.m. "Sometimes, I think you read a person's mind," she said, standing, picking up her own dishes and following him to the sink.

"No, just been there, done that." He took the dishes from her. "Why don't you go check out? There's a small flat-screen TV in your room if you'd like to watch it."

"No, I'm whipped. Eating all this food has made me super sleepy. What are your plans for tomorrow? And how can I help you?"

"Let's talk about that over French toast and bacon tomorrow morning whenever you wake up, okay?"

"That's a deal. Good night, Travis. And thank you for all you're doing to help me." Jesse wanted to throw her arms around the cowboy, but she resisted.

"Just passing it on. Good night, Jesse. I hope you have a deep, uninterrupted sleep tonight."

So, did she.

November 2

"WELL, WHAT DO you think?" Travis asked Jesse as they stood back the next afternoon, looking at their team handiwork to make the caboose livable for her. Her black hair shone with blue highlights beneath the new ceiling lamp that brought lots of light into the boxcar. They had worked tirelessly since seven that morning, after eating a big breakfast of French toast and bacon at Sue Conway's diner. It was now three p.m. Travis watched as she moved her fingers through her hair, pushing strands off her damp forehead. A hard, constant worker, it was he who had to call for a time out. They had moved in the new bed, an overstuffed chair that he had kept in the barn out back, and pale yellow curtains that Jesse chose to put up in the kitchen window. The other windows in the car were double-paned to keep cold from seeping through them. He liked her color choice of drape fabric for these: a pale lavender brocade with nearly invisible white flowers, reminding him of the meadow where the boxcar sat.

"I think it's a palace," Jesse said, tilting her head in his direction. She gestured to the overstuffed leather chair. "And I'm so glad you kept your grandparents' duplicate chair. It makes it look more like they had it when they lived here."

Earlier, they had stopped at the Hamilton hay and feed store. Even though it was November, Dorothy and Jim Hansen, the owners who were in their sixties, always had a display of potted flowers that they sold throughout the year. Dorothy had a green thumb and there was a wealth of buyers who wanted the red, pink and white geraniums she sold in clay pots. They were a hardy flower and provided greenery throughout the winter months, reminding all that spring and the thaw was coming. Travis saw Jesse go over to the plant stand and found out she loved flowers. He'd bought her two pots. She'd placed a pink one on the table and the other, a red one, on the wide kitchen window sill. It brought new life into the car. *A woman's touch*. Something that was sorely missing from his life.

"Well," he said, looking around, "I think we're done. You have a quiet generator outside, protected from the elements, that will provide you with all the electricity you want. And the propane tank is filled so you'll have heat for the car." Looking around, he said, "The only thing missing is a computer and internet for you. I'm going to call up the satellite company and get something out here for you. Probably in a week or two. That way, you'll be in touch with everyone and with the world when you want to be." Travis hoped that maybe, when she felt like it, she might reach out to her old team in Delta Force. He knew this would help Jesse even though she didn't look thrilled about being wired in with the world once again.

"And," she said, giving him a brief look of gratefulness, "I have wheels now."

"We don't need the other two trucks until mid-April, so it's yours."

"I'll pay you back for the groceries we bought earlier."

"Whenever you can," he said. "No rush."

"Tomorrow I start my dishwashing job."

"Nervous?"

"Yes. I don't want to disappoint Katie."

"Katie's a local, born here in Hamilton. She's twenty-six years old and created that popular café out of nothing. She won't be disappointed in you. Her brother, Gabe, is in the Army. He's two years older than her, and they're close. Both her parents were in the Army for twenty years, so she's a military brat and has a soft spot in her heart for vets like you."

"Which is why she probably hired me."

"Most likely, but Katie's got good people instincts, too, and I'm sure she spotted your quality and intelligence."

Grimacing, Jesse said, "My intelligence regarding missions has no crossover job description in the civilian world."

That was true. He could see she was worried, licking her lower lip, not connecting with his gaze like she usually did. "I know Katie will be glad you came to ask for a job."

Moving to the kitchen, Jesse touched the new coffee maker that Travis had bought for her from Cooper's Hardware Store. It was a priceless gift to her whether he knew it or not. "Katie said that if I ever wanted to work full time and learn how to become a barista, that she'd do it."

"The out-of-season help travels south out of the winter, and it's all on her shoulders. There's days when she does need help," Travis explained, picking up his hat from the table and settling it on his head. "Katie's place and Sue's diner are busy year 'round." He grinned a little. "We need our coffee and our breakfast."

"Is there anything I can do to pay you back sooner? Do you need some office help of any kind?"

He liked the idea of seeing more of Jesse. "Well, if you put it that way, yes. Sam hates computers and we have six file drawers full of clients that I'd like to put into our computer database. Are you interested?" He held his breath, hoping so. Delta Force operators were some of the most skilled and common-sensed people he knew. Jesse had that same kind of practical smarts from what he'd seen in the last two days. He saw her frown a bit, considering his offer.

"Could we settle on an hourly rate so that way I know what I need to pay you back for everything you've bought for me?" she asked, gesturing around the caboose. "And let me have the receipts so I know?" Because she had a feeling that Travis would let her completely write off everything if he had his way about it. She wouldn't let that happen. Being raised to earn her way through life, his generosity demanded that she do something equally important for him.

"Sure," he said. "What are your hours over at Katie's?"

"I'm working noon to five p.m. on Tuesday, Thursday and Friday."

"Okay, how about you come over and spend half a day on Monday and Wednesday at my office? Maybe 1300 to 1800?"

She held out her hand to him. "You have a deal."

"It's a long-term project," he warned. "We have over a thousand clients."

"Sounds doable. I'm not the fastest typist but I don't use my two index fingers, either."

He slid her hand into his, wanting to touch her, to feel the warmth of her flesh against his. Travis wasn't about to let on how drawn he was to her. Right now, as they shook and released one another's hands, he wanted to try and develop a friendship with Jesse. Lying awake for a long time last night with her under his roof, he relentlessly tried to figure out why she was growing important to him in a personal way. She had never given any signal that she was interested in him and Travis knew why: her symptoms were her focus. Or worse, maybe it was a one-way attraction. The first year he was home, he couldn't be around a lot of people, much less entertain getting involved in a relationship. Year two and three were brutal from the standpoint that he had to take over the family guide business since Sam could no longer run it as he had before. He had no time for any type of personal relationship. He was going to have to be very patient because he wanted to know her on a more personal level, wanted to know her without the veneer of the symptoms always distracting her. That was a tall order and he wasn't sure it could happen even if he wanted it too.

"If you need anything, call me." He pointed to her cell phone on the counter.

"I will."

Nodding he ambled toward the door. Travis found himself being overprotective of Jesse. As he opened the door and walked out on the platform, shutting it behind him, he laughed at himself. The day was growing cool now, the sun heading down in the west. Of all the people who could take care of themselves, it was her. She was combat trained and had reflexes that had been born of hard, constant training. Looking around, he saw a group of deer coming down to drink water from the river across the meadow. They halted, lifted their heads, their ears up, watching him for a moment. He moved around the boxcar and sauntered toward his truck at the end of it. The deer relaxed and continued their way to the bank of the river, deciding he was not a threat to them.

As he drove back to Hamilton, the protectiveness remained in him. Maybe he should give Jesse one of his grandfather's rifles to keep out here, just in case. About the only thing around would be grizzly, cougar and black bear, and the bears would be heading for hibernation soon enough, leaving just the cougars who hunted year 'round. He knew fishermen would sometimes walk the river and some would cross the area where Jesse was living. Rubbing his hand against his neck, he decided that whatever was between them was making him want to make sure she would be safe out there.

Parking the truck at his cabin, he turned off the engine and climbed out. The sky was a pale blue now, clear and the wind sharper and cutting. At this time of year, it would freeze every night in this area. As he walked to his cabin, he wondered how Jesse was doing. She had told him this morning after awakening that she'd had the best night's sleep ever. That made him feel good. He wanted to invite her to his house for another meal, wanted to put meat on her bones, but he worried that she might feel pressured by him. Not that she gave him that signal, but Travis wasn't willing to become a pest in her life. No, he was going to have to be patient. For once in his life, he didn't want to be, chaffing against the wisdom of going slow.

Getting inside, the cabin warm and inviting, Travis hung his hat on the nearby peg. Shucking out of his heavy denim jacket that had a liner in it to protect him from the cold, he thought about a dog for Jesse. A dog's bark was a warning in case someone, maybe a curious fisherman, came too near to the caboose. Hanging up his coat, he went to the kitchen sink and washed his hands with soap. They had moved a lot of furniture and worked together to set the brand new queen-sized bed up for her.

Looking around the cabin, it seemed more empty than usual. He finished drying his hands and hung the towel on a hook. Rolling up the sleeves of his red and black plaid cowboy shirt to his elbows, he decided to make a pot of spaghetti. That would last for two days. He wondered what Jesse was having for dinner tonight. Travis had his grandfather's old wooden radio. It had been repaired a number of times and he liked the instrumental FM elevator kind of music in the background. What kind of music did Jesse like? He made a mental note to ask her the next time he saw her.

The wall phone rang. Travis answered it. "Hello."

"Dammit! Where the hell are you?"

Sam's voice cut through his vulnerable moment. His hand tightened around the phone. "I've been out," Travis told him firmly, not going to let his own anger over his father's assault on him escalate the situation. "Do you need some help?"

"I've been trying to get you over at the shop and the cabin. It isn't like you to not answer your phone."

Holding on to his patience, the grate of his father's voice was like a rasp across his unprotected flesh. "You know I carry a cell phone on me, Sam. You could have called me on that and gotten a hold of me right away. Is this an emergency? What do you need?"

"I'm outta my pain pills!"

He shouldn't be. Travis frowned. "I saw you three days ago and checked the bottle. It was half full."

"Dammit! I was in pain. I took more. It didn't help!"

"I'll call the drugstore and get you another bottle and bring it over."

"Fine!"

The line went dead.

Sam had a habit of hanging up on him when angry. He dialed the pharmacy, wanting to make sure there was a refill on it. His father was old fashioned. Although Travis had gotten him a simple-to-use elder-friendly cell phone, Sam grew impatient with it as he slowly went over the instructions on how to use it. One day, about a week later when Travis went over after doing the laundry for him, he found the cell phone buried under a bunch of his father's t-shirts in one of the dresser drawers.

He shoved his personal hurt over his father's anger aside. Moments before he had felt incredibly happy and uplifted with the time he'd spent with Jesse. It was a helluva jolt to his gritty world when he allowed his imagination to dream of a possible future with Jesse. Gently, he put away his dream. Finding out that yes, his father had two refills left, the druggist would make up one and he could drive down and pick it up. His spaghetti dinner would have to wait. Besides, his stomach was knotting from Sam's unexpected call. Before the PTSD had nailed his ass, he had been able to separate his mental focus from his emotions. Operating at such a high level, it had become easy for him to suppress his emotions. Sam was the opposite of the dad he grew up with. A complete opposite.

A run-in with Sam like this eviscerated him because he wasn't expecting it. No longer was he the tough, implacable mission specialist. All of that was eaten away over time and years of operations by the encroaching symptoms. Travis knew he was vulnerable to such things and was glad he had the life he had here in Hamilton. It was about nature, the wide outdoors, serenity and calm. It had been and continued to be healing balm for his soul, putting him back together again over time.

Sam was like a tornado popping up in his life and Travis could never predict when his pain-stricken father would suddenly rear up and attack him verbally. He threw on his hat, shrugged back into his heavy winter denim coat, grabbed the keys to the truck and left. In the truck, on the way to the drugstore near Sue's diner, Travis ached to be in Jesse's quiet company. For whatever reason, she was calming to him, to his symptoms. Right now, he wished he was at his grandparents' boxcar with Jesse and not having to go visit his upset and agitated father instead.

THE CABOOSE FELT like a loving safety net when Jesse arrived back on Tuesday evening. She'd just finished her first day at Katie's Koffee Bean, learning the ins and outs of how an industrial dishwasher worked. Jesse was thankful that Katie, who had dancing green eyes, was patient with her. That was always a plus. She mounted the steps, the old, curled ones replaced by Travis the day before. There was an old wool blanket that she'd hung over the rusty rail out in the back to dry. She placed her hand on top of it, feeling that it was still slightly damp. The weather had been perfect all day long and there was no sign of rain or snow tonight, so she decided to leave it out to dry completely overnight.

Emotionally whipped from the stress of wanting to please Katie and show her that she had hired the right person, Jesse shucked out of her Army jacket and hung it across the back of one of the kitchen chairs. To her surprise, she saw on the kitchen counter, a big brown grocery bag. The air smelled good. Frowning, she turned and went over to it. There was a note next to it:

Jesse, I figured your first day at work would be pretty draining. Sue Conway always has a Tuesday special of roast beef, mashed potatoes, carrots and the best gravy in Montana. See you tomorrow at 1300. Travis.

She peeked into the bag and inhaled deeply. It smelled wonderful! She didn't have to cook tonight. Her heart warmed to Travis and his thoughtful understanding of how she'd take the first day of work. More and more, he was nesting into her world and she didn't mind it at all because they already had a built-in trust with one another forged from their mutual experience in the heat of combat. Her mouth watered as she pulled the large paper to-go box out of the sack. When she opened it, there was enough there for two lumberjacks! Laughing a little, Jesse knew she'd put at least half of it in the refrigerator for tomorrow night's meal.

The caboose was warm and the curtains drawn so everything felt safe to her. After eating she took a hot shower and climbed into a lavender flannel nightgown. There was no dishwasher but she didn't mind, enjoying the warm suds on her hands as she cleaned up her dinner plate and flatware. It was silent in the place and she missed soft, non-intrusive instrumental music most of all. The bed looked inviting and she turned out the lights, heading for it, grateful to have a mattress, sheets and blankets. It was far better than her pup tent.

November 3

THE METAL TAG on her leather collar said "Freya" with an AKC number below it. The black and white Border Collie lay deep in the woods of Montana, five new pups hungrily suckling her. The leather collar she wore had partly burned, the leather twisted. As she lay there in the early morning hours, the cold seeped around her chosen area to whelp her pups: an ancient, tall pine tree that had finally given up, fallen from natural causes, the radius of roots exposed to the world. It was there that Freya dug down between the exposed roots and made a soft soil cradle, filled with dried pine needles, as her birthing spot. She was exhausted but remained alert, knowing she was in bobcat, fox, grizzly and cougar country. The smell of blood and birthing matter would draw the attention of any predator if they were in the area.

As her lids closed over her blue eyes, the terrible crash of sixty-five days ago flashed before her once again. Her owner, Stella, was driving her back to Billings, Montana after breeding her to another champion Border Collie in Idaho Falls, Idaho. It was dusk, and Freya was in her aluminum wire dog crate in the rear of the SUV when something happened to Stella on the two-lane highway. Her mistress suddenly slumped over the wheel, the SUV veering into the path of an oncoming eighteen-wheeler truck speeding along at sixty-five miles an hour.

Everything suddenly upended. Freya was slammed against her cage, the rear door popping open. The SUV crunched into the grill of the truck. Fire erupted from an explosion, and the SUV went airborne. Freya yelped as the vehicle hit the shoulder of the road and then flipped end over end, tumbling down a steep bank. The rear window shattered and popped out.

The next thing Freya knew was that she was trapped as the vehicle groaned to a rest at the bottom of the slope. Fire tongues licked at where she was trapped. Her fur became singed and her collar blackened. Yelping, the pain of the fire consuming the rear of the vehicle, Freya frantically looked for escape. Slamming her body against the cage door, it yawned open.

The window! Without thinking, the dog leaped through it, her hair on fire across her back. She slammed to the ground, rolling several times. It put the fire out on the hair across her shoulders. The smell of singed flesh and the acrid odor of her burned leather collar surrounded her. She stumbled to her feet, disoriented and scared. Looking back at the SUV, crumpled completely in the front, the fire blazing within it, she ran and ran as far as she could get away from that crackling, popping vehicle. As she sped down to a grove of trees, racing as fast as she could, another massive explosion rocked and thundered through the area behind her.

The pressure wave from it tossed Freya into the wet, long grass. It slammed her into the ground, knocking her semi-conscious. She yelped again, her body twisting and tumbling until the grass finally halted her forward movement. Frightened, she jerked a look back, seeing a huge plume of black smoke rising in a deadly column, the SUV no longer visible. Shaking her head, she got to her feet. She had to escape! The smell burned her sensitive nostrils as she lunged forward, moving deeper into the forest, sensing that she would have some kind of safety away from this fire monster who was belching and exploding behind her. She had cut her right paw on sharpened glass as she'd leaped out of the SUV. It left a trail of blood, but she never felt the pain of her injured paw or the second-degree burns across her neck and shoulders because of the adrenaline anesthetizing her bruised body.

All Freya wanted to do was survive.

CHAPTER 4

November 3

FREYA SLEPT OFF and on, her black ears moving up like hairy triangles when she heard a noise that might mean danger. Her pups were now sleeping. Something niggled at her well-honed survival instincts. She was a herding dog by breed and nature—one of the most intelligent dogs on Earth—and she felt something, a predator, creeping around in the darkness of the forest, following the scent of blood and afterbirth that was still lingering in the air.

She had to move her pups.

Now.

Getting up, she oriented herself. Off to the west she sensed an opening, a way to escape. The smell of water was in the air, as well. She was dying of thirst, not having drank any water in the last twenty-four hours. Deep in the woods, there was only pine trees, downed branches and drying pine needles. At least it wasn't raining or snowing.

She turned, getting her internal bearings, knowing the wind direction and wanting to move away from it, to get upwind of it if possible. The tops of the pines sang with strong winds that came and went. *What to do?*

Her guidance told her to take her pups, one at a time, west. She sensed safety there. Picking up the first little black and white charge gently in her mouth, she turned and pawed dried pine needles over the rest of her brood, hoping to keep them from a predator's eyes that could see through this darkness.

Running, weaving in and around the thousands of trees, she had no idea of how far she'd gone. Suddenly, the tree line disappeared and she halted, breathing hard, the pup hanging in her mouth. There to her left was a wide river, the water tempting her. In front of her was a huge, oval meadow, with more woods on the other side of it.

Her gaze settled on a red-colored box house that sat at the edge of the meadow. Because she was raised by humans, it was natural for Freya to study the darkened, rectangular house. It looked different from the homes in Billings where she had lived with her mistress. This one was long and narrow, and not very large. Spotting a blanket hanging on a metal railing on the rear of it, she trotted quickly toward it, sensing it could mean safety for her pups.

Taking the wooden stairs, she looked to her left. There was a curtain over the window but it was too high and she couldn't see into it. She smelled a female human in there, however. Humans meant protection to her. Gently setting her pup near the door, she turned, sniffing the green wool blanket hanging over the rail. She turned, allowing her pup to lay on the wooden platform. Moving to the other side, she leaped up on her hind legs, grabbing an edge of the cloth with her teeth and with her downward weight, hauled it off the rail. The blanket fell into a large, jumbled heap in front of her. It was large, lumpy and could be warm enough for her and her pups. Using her paws, she opened it up.

Going over to her pup, she picked it up and nosed it deep into the warm folds of the blanket.

In an instant, she leaped off the side of the platform, making her way to the bank of the river, eagerly lapping up a lot of water. Sated, she sped back into the woods to retrieve her next pup.

Each time Freya returned for one of her pups, the hackles on her burned fur along her shoulders raised in alarm. There *was* a predator nearby and it was following the scent of the birthing matter. Could she get all five of her pups out of the hidey hole in time?

It was near dawn, the gray ribbon along the eastern horizon barely appearing as Freya brought her fifth and last pup into that woolen blanket. The pups were whining in little squeaks, their eyes closed for at least seven to ten days. They pawed around, over the top of one another, hunting for their mother.

Freya ran back to the river and took another load of water into her heaving body. She was panting heavily, exhausted by the birth and having to run for miles back and forth to keep her pups from whatever predator was closing in on them. She ducked beneath one part of the blanket and with her long nose, pushed the material here and there until her back was against the metal rails, the blanket between her and them. Settling down, she nosed each pup, bringing them to suckle the milk they were looking for.

Always alert, laying back, eyes open, ear pricked, Freya felt the warmth of the blanket around herself. There was only one opening, which was right in front of her and the door to this odd-shaped home. The scent of the woman was on the fabric as well, and Freya felt some of her anxiety dissolve. Her mistress had been a woman, had loved her affectionately, and Freya had loved her. The last sixty-five days, wandering through the mountains, trying to find food, her belly growing larger and larger with the pups she carried, was her only focus. She did not have time to grieve over the loss of her human. The crash sometimes jolted her out of a deep sleep, replaying the fire and explosion in front of her. It always left Freya confused and lost. The home she'd had before was wonderful. She'd been raised with love, care and patience. She'd never been a dog of the land, having a rich green lawn, an acre in size, to run and play upon. Her mistress had driven her around the United States, showing her at major dog shows. Freya liked the activity, loved the travel and loved the excitement of the dog shows. She always made new doggie friends.

Most of all, she loved the contests where she had to herd a group of sheep from one place to another. Stella would give her signals and she'd race around, nipping at the heels of slower sheep, and get them to go where her mistress wanted them to go. She won many championships for her efforts and her human was happy, too—so was she.

Until the crash.

Closing her eyes, fatigue allowed her to sleep while her puppies suckled. Her herd dog brain told her she was safe with humans and houses. But that didn't stop a predator from finding her, either. She was still leaking fluids from the whelping, and any one of them could follow that trail and find her. It was only a matter of time. Her senses told her the human inside this house would protect her. But how was she to let the woman know she was here and needed her help?

November 4

THE GRAYNESS IN the caboose woke Jesse up. She felt drugged with such a deep, healing sleep. The mattress was firm, the pillow soft, and she was warm and cozy, her nose not numb from the cold. She felt delicious. Barely opening her eyes, she saw the clock on the wall read five-thirty a.m. It had been a dreamless sleep, and Jesse was grateful for that, having been awakened so many times in the past by nightmares and flashbacks.

Slowly, she opened her eyes and looked around. *Home.* She had a home. A real one, thanks to Travis and his ongoing generosity. And she loved this little boxcar as never before. It brought tears to her eyes momentarily because human kindness didn't always surface in those months she'd wandered lost and without purpose. Now, her life was starting to come into focus once more. She had two jobs. She'd successfully handled the first day of dishwashing at the Koffee Bean. This afternoon, she would see Travis, which made her feel excited, and she would learn to transfer fishermen's names to a database at the office. None of this was beyond her intelligence. But it looked easy and low stress, which she needed more than anything else. It had been a brutal downhill fall from grace, from the life she'd known in the military.

But now, Travis was helping her like the guardian angel she saw him as to get her back on her own two feet. Just having a job, a way to pay for food and rent, meant everything to her. She sat up, the covers falling away, stretching her arms above her head, yawning.

There was a strange noise outside her bedroom, the door partially cracked open. Frowning, Jesse honed in on it.

It sounded like scratching. Was it a mouse in the caboose? In her room? Getting up, she turned on the light, looking around the bed and in the small clothes closet.

Nothing.

Frowning, she looked out into the gloom, all the curtains shut, the warmth wonderful to her bare feet as she went to the bathroom. She'd put her clothes she was going to wear in there, along with her tennis shoes. A quick, hot shower would wake her up. And then, she'd make a cup of delicious, hot coffee. Her world was looking up. And it filled Jesse with hope as she shut the door to the bathroom.

Emerging half an hour later, it was six a.m. and there was light filtering into the caboose from the coming dawn. She had washed her hair, combed it into place, dressed and walked out into the main area of the caboose, opening the curtains as she went. The sky was wide and a pale blue above the meadow. Hoping to spot some deer coming to the river, she glanced out at the yellowed grass, seeing nothing moving. The place was quiet this morning.

As she opened the curtains toward the tree line, she froze.

There, just inside it was a huge cougar standing, looking toward the caboose. Her skin crawled with danger.

There was frantic scratching at the back door.

Frowning, Jesse took one last look at the cat who remained motionless, just watching the caboose. Hurrying to the back door, she pulled the curtain back. Her eyes widened in surprise. A black dog with a white blaze, with brown eyebrows above her blue eyes, was frantically pawing at the door, up on her hind legs.

Good grief! What was going on? Jesse opened the door.

The dog whined and sat, thumping her tail, looking up at her.

Jesse leaned down, "It's all right," she crooned, petting the dog's head. Her gaze riveted on the cougar who stood like a statue, watching them through amber eyes. The cat was less than three-hundred yards from where she stood with the dog.

The dog whined, turning, pawing into the blanket that had fallen off the rail sometime during the night.

"Get inside," she told the dog, pointing toward the opened door. Why was she anxiously digging at the old wool blanket? It made no sense to Jesse.

The dog whined louder, digging harder, refusing to move into the caboose. Part of the corner flew back from her efforts.

Jesse gasped. There were five newly born black and white pups!

Rapidly, she put it together. Leaning down, she gathered the huge, bulky blanket between her arms, swiftly carrying it inside the caboose.

The mother followed.

After laying the blanket near the table on one side of the home, Jesse hurried to the back door, slamming it shut and locking it. Her heart was beginning a slow beat as she turned, grabbing her cell phone off the kitchen counter. Leaning down, she saw the cougar move—toward the boxcar.

Damn!

Fingers trembling, she punched in Travis's phone number.

It rang three times before he answered.

"Yeah?"

"It's Jesse. Travis, I need help. I found a mother dog with puppies on the rear of the caboose and a cougar is following them. I've got the dog and pups inside with me. I've locked the door. The cat is moving our way. Is there a pistol or gun in this place?" She heard his slurred, drowsy answer, feeling bad that she had awakened him.

"There's no weapon," he grunted. "Stay there. I'll be out in ten minutes. I'll have a rifle with me. Stay away from the windows. Do you hear me?"

"Yes," she answered, hearing the sleep torn from him.

The phone clicked dead.

Putting the cell phone on the counter, she saw the cougar walking toward the rear of the caboose. The cat had probably been following the mother. Turning, she saw the dog standing in the center of the boxcar, a low growl in her throat, her hackles, or what was left of them, were standing straight up on her shoulders and all the way down her spine. The pups were okay, nestled in the warmth of the blanket, sleeping.

Jerking open one drawer, Jesse gripped a huge butcher knife. It was all she had. Would the cat attack? Try to break a window and get in? Her mind skipped through many scenarios. She didn't know the habits of a cougar except that this one had followed the dog here, to her home.

The dog's growl increased, her body stiffening.

Jesse lost sight of the cougar. Where was it?

Panic struck her. She felt as if she were back in combat. Her hand tightened around the wooden handle of the ten-inch butcher knife. She walked up to where the dog was at, her gaze riveting to the rear window.

Suddenly, the cat's face appeared in the window, it's huge paws on either side of it, amber eyes looking in—at them.

Gulping, Jesse felt the power of the cat's intense focus.

The dog leaped into action, throwing herself at the back door, trying to attack the cougar on the other side of it. Her barks were sharp, ear splitting and her growl deep and filled with hatred.

The cougar dropped back down on all fours, disappearing from the window.

Jesse blinked. What could she do?

Nothing. Oh, God...

The dog barked furiously, throwing herself again and again at the back door, the hair all along her neck and back standing straight up. The barks and growls were savage.

Jesse forced herself to walk to the rear door. Was the cougar still on the platform? Waiting? Figuring out how to get into the caboose? She swiftly turned, gaze snapping from one window to another. The easiest way to get in was through this back door. The window was too small for the cat to actually get in through it, but he could cause a lot of problems for her, the dog and the pups.

The dog whined, spun around, racing toward the window where the pups were in the blanket.

Jesse saw the cougar about ten feet away, in the meadow, studying the window.

This was a window the cat *could* get through. Her mind moved swiftly, looking at it more closely. It was a single-paned window. Yesterday, Travis and she had discussed replacing them with double-paned windows to keep the heat in the boxcar.

This cat looked to weigh near a hundred pounds, well-fed from what she could tell.

The dog was barking frantically, up on her hind legs, pawing at the frame of that window.

Where was Travis? Had ten minutes passed? Jesse knew from being in combat before that everything slowed down like slow motion frames in a movie. And it felt like a tunnel to her as she watched the cat twitch its tail, looking right and left, and then centering its full attention once more on the window. The caboose echoed with the sharp barks and growls of the mother, who was frantic to protect her brood. So was Jesse.

She pulled a chair from the table away from the window, standing before it. Maybe if she appeared, the cat would be afraid of seeing a human in it. At the same time, she knew the cat could hear the mother dog barking at him. And she knew instinctively that the cat understood the five puppies, a nice meal for him, were inside this boxcar.

The dog suddenly turned, her ears up, looking toward the bedroom.

Was Travis here?

Jesse looked toward the bedroom window.

The cougar suddenly took off, running hard out of the meadow, disappearing from her sight, aiming itself for the tree line.

It had to be Travis!

She ran into the bedroom, pulling back the curtain.

There he was! He was climbing out of the truck, rifle in hand, his gaze on the cougar who must have run into the woods and disappeared.

Heart pounding, Jesse ran to the back door and unlocked it. She first made sure there was no cat around before opening it. As Travis took the stairs, she saw the hardness in his expression, the Delta Force operator, not the man she'd met before.

"He's gone," Travis said as she opened the door. "Ran into the woods."

Gulping, she gave a nod.

The dog came up beside her, panting heavily, wagging her tail at Travis.

He looked at Jesse. "You okay?"

"A little shaken, but yes. Come in?" She turned and put the butcher knife away in the drawer.

The dog trotted over to her puppies, pawing at the blanket. Jesse went over and opened it up so she could be with them.

Travis shut the door, put the safety on the rifle and set it in the corner. He took off his Stetson, staring at the dog and pups. "Helluva morning?" he asked her, grinning sourly.

"Yeah, just a little." Jesse told him about the cat rising up on its hind legs to stare in the rear door window. Travis had not shaven, the darkness giving his face a more dangerous look, but he was also an operator and she could feel him trying to ramp down just as she was trying to do, from the crisis.

Travis moved to the window at the kitchen, staring hard at the tree line. "Don't see him. He's probably laid down, hiding, and going to wait you out."

Shivering, Jesse said, "I never expected something like this, Travis."

He straightened and eyed the dog. "Do you know this dog?"

"No, never saw her before." She wiped her damp hands down her jeans and went over to where Freya lay suckling her pups, still panting. "There's a dog collar on her. Maybe she's lost?" She knelt down, crooning to the dog.

"People sometimes drop animals off here because it's so out of the way," Travis muttered unhappily, walking up to where Jesse knelt, eyeing the wriggling brood of puppies.

Turning the darkened, somewhat twisted leather collar, Jesse said, "There's the name Freya on it, and a number. Gosh, the collar is partially burned, Travis." She gently eased it off the dog's head, handing it to him. What do you think?"

"Look at her neck and shoulder," he said. "Looks like she lost a lot of hair in that area." Taking the collar, he looked closely at it. "I think that's an AKC number on it. Wouldn't be surprised if the dog has an identifier chip in her shoulder with a lot more intel. She looks pretty thin."

"Freya?" Jesse said, petting her gently.

Instantly the dog perked up her ears, looking up at her with adoration.

"That's her name," she said. Taking her fingers, she gently moved them along the animal's neck and back where it was almost hairless. "Travis? This looks burned." She leaned down, sniffing it. "Yes, it's been burned off her. What happened to her?" She slid her hand gently across Freya's broad black and white skull.

"Dunno, but maybe later we can find out." He scowled and studied the tree line outside the boxcar. "I was thinking of giving you Hiram's 30.06 last night. I guess I was picking up that you might need it out here."

"Believe me, I wanted one," she muttered, rising. "We need to get her some food to eat. I have nothing here for her."

Travis turned, studying them. "For now, let's move all of you into my home." He pointed toward the tree line. "That cat knows Freya and her pups are in here. It will wait you out. You're not safe here for now, Jesse. You don't know how long the cat will hang around, or where it's hiding. It will see you before you see it. The minute Freya goes outside to do her business, he could attack her. And then what?" He pointed to the puppies.

"Damn," she said, nodding. "You're right. Will the cat ever leave?"

"Probably when the snow sets in, which will be another two weeks. This is probably either its territory and he's got a lair nearby. But he'll always be hunting in this area."

"I don't want to kill him," she said more to herself than him. "Not unless I have too."

"Freya belongs to someone. I want you to come and stay with me at least for a couple of days until we can sort this out. I can take her over to our local vet and she'll have a device to check and see if she has a chip in her neck or not. We should be able to contact the owner that way."

"Good idea." Jesse's voice dropped. "She's so pretty and her pups are just adorable."

Travis chuckled. "Yeah, nice looking for sure. But if something happened to the owner, Freya already has a home. And I'm sure the owner would be looking for her. Those are Border Collie pups she had, so something tells me she was bred to her own kind for a reason."

Jesse couldn't disagree. "Okay," she said, sighing, looking around at her wonderfully warm, snuggling home. "I hate to leave the caboose, but you're right."

"Have you had coffee yet?"

"No," she said, looking longingly at the coffee pot.

"Let me give Freya a dish of water she can lap from. You make your coffee and I'll help you pack your stuff."

Travis was right. "Crazy as it sounds, I'm already attached to Freya. You should have seen her when the cougar was at the back door. She was literally throwing her body at the door. I've never heard a dog snarl and growl like she was doing."

"Border Collies are herding dogs, protectors of the flock," Travis told her, handing her the coffee pot. "Their instincts are to attack a predator. They're not afraid if it's a bear twenty times its size or not, they'll go after it to defend the lives of the herd. In this case, she was protecting her pups and you. They're bred to do that."

"Well, she was so courageous, Travis. It stunned me the ferocity in that body of hers. Her lips were drawn back and her white teeth are sharp. I was afraid she'd try to break that window to get at the cougar."

Chuckling, Travis pulled the coffee from the cabinet, handing it to her. "I have a friend in town who has a Border Collie, and he's told me some of the fights his dog has gotten into from time to time. Jacob is about eighty, and he and his dog, Sol, are always fishing the Bitterroot River. There've been times over the past five years, especially in the spring, when the grizzly were coming out of hibernation and smelling Jacob's creel filled with trout. His dog Sol would attack them and chase them off. A Border Collie will go up against any predator. Doesn't matter the size, they're absolutely fearless when their protection genes get triggered."

"I almost find myself hoping that I can keep her. I know that isn't right because someone else loves Freya, too."

"She's prettily marked," he agreed. "And those pups are too."

Plugging the pot in, Jesse turned, glad to have Travis in the boxcar with her. Just his size, never mind the rifle he brought with him, made her feel safe. "I'm sorry I kicked you out of sleep this morning."

Shrugging, Travis said, "It was for a good cause. While the coffee's perking, let's get that luggage off the top shelf of your bedroom closet. You need to pack some clothes before we leave."

"You're right." She shook her head. "I woke up this morning thinking how my life was going to quiet down now. I have two jobs. I can pay my rent and buy groceries. And by the way? Thank you for that grocery sack filled with supper for me last night."

"You're welcome. And then this happened. Well, welcome to Hamilton, Montana. This is another side of it you probably would not have seen as a tourist," he teased, his smile warm.

The rest of her anxiety dissolved beneath his low, warm voice and the tender look he shared with her. "You're right."

"Still want to stay in Hamilton?"

It was her turn to grin. She halted at the door to the bedroom. "You couldn't chase me away."

CHAPTER 5

November 4

J ESSE FELT GOOD that Freya took to the ride to Travis's cabin. Travis had put her and the pups in the super-cab truck he'd driven to the boxcar. She was happy to have her pups in that old wool blanket placed on the back seat. What bothered Jesse the most was Travis saying he was going to make a call to Fish and Game because the cougar's behavior was way out of normal bounds. It did not seem to be frightened of humans. She'd seen his scowl deepen when she told him how the cat had risen up on his hind legs, paws on either side of the caboose door window, looking in on them. Something wasn't right.

Once at the home, Freya leaped out of the truck, expectantly waiting for Travis to carry her pups inside. She followed him after going for a pee nearby, rushing inside the opened door to meet Jesse, wagging her tail, and looking adoringly up at her once again.

Smiling, Jesse leaned over, gently patting her head.

Inside, Travis was all business, carefully carrying the pups in the blanket.

Freya raced ahead, galloping across the living room and down the hall to Jesse's bedroom. She skidded to a halt on the shining wooden floor, turned and looked expectantly up at Travis as he followed her.

"Guess she wants her litter in your bedroom," he said, tossing Jesse a glance to the right. "You okay with that?"

"Sure."

"Good." He nudged the door fully open with the toe of his boot.

Laughing, Jesse said, "I think her owner was a woman."

"I do too." Travis watched the Border Collie snoop quickly around the large, rectangular room. She went to the darkest corner, away from the door and window, on the opposite side of the bed. "She's wanting a cave-like environment," he said, carrying the litter over to the corner where she stood, giving him a pleading look.

"She's probably still scared that cougar is going to come after us again,"

Jesse said, helping to open up the blanket once he'd placed it on the floor. Tucking it in here and there so that it looked a bit like an open maw of a cave, Jesse was satisfied. Inside, the pups slept in a pile, oblivious to the world and what was going on around them.

But Freya wasn't. She immediately nosed her way inside the rear of the blanket and began cleaning up and licking each of her babies, doing her motherly duties.

Jesse smiled as Travis stood at the end of the bed, watching them. "Those puppies are so cute. Just endearing."

"They are," he agreed. "I'm going to go over to the office. My father's dog, Cyrus, has a huge, comfy dog bed he uses, and there's also some kibble over there. I'll pick up the big dog bowl, too. We need to get her something to eat. Has she eaten since you brought her into the caboose?"

"No," she said, worried. "I'll go get her a bowl of water from the kitchen in the meantime."

"I'm also going to call Joe Varner. He's with Fish and Game. And I'll get Emily Hardy, our vet, over here to check Freya and her puppies out, so be expecting a visitor."

She reached out and briefly touched the coat sleeve. "You've saved their lives."

"No, you did." He caught her hand and gave it a squeeze. "I'll be in touch. You just stay here and keep Freya company."

His hand was warm, dry and roughened. Jesse tried not to enjoy the contact as much as she did. Following him out, they left the bedroom door open so that Freya could come and go as she pleased. "I'm glad we're not out there at the boxcar right now. That cougar scared me," Jesse admitted.

"I was scared for all of you," he said, sliding her a glance. "How are *you* doing after this attack?"

"A lot of my old combat ways of doing things resurfaced. Muscle memory. I was clear headed, looking for any kind of weapon I could find to protect us. I had a sense that the cat would come up on the platform, and he did."

"That's crazy stuff," he muttered, halting at the front door. "I'll be back in just a bit. Just take it easy, okay? You'll crash after that adrenaline stops running through you."

"You're right."

"I'll be back soon."

Those words were solace to Jesse. She got busy after Travis left, finding a large aluminum bowl, filling it with water and setting it near the puppy brood in her bedroom. Freya was feeding her pups, eyed the water appreciatively and gave, what Jesse thought, was a grateful look. She was falling hard for this courageous mother. She'd never seen any dog throw herself bodily against the door to attack a cougar who stood on the other side of it. Shaken more than she wanted to admit, Jesse got busy in the kitchen making up a batch of scrambled eggs for Freya.

Travis returned with a huge, red flannel dog bed, large enough for Freya and her litter and she helped him carry it into the darkened corner of her bedroom. Freya was up, eagerly lapping water from the bowl when they brought it into her. Travis arranged it such that the familiar blanket was spread across it. She was fine with him doing that and Jesse gently removed the puppies, covering the doggy bed and then placing her puppies on it. Immediately, Freya went back to it, laying down on her side, all her pups making little grunting and snuffling sounds as they blindly headed right for the milk.

"I got the kibble," he told her. "I'll bring it in. The vet, Emily Hardy, is on her way over here. I also talked to Joe at Fish and Game. He's going right now to check things out around the caboose."

"Is he going to kill that cougar?"

"I don't know. No one knows the wildlife in our region like Joe does. He said all things being equal, the cat behaved oddly and he's concerned that it might have rabies. He's going to come here and see us when he gets done with his investigation. And until he's made a determination, you, Freya and the pups are to stay here in town with me."

"I can do that," she assured him. "Let me get Freya fed. I'm sure she's starving. I cooked up scrambled eggs for her." She pointed to the skillet sitting off to the side of the stove to cool.

"Great idea," Travis congratulated her. "Let me get that kibble and food bowl."

Jesse had never felt better. Being able to help and support Freya meant everything to her. It brought back so many memories of her childhood with her best friend, Tag, a yellow lab. Soon enough, Travis arrived with the sack of kibble, placing it on the counter. She quickly put two cups into the bowl and mixed it with the freshly cooked, but cooled, scrambled eggs.

Freya leaped up when Jesse placed the bowl of food next to her water. She stood back, watching the dog gulp and swallow until it was all gone. She licked her lips with her pink tongue and then trotted out to the kitchen door to be let outside.

Laughing to herself, Jesse thought that Freya was training them up. She opened the door and followed her out into the cool morning air. Freya had found a corner of the lawn near the driveway to do her business. As soon as she was done, she ran inside, straight to her pups. She liked the dog's high intelligence and it made her feel happy inside to be keeping her and the pups safe.

About twenty minutes later, there was a knock at the door. Travis answered it because he was closer. It was Emily Hardy. Jesse instantly liked the woman—she was tall, lean and wearing jeans and a green and black checked flannel shirt beneath a purple nylon down coat that fell around her hips. Travis introduced them, carrying Emily's vet bag for her and shutting the door behind them.

"Wow," Emily said, shaking Jesse's hand, "word gets around Hamilton fast! You and Freya faced down a cougar at the caboose door. How are you doing, Jesse?'

Liking the woman's low, husky voice and her care, she smiled. "I'm fine. Freya and her pups are in my bedroom."

"Lead the way. Travis, by any chance do you have some coffee around?"

He chuckled. "Yeah, I'll make us a pot. You two ladies go see the dog and pups. I'll bring you in some mugs, later."

"Remember, I like it sweet and blond, Travis." She tossed a smile over her shoulder, following Jesse across the room.

"Got it," he laughed. "Go have fun with our new furry friends."

JESSE WATCHED AS Emily gently and thoroughly examined Freya and then carefully checked each of her sleeping pups, writing down notes as she went. Jesse felt like the dog was in good hands. She liked Emily's natural warmth and maternal way of working with Freya, who looked absolutely happy to have another woman around her.

"Okay," Emily said, handing her a piece of paper. "Here's the chip info that Freya carries. There's a phone number. Can you call it for us and see what you find out?"

Travis stepped in with two steaming cups of coffee in hand. "How's it going?"

"Fine," Jesse said, sliding off the bed, paper in hand. "Emily found a chip in Freya's neck. I'm going to call the number and see what I can find out, maybe I'll be able to contact her owner."

"Good," he said, handing her the coffee cup as she headed for the hall. "I'll stay here with Emily and keep her company." Leaning over, he handed the vet the other cup of coffee.

"You're a life-saver, Travis. Thank you."

Glancing around, he saw Jesse disappear down the hall. "So, how is Freya?"

"She's about fifteen pounds underweight. I'm surprised she was able to continue to carry these five pups in this kind of condition. She's been on her own for a while." Emily was on her knees next to the doggy bed and barely touched the short-haired area around the top of Freya's neck and shoulders. "She's got second-degree burn scars here and here. It's as if she was in a fire or something, and got burned. Even her coat hair hasn't completely come back to that area. I hope Jesse can shed some light on this with that phone call."

"And she's healed now?"

"Yes, but I'm going to leave some wonderful calendula ointment with you, which will soften that scar tissue and help her overall." She pulled a jar out of her black leather bag and handed it to him.

"And the pups?"

"All fine. Smaller than usual, but with Mom being fifteen pounds under weight, they aren't going to grow to normal size during gestation, either."

"So? They'll all be stunted in growth? Never be as large as other Border Collies?"

Wrinkling her nose, Emily said, "Well, not necessarily. You're feeding her now, and I want to leave some bottles of vitamins for her that you can drop into her kibble each day. Those vitamins and minerals will get into her milk and transfer to the puppies. They were just born, maybe two days earlier, so they have a chance to be full size if they stay with you and Jesse and get fed properly."

Nodding, he said, "I used to be alone and now I have two women under my roof, not to mention, five puppies." He grinned over at her.

Laughing, Emily tucked her stethoscope away in her bag and peeled off her latex gloves, dropping them into a bag and snapping it shut. "I like Jesse a lot. I talked to Katie yesterday and she raved about her, about how hard she worked and how well she did her job at the coffee shop. I think Jesse is a definite fit for our town." She tilted her head. "I heard through the grapevine that you're sprucing up Hiram's caboose. Is that true?"

"Yep," he murmured, watching Freya close her eyes and go to sleep, her pups' tummies filled with milk once again. "Come on, let's go out in the living room. We can talk there and leave the dog in peace. She's had a helluva morning."

"Isn't that the truth?" Emily gathered up her bag and stood. "That coffee was good, Travis. Can I get a second cup?" She looked at the watch on her wrist. "I've got to be in surgery in an hour. Got three of them lined up this morning at my clinic."

"Come on," he coaxed, standing to one side, motioning her out the door. "We'll get you primed with caffeine and you'll be fine for the day."

He saw Jesse get off the wall phone in the kitchen as they approached her. The look on her face made him frown. Something was up.

"Find out anything?" Emily called, sitting on the couch, medical bag at her feet.

Jesse glanced over at Travis, who stood nearby. "Yes. Plenty." She brought over the notes she'd jotted down. "Freya is a working dog champion on the national AKC show circuit. Her owner, Stella Caldwell, was bringing her back from being bred to a champion Border Collie in Idaho, when there was an auto wreck. Mrs. Caldwell was killed. At the autopsy, they found she'd had a stroke at the wheel and careened into an eighteen-wheeler truck coming the other way." Shaking her head, her voice lowered. "The firefighters were called and they put the fire out. They saw the charred remains of a dog crate in the back of the totaled SUV but no dog. The person I spoke to was the executor of Mrs. Caldwell's estate in Billings, Montana. She has no living relatives left. In her will, she asked that Freya get a good home."

"Wow," Emily said, taking the cup of coffee from Travis. "The burn scars on Freya's neck must have occurred at the time of the crash."

Jesse sat down on the couch, worried. "You're right."

"I gave Travis some ointment to put on the scars. They should heal fine and she should get all her hair back in that area. He can fill you in on the rest of what I told him."

"Good," Jesse said.

"What did the executor say about you finding her?" Emily pressed.

"She asked if we wanted to keep Freya or not. She said that there are several other breeders who would like to have her, too." Jesse looked up at Travis who was listening intently.

"How do you feel about that?" Travis asked Jesse.

"I'd love to keep her and the pups. I've been missing a dog in my life. I don't mind taking care of her and the pups at the boxcar."

"Well," Emily murmured, "those pups are probably worth an awful lot of money since she's an AKC working dog champion."

Grimacing, Jesse looked at both of them. "I have this crazy idea that maybe, if Travis is okay with it, I could keep Freya after her pups are weaned. Maybe five people in Hamilton would like them? Give them a real life outside being on a dog show circuit? What do you think, Travis?"

He smiled briefly. "I like the idea. Freya's been through enough. Let's give her a dog's life with someone who wants her to enjoy her freedom, not be stuck in a crate, driving from state to state to compete for trophies and ribbons."

There was a knock at the door.

Travis turned. "I'll get it."

Relief surged through Jesse. She would get to keep Freya! That meant so much to her and she didn't know why. Maybe it was a piece of home, a distant, wonderful memory of her growing up years with Tag. Right now, at her stage of recovery and with her symptoms, Freya and her puppies were a healthy distraction for her.

"Hey," Emily called, waving, "Joe!"

Joe Varner entered the home, shook Travis's hand and came in. "Looks like the whole town is here this morning, Emily."

Travis led him into the living room and introduced the Fish and Game agent to Jesse, who shook his hand.

"Have a seat, Joe. You must have done your snooping around out there for that cougar?" Travis asked.

Sitting down in the chair opposite the couch, Joe set his report papers on the coffee table between them. "I did." He raised his blond brows, eyeing Emily. "I found the cougar about a quarter of a mile inside the tree line. It's dead."

Gasping, Jesse said, "No! What happened to it, Joe?"

"Best guess," he said, shrugging, "is the cat had contracted rabies. That would explain its abnormal behavior at the caboose where you're living."

Clapping her hand against her mouth, eyes widening, Jesse looked up at Travis. He was grim looking.

"Rabies?" he demanded.

"Can't be sure. I've taken some swabs from its mouth and I'll know for sure at my office later today. I'll get back to you on that."

"Skunks sometimes have rabies, but so do raccoons. Both are around the river," Emily said, "where all predators hunt for food."

"That's what I'm thinking," Joe said. "The cougar may have caught and killed a coon who was infected, and in turn, he got infected by the virus and died from it."

Shaking her head, Jesse muttered, "If that's true, then I need to wash everything on the steps and platform of the caboose with bleach, as well as that door. Rabies virus could still be hanging around."

"Yes," Joe said, his attention shifting to her. "But I don't want you going anywhere near that caboose or meadow until we know for sure what killed the cougar."

"What do you suggest if it had rabies, Joe?" Travis asked.

"Well, you told me earlier that Jesse and the dogs were staying with you, here. I think that's a good idea. If it pans out that the cat contracted rabies, I'd wait at least a week and then go out with latex gloves, boots on, pails of bleach, water and throwaway sponges. All those cleaning items you use to wipe the surfaces down have to be burned. You can always wipe off your boots with bleach and kill anything on them. The latex gloves you can also burn after you're done cleaning up the area around the caboose."

"Ugh," Jesse said. "Who'd have thought this whole crazy situation could happen?"

Joe nodded. "Rabies is always around. You've got wild animals living all around Hamilton. It's up to Fish and Game, as well as the state health department, to keep tabs on rabies. I'll be coordinating with them, too, as soon as I get back to my office."

"But it doesn't make my boxcar unlivable, does it?" Jesse asked, wanting so badly to go back there to live. She wouldn't admit that being with Travis here in his cozy home helped her in so many ways. Not only did he make her feel less anxious, but so did Freya. She couldn't explain it, but if she had her druthers, she'd like to have both man and dog in her life. But so much was happening to her she couldn't sort it all out.

"No, it won't stop you from living in it," Joe told her. "It's just temporary for a week. The health department will have to come out to check it after you get it cleaned up. I'm sure they'll give you a good bill of health and then you can move back in and pretend none of this happened."

"I'll never forget it," she admitted, wryly. "And I'm sure Freya won't either."

"All's well that ends well," Emily said, finishing off her coffee and standing. "I gotta get to work, gang."

Joe stood also. "I'll walk you out to your truck."

Jesse saw something in Joe's eyes, but said nothing. Emily was a fount of positivity for everyone. A live wire. She looked at herself and came up wanting, knowing that the old Jesse would never return. It was a downer, but she shoved it aside, standing up and giving Emily a quick hug of farewell.

Travis came over, standing near her after they said goodbye to Joe and Emily. Once the door shut, he turned to her. "I know you're probably all set to come to the office at 1300, but I want you to stay here and be company for Freya today, instead." He touched her shoulder. "Besides, it's been a helluva morning for you, too, Jesse. Take some downtime to collect yourself?"

"Thanks, I'll take you up on that. I think we need to give Freya some constancy in her life, don't you?"

"Unlike us?" He shared an amused look with her. Only vets with PTSD would get that inference.

"Yes, like us. But I'm finding, Travis, that I love that little caboose. It gives me a point of stability."

"I understand. Once we find out about what that cougar died from, we'll know what chess move of life we need to make next."

"Are you all right with Freya under foot?"

"Sure." He looked around the cabin. "Kinda makes this place a home, not just an empty shell. Growing up, I had a dog around all the time. It feels good having another one around."

"I feel the same way," she whispered, feeling the heat roll off his tall, powerful form. "I was never so glad as when you drove up to the caboose and that cougar ran off."

"We need to have one of Hiram's rifles put out there for you. We'll take care of that in a week or so."

"Until then. Maybe today I'll take some down time, but tomorrow I need to work at Katie's place."

"That's fine. Since you'll be gone half a day tomorrow, I'll pop in every couple of hours on Freya and make sure she has her needs met. That way, she won't feel abandoned."

"Gosh, can you imagine what this poor dog has been through?"

"No, but it was a lot. I think after the crash, she ran off for the mountains and just kept on going west, running into Hamilton and the caboose. She ate off the land, which explains her weight loss."

"I'm glad she ended up at your grandparents' boxcar. I know from what you told me earlier, they loved all of nature."

"Yes, they did." Travis smiled a little. "He'd have howled his head off over that cougar at his back door. That's one for the history books. Hamilton will be buzzing about it for at least a few weeks."

"And it looks like gossip flies through Hamilton like a wildfire," she mused sourly.

"It's not all bad," he counseled. "It's a small town with a big heart. Neighbor helps neighbor out here. I've got to get to work. You know where I'm at if you need anything. Just call. I'll drop back here for lunch."

"I'll make us something to eat."

"Sounds good to me." He headed for the door, picking up his Stetson from the nearby wooden peg. "Thanks…"

Jesse didn't want him to go, his larger-than-life presence always calming to her. She'd never looked at a man—ever—for protection. Because she felt so awkwardly vulnerable, he was like a masculine umbrella of sorts, sheltering her life presently, and shielding her in many respects. She didn't want to be like this the rest of her life and put that shameful awareness aside. There was lots to do in the cabin and the least she could do was clean it up, plus take care of Freya. How she looked forward to holding each little puppy! They too, gave her a sense of calm from her anxiety.

Life was looking up despite the unexpected ups and downs. Most of all, she was with Travis and loved his home. Psychologically, Jesse knew it was helping her and she was incredibly grateful.

CHAPTER 6

November 4

TRAVIS LOOKED FORWARD to coming home at noon. He was bored to death at work. He missed Jesse's quiet presence. She was rock steady in a crisis, but he expected that given her combat background. Never would she panic or lose her head in the middle of any kind of chaos. But afterward was when she'd shake and crash, just like they all did. Taking off his Stetson as he entered the cabin, he saw her in the kitchen.

"Hey," he called, "whatever you're making smells good." Her hair was tousled and he tried to imagine what she would look like if she allowed it to grow longer.

"Egg salad. You had a lot of cartons of eggs in the fridge. I decided to do something with them."

Freya bounded out of the bedroom, racing across the living room and into the kitchen, wagging her tail at the people who cared for her and her pups.

Leaning down, Travis petted her head. "How's the brood doing?" he teased.

"Oh, fine," Jesse laughed. "I put a water bowl out here near the pantry." She pointed in that general direction down at the other end of the long counter. "I checked on her pups and they're roly-poly and full of milk."

"Anything I can do? Set the table?"

"Sure, go ahead."

"You look more settled."

"I think it's the house, the dogs."

He pulled plates from the cabinet near where she was working. "I think Freya and her pups are going to be good for you."

"They calm me. I remember Tag, my yellow lab, growing up. He was always with me. He slept in my bedroom. We did everything together."

He set the flatware on both sides of each plate, adding a couple of paper napkins. "Animals have a magical effect on us," he agreed. Hell, Jesse had a magical effect on him! Travis was past denial at this point regarding how she affected him. This morning seeing that cougar stalking around the caboose ended him trying to insist he wasn't drawn to her. At the office, with little to do, he had done a lot of thinking over the past few days. There was nothing wrong with Jesse that he could fathom. Wounded? Yes. But so, what? So was he. So was Nick Conway, who had been an Army Ranger before getting discharged for PTSD. Life didn't work out like he thought it might, like he'd seen for other people. Those military people coming back from combat had their life path destroyed. Now, like Jesse, himself, Nick and so many others, they had to cobble together a new life journey. One with a lot of hidden WMDs thrown here and there. Despite all of it, Travis came away with the fact he genuinely liked Jesse. There was nothing to dislike. Despite her emotional and psychological wounds, she had a good heart, she was self-aware, and she had compassion for others. That, in Travis's book, was as good as it was ever going to get.

Having Jesse under his roof, plus the dogs, settled him in a new and sur-prising way. He found himself opening up around her. The dogs were trustworthy and Travis enjoyed having them around. Even more, he was desiring a serious relationship with Jesse, but he wasn't sure she was at a place in her healing where she could even think in that direction. A long time ago, he'd learned patience. It often brought good things to him if he reined in his impulsiveness. This was one of those times. He had no wish to lean on Jesse, flirt or let her know of his growing feelings for her. They had enough time and he was grateful knowing that.

The phone rang.

Travis picked it up. "Hello."

"Travis? It's me, Joe. I just got back the results from the lab on the swab I wiped in that Petri dish here at the office. It's confirmed rabies."

"Good to know. Well, we have a plan in place."

"Jesse had given me the phone number of the executor to Stella Caldwell. I called her and asked if she had the vet information on Freya. She did and is emailing me a copy of it tomorrow. Freya has her rabies shot in order, so she's protected. I called Emily to ask about the pups and she said that they would have to wait, that they're too young to have that shot."

"That means we have to do a really good job of cleaning up where that cat was at around the caboose so the pups don't get infected."

"Right. There have been very few scientific tests to find out how long the rabies can exist outside the body. One test showed the virus living six days at 41F. At 68F, the virus lived twenty-four hours on glass and leaves, and forty-eight hours on metal. A third test showed rabies at 86F under sunlight, lasted an hour and a half. And twenty hours under the same temperature without sunlight. My advice is to wait seven days. It freezes at night, so based upon these studies, the virus will probably be dead by the time you let Jesse go back to the caboose. That and scrubbing all surfaces down with bleach and water. Make *sure* she has no open skin, wear long plastic gloves and put a mask on her face so she can't inhale anything nearby."

"I'll make sure. Good that rabies has a short life span outside the body of human or animal."

"Yeah, for sure. And with winter coming on, I think the freezing will take care of it, but we want to be conservative about it and protect Jesse and the dogs."

"What about that yellow grass out in the meadow where the cougar was at when I drove up?"

"I wouldn't let Freya go snooping around out there yet. The cat's saliva holds the virus and it probably fell into that dead grass. Just to be on the safe side, I'd suggest keeping them at your place for fourteen days. By that time, we usually get some snowfall in here and that will kill any virus that might still be left hanging around."

"I can do that. Over here, Freya has a huge yard to run around in and she'll be safe."

"That's what I was thinking. Okay, I gotta run. See you later."

"Yep, thanks."

Travis hung up the phone and saw that Jesse was listening as she put the finishing touches on their lunch. He told her what the conversation was about. "Are you okay staying here two weeks instead of one? We can go out to the caboose and clean it up at the seven-day mark with water and bleach."

She handed him his plate and walked to the table. "That's a good idea if you're okay with us underfoot that long." Sitting down, she saw him grin as he pulled out his chair and sat.

"I was thinking this morning at the office how good it felt to have you and Freya here under my roof," he admitted, picking up one part of the sandwich. "I'm fine with you here, but it's up to you, Jesse. You're more than welcome to stay."

She munched on the sandwich, thinking through the situation. "In my case I need some rut routine to keep me calm and focused. I have my dish washer duties at the Koffee Bean and the job at your office. It's nice to know that Freya and her babies are safe. That means more to me than anything."

"Putting them at risk is a stress," he agreed, trying to keep the joy out of his voice. He could see her thinking and he appreciated her doing it out loud so he didn't have to guess where she was at. In fact, if Travis wasn't seeing things, there was relief in her eyes over his offer of a two-week stay. "And the best thing for our type is the rut routine. It helps us so much."

"Yes." She smiled tentatively. "You're okay then with all of us being here? It's not going to stress you, Travis? I know a lot of vets who want to live alone. They can't handle situations like this."

Trying to sound serious, keeping the bubbling happiness in his chest at bay, he said, "I'm okay with all of you here. I honestly think it will be good for all of us."

"We just have to keep communicating, Travis. I worry about that. Men aren't good at it."

"I'll get very good at it. I'll try to stay open and I'll always be honest with you."

"Same here," she said between bites, picking up her cup of coffee and taking a sip.

Travis felt something around her, but he couldn't put his finger on it. There was lightness in her eyes and he'd known her long enough to translate that to the fact she was happy and calm. "Well," he teased, "maybe this old log cabin will work its magic on you like it did me. The first year after coming home, this place was like a protective haven for me. I hope it will be that for you and Freya, too."

TRAVIS BOUGHT A dog brush and comb from Libby Johnson, whose family owned Cooper's Hardware Store, the only one in town. She had a small pet section and had guided him on the purchases. He felt good about this. He liked being able to make Freya feel loved and cared for. He'd also stopped at the Las Palomas Bakery and bought some dessert from Alex Delgado: a pumpkin pie. When he'd handed Jesse the sack and she saw it was a comb and brush, she smiled. Her smile grew even larger when he produced the pumpkin pie, which they would have for dessert after the meal.

Freya came out of the bedroom when she smelled dinner on the table. Because she was so thin and underweight and feeding five pups, Jesse had relented. She'd made the dog her own kind of egg salad, without the spices in it. After dinner, Jesse had made her up a handful of dry kibble, spooned on the special egg salad into the aluminum bowl and put it on the rubber mat near the pantry door for Freya. The dog gobbled it up, giving Jesse an appreciative look as she licked her muzzle afterward.

The evening temperature was dropping and Travis went to work starting a wood fire in the fireplace. He saw Freya checking it out as he put the protective grate in place so the sparks couldn't fly into the living room.

"I wonder why she's studying the fire so intently," Jesse said, sitting down on the couch.

"Probably because it reminds her of escaping the fire in that car when it crashed?"

She nodded. "You're right. She doesn't seem to be afraid of it exactly. Wary, maybe?" Freya turned away, trotting down the hall, going back to her pups.

"Yes," he agreed. "Want that pumpkin pie with some whipped cream?"

"That would be great. Want me to help?"

"No, just relax. I'll bring it to you."

"You're really spoiling me."

He gave her a warm glance. "You've more than earned it, Jesse." In a few minutes, he brought over two plates and a fork with each of them. Handing one to her, he said, "This is my favorite time of the day," and sat down at the other corner of the couch.

"Why is that?"

"Something about the fire, the sound of it, I guess." He spooned the pie into his mouth, making a low sound of appreciation. "Alex's parents came here from Mexico in the 1930s and built Las Palomas Bakery."

"I passed by it a week ago. Everything looked so good, but I didn't have two pennies to rub together to buy anything."

"Well, you will now," he said. "Like the pie?"

"Delicious."

She was also delicious looking in his eyes but he was careful not to stare at her too long for fear she'd pick up on his true intent and need for her. Not fooling himself, he knew those who had experienced combat sometimes had nearly scary psychic abilities to sense others or a situation gathering around them. Under no circumstance did Travis want Jesse to feel stalked, threatened or stared at.

His cell phone vibrated in the leather case attached to his belt. That didn't bode well. He set the plate on the coffee table and stood up, pulling it out. Excusing himself, he went into the kitchen seeing the number of the caller. It was his father.

What now?

JESSE SAW THE relaxation in Travis's face disappear as he talked in low tones in the kitchen on his phone. Frowning, she continued to eat, eavesdropping. Just the tenor of his voice, lower and grimmer sounding than usual, made her worry arc. Whoever was at the other end wasn't a happy camper.

He hung up and shoved the phone back into the leather carrying case. Turning, he said, "That was my father. He needs me over at his cabin. I'll go over and see what's going on and come back later."

"Is there anything I can do?"

"No, just stay here, feed the fire and enjoy the dogs. I'll see you in a bit." He pulled his jacket off one peg and his Stetson from another.

Jesse felt a lot of stress suddenly surround Travis, but she stopped herself from being nosey. She remembered him telling her that Sam wasn't the most pleasant person to be around because of his painful joints and that he was in constant, unrelenting pain. She saw Freya pop out of the room, standing at the end of the hall, her ears up, her gaze falling on Travis. She felt and heard it, too.

The front door closed.

Freya came over and sat down next to her leg. Patting her, Jesse said, "I hope you like being combed and brushed. As soon as I'm done we're going to start getting some of that fur of yours unknotted."

Licking her hand, Freya thumped her brushy tail, her blue eyes dancing with life.

Laughing softly, Jesse loved sliding her hand down her wiry coat. "You know, in about a month from now after taking all those good vitamins Emily left you, your coat is going to be soft, shiny and silky again, Freya. Plus, maybe in a few days, Travis and I will give you a bath."

The tail thumped even harder.

Tag had been her buddy but Jesse liked that Freya was so much more affectionate. Was it because females were nurturing and maternal? Jesse thought it might be so. Estrogen versus testosterone. Right now, she needed this extra love from Freya, amazed that she had it to give, considering the terrible life-threatening circumstances she'd just come through.

Her mind and heart turned to Travis as she put her empty plate on the coffee table. She wished he didn't have an angry father, but she understood what pain did to a human being. Their own pain was emotional and mental. But it was pain just the same, and she was learning how to handle and deal with it. Never did she want to drug herself up to her eyeballs and feel like an automaton, empty with no feelings at all. Jesse didn't judge those who wanted to take them, but the drugs on her sensitized body left her feeling like a robot and all her life, she'd relied on her sensing and feelings like a GPS unit within her. Drugs took that ability away and she felt lifeless and rudderless in that state. No, she'd rather feel the pain, mostly the anxiety, and still be able to feel other more positive emotions that were slowly coming back to life within her, instead. Travis brought out those good feelings in her, and so did Freya. The last week of her life made her feel as if she had been whiplashed. But at least it was mostly in a good way this time.

Sitting there and loving Freya with long strokes across her fur, her mind moved to Travis going over to see his father. Did Sam call every night like this? Was there something wrong? She hoped not. Her senses told her that this was something that happened fairly often. She felt sorry for Travis, without knowing why.

TRAVIS GIRDED HIMSELF as he entered his father's log cabin. He quietly closed the door behind him, seeing his father in his electric wheelchair, wearing loose gray workout pants and a gray sweatshirt. At one time, he'd been a tall, lean hombre, always wearing a straw cowboy hat, a pair of leather patched cowboy boots, jeans and a yoked plaid, long-sleeved shirt. Now, his face was leaner since the joints in his knees had rendered him to a chair, and he'd stopped eating like he used to. He'd lost nearly fifty pounds in the last two years, half the man he'd remembered as a kid growing up. He saw Cyrus, the fifteen-year-old hunting dog laying down on a brown and white braided rug near the fireplace. If it wasn't for this calm, affectionate mutt, Travis was sure his father would be in a lot fouler mood far more often as a result. The old dog had gray on its long muzzle and Travis had always thought he might be a mix of black lab, a bloodhound and God knew what else. He wasn't a pretty dog except for his curly black-haired coat. Maybe there was some curly dog breeding in him, but he couldn't guess which breed.

His father hadn't always been the angry old man he saw before him now. As a young boy, his dad was a man with a good sense of humor and always thoughtful of others. Not anymore. He noticed food out on the table that hadn't been put away and the smell of something rotting—it was some blackened bananas sitting on the counter. Where was his latest in-home help? Word had gotten around Hamilton in a hurry to the women living here that working as a caretaker for Sam Ramsey was a losing proposition.

"How are you doing?" he asked his father, coming up to him in the living room.

"Elena quit, dammit!" Sam jabbed a finger at the kitchen. "I need some help. I haven't eaten dinner, yet, and I can't make it for myself tonight. My damn knees are too painful to stand up on today."

"I'm sorry to hear that." Elena was an undocumented worker, her family coming north to Montana from Guatemala, to make a life for themselves. Her husband, Ernesto, worked at the local grocery store. He had a good reputation, was a hard worker and together they had three young children. Knowing they needed money, despite the gossip around Hamilton, Elena had applied for the job. Travis had hired her a month ago, hoping it would work out. It hadn't obviously. He saw the anger rising in his father's narrowed eyes and tried to protect himself from the coming explosion.

"She was thin skinned."

He wasn't going to ask why because he already knew. Sam bullied and berated everyone, it didn't matter if it was a man or woman. "What do you need, Sam?" Calling on his patience, Travis wasn't about to go there with him. He would hear the same spiel he heard every time.

"I'm hungry! Those bananas are rotten! I can't reach 'em to throw 'em into the garbage."

"I'll take care of it." Travis went to work. Mentally, he made a point to call Elena tomorrow at a decent time, find out what happened and cut her a check for the hours she put in, and apologize for Sam's behavior toward her. Feeling badly for the woman, he opened up the refrigerator to see what was there. Privately, he wished he were still home with Jesse and Freya. Only good feelings there. Calm. Peace. Nothing like here.

"I'll make you a roast beef sandwich," he told his father.

"Sounds good," he muttered, driving his wheelchair up to the table. Cyrus followed at a leisurely pace, laying down on Sam's right side where he could get his tidbits from anything his master ate.

Travis didn't expect any thanks. "I'll put an ad in the paper for a caretaker tomorrow morning. Until then, I'll come over and see you have what you need three times a day."

"Yeah," he muttered, glaring around the silent house. Reining in his frustration, he put the sandwich on a plate, cut it in half and grabbed a bag of potato chips, taking them to the table. Sam wasn't a total invalid. He could get up and walk when there wasn't so much stiffness in his knees, take a shower and do all kinds of things. Sometimes, Travis felt used and manipulated by him. He was glad that their homes were on opposite ends of town, at least he got some of the breathing space he needed from his father. It grieved him to this day that the loving relationship he had with his dad as a child had turned into this.

He knew potato chips were Cyrus's favorite food. At least the dog, which he regarded as a saint to live with his father, would be happy for tonight's hand-outs.

"What's this I hear from the gossip goin' around town that you're fixing up Hiram's boxcar? You shoulda let it rot! And what's this about a girl renting that boxcar?" he snapped, glaring up at Travis as he pulled the plate toward him.

Barely glancing over his shoulder, Travis told him the story in as few words as possible. He braced himself for a coming explosion.

Sam merely curled his lip, but hunger got to him and he eagerly began to consume the sandwich.

"It's rent money coming in," Travis added, knowing that Sam was always concerned with the bottom line.

"I said, you shoulda let that boxcar rot!"

Travis stood there, torn. When he was small, he and his younger brother by two years, Kyle, would go visit Hiram and Inez at their home. Their cabin was located near the office. As close as he was to his warm, affectionate grandfather, Kyle had been Inez's favorite. There was just something special those two shared and he was okay with it. Kyle was very much like their mother, Sheila. She was tall, thin, somewhat pale and weak looking compared to his father, Sam. Kyle took after her. He took after Sam. Kyle was diagnosed with autism, had trouble in school and it was Inez who patiently taught him how to read and write as a youngster. Severely shy, Travis didn't know how to relate to his brother who would never look anyone in the eyes. He would hide in his room, read books, play computer games, and be happy. Sports never appealed to him. Or girls. Or being a member of one of the clubs in high school.

Over time, Travis learned Kyle's code for what made him feel safe and somewhat happy. He knew, looking back on those childhood days, that Sam couldn't understand his second son, which caused a lot of tension between the two of them. As soon as Travis understood what was going on at the tender age of nine, he would take his shy brother on long hikes along the banks of the Bitterroot River. And often, especially on weekends, they would stay in their grandparents' home. Even if Hiram was out on railroad work, the door was always open and Travis and his brother could wander into their cabin. Inez would pinch-hit and make sure Kyle was well fed, his knapsack packed with lots of books because that is the world he dove into and was happiest within.

Pulling himself back to the present, Travis felt old grief stir in his heart. Kyle died in a car crash at twenty-four, on his way to Missoula. His father went berserk with grief. They'd already lost their mother, Sheila. Now, Kyle was ripped away from them. His younger brother had been a kind, super-sensitive, and caring teen. He cried when he would see a dead butterfly on the side of the road, struck by a car windshield. He would care for a baby bird that fell out of its nest, hunting up food for it. Another enigma was why Sam hated his own father so much. Everyone in Hamilton loved the red-bearded Irish Viking and his outgoing wife, Inez. Kyle had adored and loved them, too.

Life was hard, as Travis knew too well. He tucked all those memories and feelings away, cleaning up the kitchen counter and getting his father's rumpled bed made. When he was done, an hour had passed. "Do you need anything else before I leave, Sam?"

"No. But you gonna come over and make me breakfast tomorrow mornin'?"

Travis shrugged on his coat and threw the Stetson on his head. "I'll be here at eight a.m."

CHAPTER 7

November 10

"WE NEED TO give Freya a bath," Jesse told Travis as they cleaned up the dishes from breakfast. It was Saturday morning and she looked forward to not having to work for two days. Travis's father now had a new caretaker and she hoped it would work out for everyone. Tomorrow, they would go to the caboose and start the water and bleach clean up. Outside, the Indian summer continued and she loved the colorful fall leaves twirling magically across the blue sky in the inconstant morning breeze.

"I'm sure she's used to baths if she was a show dog," he said, putting everything in the dishwasher. "Should be straightforward with her."

"Do you have a place to wash her?"

He smiled. "I have an old bathtub down in the basement. We could wash her there?"

"Is there a dog groomer in Hamilton?"

"No. It's us or nothing. How about now? Do you have anything else planned?"

As if on cue, Freya came out of the bedroom, trotting across the living room and joining them. "Want a bath?" Jesse asked the dog, petting her head.

A wagging tail was her response.

"She's a mind reader too or she understands English. Let's go do it, then," he said, straightening. "I've got old towels and there are two rugs on either side of the tub we can kneel on. Should be fun, huh?"

They both eyed Freya, who had tilted her head first one way and then the other, as each of them spoke in turn. "Sounds like we're going to be wet, too, by the time this is all over."

"I don't think you'll melt," he teased, chuckling.

Her lips pulled into a wry smile. "No, been through more than rain and never melted."

"You're letting your hair grow?"

She washed her hands in the sink and dried them off. A nice feeling rolled through her and she noticed a glint in his eyes as he'd said it. No, it wasn't teasing. It was something else. Something she'd not seen before. Picking up a slight curl of her hair near her temple, she said, "I don't have to keep it short anymore. It's growing like a weed. I used to have hair that touched my shoulders and that's what I'm aiming for again."

"Part of getting back into civilian life. Right?"

"In a way." She reached over, touching his temple. "You still have military short hair. I don't see you wearing curls." Jesse knew that would get a big rise out of him. Most military vets, with some exceptions of course, continued to wear their hair short after getting out of the service. His eyes grew large for a moment and she enjoyed his reaction. It was nice to be allowed into his world of trust where he could be vulnerable and open with her. Truly, it was one of the greatest gifts one person could give another.

"Touché," he said. He gave Freya a pat on the head because she'd come over to greet him next. "Not to get off topic, but we're going to have to move her and her pups out of your bedroom. They started opening their eyes on the seventh and now, they're all over the place. I worry about one of us accidentally stepping on one of them."

"I know." She sighed and looked around the large living room. "Do you have any ideas, Travis?"

"I was thinking of putting them down into the basement. It's clean, warm and dry. Plus, there's lots of light from the windows. I can put up a fence of sorts in one-third of the area. That way, as they start peeing and pooping, we can clean it up. They're too young to potty train yet and any day now, I'm afraid we're going to start getting snow. We can't put them outside in this kind of weather."

"You're right. The basement sounds like a good place." She glanced at Freya. "I wonder if she'll be okay with it?"

"I guess we'll find out. Come on, let's go down there and look around. She'll follow us."

Jesse had not been in the basement before and her expectations rose as they took the old, solid cedar staircase down to it. She'd been worried it might be dank and dark, but it was just the opposite. Just as he had promised, it was filled with light, spotlessly clean, with two-thirds of it covered in a nubby carpet and one-third of it concrete floor. Freya followed and seemed sincerely interested in the huge, bright, rectangular area.

Travis watched her snoop around. "I think this is a perfect place for her. She seems to be favoring that one corner under the window. Good light there and it's in a corner where she feels safer than being out in the middle of this place."

Nodding, Jesse watched the dog navigate the entire basement. "She's definitely checking it out."

Travis walked up to a cupboard near the old tub. "Let's get her cleaned up." He handed Jesse some old, but clean, dry towels. He went to another cupboard and pulled down a bottle of shampoo that Emily had given him the other day. There were two rugs on either side of the tub. He put the plug in the tub and turned on the water, keeping it warm, but not hot.

Freya came over to the tub, ears up, interested.

"Maybe she wants a bath," Jesse said.

"Some dogs like water. Others don't. We'll find out which type she is in a minute." He rolled up the sleeves on his red and black checked flannel shirt. "Be prepared to get wet," he warned her with a grin.

Laughing, she pulled the orange sleeves of her tee up above her elbows. "I'm ready."

"Okay," Travis said, gently picking up Freya, "let's see how she likes this…"

There was no need to worry. Jesse watched as he placed Freya's paws on a long, thick rubber mat that would stop her from slipping and falling. The warm water was knee high. The dog stood there, looking at them expectantly.

Jesse took a nearby plastic drinking cup that Travis had given her along with the towels, and began to wet her down from her neck and across her back and hind quarters. Soon enough, their hands were meeting here and there. Freya stood obediently, not trying to avoid the water or them massaging the shampoo into her dirty fur.

"Yep, she sure knows what a bath is all about," Jesse said, enjoying the unexpected contact with his hands. They scrubbed her, gently picking up each leg one at a time, and washed the dirt off her white fur and moved on. The last to be cleaned was her black and white tipped tail. Travis then drained the dirty water and put in fresh warm water. They began to use the two drinking cups, pouring it over her sudsy body, washing away at least three months' worth of grit and grime.

"She's so beautiful," Jesse sighed, giving him a glance as they finished with the first rinse. He drained the tub and filled it again.

"She has brown on her legs that I didn't see before," Travis said, starting the second rinse. "That's how filthy she'd become. I'm glad we're giving her a bath."

"Poor dog," she whispered, giving Freya a sympathetic look.

Freya wagged her tail.

Yipping, Jesse got swatted with a tail full of water.

Laughing, Travis caught her tail, and then she shook herself, droplets of water flying in every direction.

They were both good and wet by the time everything was done. After draining the water after the second rinse, Freya stood and enjoyed the towels being rubbed all over her, soaking up the water on her fur. Finally, she was dry! Travis lifted her up and out of the tub, setting her on the nubby carpet on the floor.

Instantly, Freya shook herself good once again.

"She's ten colors lighter," Jesse said, mopping up the water around the tub with one of the spent towels.

"She's smiling." Travis looked down at the dog trotting around, stopping, shaking and trotting on once more.

"I'm sure she is. The poor thing." Jesse finished cleaning up the tub and stood. Travis gathered everything else and took it upstairs to be put into the washer.

Freya's fur was barely damp as she bounded up the stairs after them, ran to the water bowl, lapped a lot of it up and then headed back to her pups in the bedroom.

Within a few hours, with Jesse's help, Travis had cordoned off one-third of the basement for Freya and her pups. The area didn't have the nubby carpet, but rather, was smooth concrete, making it easy to clean up after the pups. Jesse felt as if another barrier between her and Travis had melted away. They'd had a lot of fun, laughter and good times washing Freya. Most of all, she liked the unexpected contact with his hands. Every day, she was growing closer to him in every way. And only this morning, she wondered if she had seen that glint in his eyes that told her he was interested in her. Was it her imagination? They got along well with one another. There was a natural ease between them and she liked his sensitivity toward her and the dog. Every day she slept under his roof, she felt marginally better, like taking baby steps forward toward a better kind of life. Being with him was a positive, no question.

November 10

"DO YOU HAVE a sister or brother?" Travis asked Jesse. They were sitting cross-legged in the puppy enclosure in the basement, playing with the five puppies who were more than happy to have human contact and affection. Freya lay nearby, alert and watching the interplay. He saw Jesse shake her head.

"No. Only child." She picked up the only male, kissing its noggin and setting him back down. "You mentioned once you had a younger brother named Kyle."

He stirred. The time here with Jesse only intensified his yearning to go deeper, to be on a more intimate level with her. He'd lost sleep at night thinking of a way he could do it. Travis had finally decided the only way was for him to open up—not something he was very good at. Meeting her gaze, he said, "I did." He saw her digest his statement as two of the female puppies went racing from him to her. Travis liked the way she met them, bringing each one upward, holding them against her chest and nuzzling them. He smiled. Jesse was good with people and animals—maybe it came from being a translator because they had a lot of psychology blended into their daily work.

Placing the pups back on the floor, she asked, "You said that past tense." She dug into his gaze, asking without asking the obvious question.

Uncomfortably, he moved and his lips pursed for a moment. "Kyle died in a car crash when he was twenty-four."

"Oh...I'm sorry..."

He winced inwardly, her heartfelt words tackling his desire to protect himself. He didn't know why he got defensive because Jesse was sincere. It was about him. About buttoning up. Somehow, Travis knew he had to break that logjam within himself and allow Jesse entrance into him, into what he really needed with her: intimacy, like the kind that he saw between Nick and Holly Conway. One of the little female pups toddled over to him, climbing up on his crossed ankles and he eased her over to his denim clad thigh. Happily, she flopped down on her belly, exhausted, her hind legs hanging over his leg. "I have real problems opening up personally," he managed, giving a one shouldered shrug. "Kyle was autistic. He was diagnosed in kindergarten. I was in the second grade. I knew my brother was different, but he was sweet, and sensitive and a good person. He'd always wave his hands when he was stressed out, did this even as a baby as far back as I can remember, and I took it as normal." He took a deep breath and held her compassionate gaze. "He was very, very shy. I thought nothing of it. The boys in his kindergarten started bullying him. I saw it happen one afternoon when I was going to pick him up and walk him home. I grabbed the kid, chewing him out. I told them if I ever caught them making fun of Kyle again, I'd do worse the next time around."

"Did it stop?"

"Yes. They left him alone. He was having a hard enough time because he was shy. My father didn't understand him. Kyle loved to read, Jesse. My mom read to both of us from the time I was three years old, onward. She'd put Kyle up on her lap in the rocking chair and I'd sit at her feet and listen. I loved those evenings when she had time to do it. I always slept well on them, and so did Kyle."

"What happened after he was diagnosed?"

Travis took another little female into his large hands after she came romping up to him, tugging at the cuff of his shirt. "My mom was devastated. My father said he always knew Kyle wasn't normal. They got into a bad argument and I remember Kyle coming to me to be held. He'd do that when he felt really threatened. I took him to his room and I got him to start reading one of his books. If he could read a book, he would calm down. I learned that when he waved his hands, that it meant he felt stressed or frightened."

"Because the book took him away from whatever the threat was?"

He frowned. "How did you know that?"

"There were kids in some of the Afghan villages, mostly boys, who were autistic. As an interpreter, during schooling, I was made aware of such kids, and how to work with them." Quirking her lips, she said softly, "Travis, these kids are not stupid, nor are they mentally ill. They are very, very bright. They just need the right kind of environment to thrive in, is all."

"Well, my family dynamic wasn't helpful to Kyle at all. My mother was broken-hearted over his condition. It was my grandmother who came to the rescue. She showed my mother how best to learn how to help Kyle cope. She taught me how to help him, too. She and my mother then went to his kindergarten teacher and enlisted her help. All those things supported Kyle and with time and maturity, he did a lot better. Later, when he hit twenty years old, he began to thrive."

"What about your father?"

"Sam tried to learn how to deal with Kyle. They had a patchy past with one another from time to time. As Kyle got older, they got along much better and had a good relationship."

"What about your grandparents? How did they react to this information and diagnosis of your brother?"

"Kyle was always Inez's favorite and when he was young, she would sit with him in a rocker that was in his bedroom at their cabin. She'd read to him nightly, which he loved. My grandparents loved him. They never thought there was anything wrong with him and accepted him just the way he was."

"I'm sure they loved you, too, Travis."

"Sure, they did, but there was a special, loving bond between Kyle and my grandma. She was so gentle with my brother, never using any fast hand movements, and always talking with him in an even tone of voice. Kyle got stressed out if someone was yelling or raising their voice at him, which happened often enough during grade school, and later on. Kyle loved going out on weekends to be with them. I think intuitively they knew there was something different about Kyle than most other kids and they were protective of him."

"Did any of the other kids bully him after that first time you waded into them?"

"No, because there's only one school here in Hamilton and at that time, it had all twelve grades, plus the kindergarten, contained in it. Word got around fast about me shellacking those bullies.""

"That's so stressful to anyone," she murmured. "It's tragic about the car accident."

"Yeah," he muttered, running his fingers through his short hair, "I think it killed my father in so many ways."

"Oh?"

"My mom died of cancer when I was 16 and Kyle was 14."

Reaching over, Jesse laid her hand on his arm. "What a horrible thing to happen. I'm so sorry, Travis. And poor Kyle. How did he take it?"

He patted her hand. "None of us took it well, as you could expect. Our grandparents picked up the slack after that and Inez made sure there was a woman's presence in our lives. She would come over and clean house, do the washing, and take care of us kids. I don't know if we'd do as well as we did if she hadn't been part and parcel in our lives. My father was devastated. He loved my mother with every fiber of his being. He withdrew from us for a couple of years. At that time, as a teen, I didn't understand mature love between two adults or the loss it created when one of them died. Sam had always loved us. But those years after our mother died, were tough on every-one. Sam withdrew and he wasn't available like he'd been before. Hiram would make sure on weekends that we went fishing or hiking. During the winter, he taught us how to snowshoe and ski. It helped us a lot because they provided us with stability."

"You lost half your family." She looked toward the ceiling, holding the male pup—the only one with blue eyes—between her hands. "I don't know how I could go on if half my family was gone, either."

"You talk weekly with your parents, and I think that does you a lot of good. Doesn't it?"

"Yes, it means the world to me. We've always been close." She rolled her eyes. "And now with these symptoms, I can't be around them because it's too hard on all of us." Giving him a tender look, she added, "Being here with you the last ten days, as kindred spirits of sorts, has been a real blessing to me. I've slept every night. I wake up with new, wonderful energy. I'm feeling hopeful again."

"I can see the changes in you, Jesse, and they're good ones from what I can tell."

"You and the dogs are my touchstone," she teased, giving him a wobbly smile. "Were you on deployment when Kyle died?"

"Yes," he sighed. "I didn't get home until four months after it happened because I'd been on an undercover assignment in Pakistan. My father was an emotional wreck when I finally got home."

"I'm sure he was devastated by it."

"I felt guilty as hell for not being there for Kyle's funeral or being a support for Sam…"

"You had your own grief to work through once you found out about it," Jesse pointed out gently. "Did you ever get time for yourself when you were home on that thirty-day leave?"

Shaking his head, he growled, "No…not really. Sam had let the business slide and I had to step in and get it back on track. When I arrived back to Jalalabad after the leave was up, they offered me a huge sign-up enlistment bonus. I decided to leave the Army and go home. Kyle dying just took a huge chunk out of me and I no longer had the drive to do undercover work anymore."

"The grief?"

"Yes, I think so. I was a mess inside, anyway."

"That didn't help you at all when you came home with the PTSD symptoms," she said quietly, giving him a concerned look.

"It was a rough landing. My father had not taken care of the boxcar, or kept it livable, either."

"Maybe out of grief?" she wondered, giving him a sympathetic look.

"I've thought that. So much of what Sam loved was taken from him in such a short amount of time. That caboose was a symbol of grief and bad memories for him, I think. He's never spoken about it, but he let the boxcar go, never wanting to go out there."

"You had a terrible first year home, then. I don't know how you got through it."

"I kept busy because Sam couldn't care for the fishing guide business due to his mounting knee issues. I was too busy to try and keep my grandfather's caboose clean and prepared for the winter." He gave her a glance. "And here I am three years later, still unable to fix it up, paint it and keep it up like it used to be until you came along and breathed new life into it."

She reached over, squeezing his hand resting on his thigh. "Maybe the spirits of your grandparents led me to it?"

"That's a nice thought," he said, turning his hand over, lacing his fingers between hers. "You've brought a lot of goodness here by coming to Hamilton, Jesse, and I feel you're like a guardian angel of sorts to us. I felt so damned guilty about not caring for their home. It ate at me. You finding it and then helping me clean it up has taken a load off my shoulders." He managed in a gruff growl, "You're important to me, too. I just want you to know that. You've brought light into my dark world."

She managed a weak smile. "I brought the dogs with me, too. I wasn't sure you'd welcome them."

He reluctantly released her hand, seeing a yearning in her eyes for the first time. It fed him hope. That look was of a woman desiring her man. Could he dare dream that she felt similar to how he felt toward her? It was a dizzying, shocking possibility. "You're all welcome in my house," he told her, his voice laced with emotion. "I wouldn't have it any other way."

November 20

"HEY," TRAVIS SAID, getting off the phone at his office, catching Jesse's attention, "that was Nick Conway."

"Yes?" she replied, poking her head up from her computer on the opposite side of the room.

"He and Holly have invited us over to Thanksgiving dinner. Want to go?"

She had met Nick and Holly a few days ago at their Delos charity in town. "That would be wonderful. You okay with it?"

"Sure."

"I know Holly is pregnant. Does she want us to bring anything? Dessert? A casserole?"

"Why don't you call her and ask?" He stood and walked across the office, handing her a piece of paper with their phone number on it.

"I will at lunch," she said. "I really want to finish off this data list for you."

He stood to the side of her desk. "You're a fast typist."

"Not that fast. Maybe eighty words a minute or something like that." She had the files on one side of her desk and had to open each one to put the name, address and contact number into the program.

He looked around the quiet office. "Wait until next April, Jesse. This place is a beehive of business. A lot of nonstop activity."

She stopped typing and looked up at him. The snow had fallen a few days ago, maybe a foot, and it had gotten very cold in the area. Since then, he had been wearing a dark brown leather vest over the flannel shirts he favored. "I think I'll be ready for it."

"You're looking more relaxed every day," he agreed, stuffing his hands in the pockets of his Levi's.

"Having a warm house, a roof over my head, you and the dogs? It has helped me so much. I guess I never realized until a day ago, how much we all need family or friends after returning home from combat. I was wondering last night before I fell asleep if maybe I should have stayed home with my parents and gutted it out."

He nodded. "Most of my friends left their family home shortly after their return stateside. Those that didn't were married and within a year, usually, they got a divorce."

"I got lucky," she said. "You were a survivor with symptoms like me and you knew what I needed, gave me the space and understanding."

"I'm glad I could hold that space for you, Jesse. You deserve it."

She gave him a tender look, fighting the need to stand up, wrap her arms around his broad shoulders and hug him. And kiss him. Quelling those needs, she said, "You've been a life preserver for me."

"That and those frisky pups of Freya's."

Laughing, she said, "Hey, they are frisky! Galloping all over the place, finding their legs and balance. They're a real joy in our lives."

"They are. I was talking to Nick yesterday and he said to start training the pups to go to a newspaper to do their business. We should start doing that."

"Good idea."

"I've gotten several calls from people here in Hamilton who would really like one of these pups when they're six weeks old."

"I'll talk to Holly about this and get some info from her on who these folks are. I'll give her a call after lunch."

At noon, they went home for lunch, got Freya outdoors for a bit, cleaned up after the pups who had found one particular area to do their business, and then, went upstairs, washed their hands and ate lunch together. Of course, Freya always sat near Travis, who spoiled her with tidbits. The dog knew who to beg from.

JESSE DECIDED TO drive over to the Delos charity in town after lunch to see Nick and Holly. Even though Holly was decidedly pregnant, Jesse found both of them on the first floor, helping the volunteer staff start dinner for the elderly shut-ins they served. She spotted Holly working at the gas stove stirring a huge pot of soup.

Nick waved hello to her. He was busy putting slices of bread into a baggy for each food tray coming his way from a volunteer. Waving back, she headed over to where Holly was standing. Her crinkly red hair fell below her shoulders, glinting in the overhead lights as she approached from the side so that Holly would see her coming.

"Hi, Jesse!" she said, setting the spoon down. Turning around, she hugged her.

"Busy as always, I see."

"Yes." She beamed releasing her. "Nick called Travis? Are you coming to our place for Thanksgiving? We'd just love to have you two over there with us."

"We are. But Travis forgot to ask if we could bring anything over for the meal?"

"Oh, heavens no, Jesse. Just bring yourselves and don't dress up, okay? You're family."

She warmed to that thought. But then, Holly was a super-mother type. "How's the pregnancy going?"

She moved her hand across her swollen abdomen beneath a pink flannel shirt that hung to her hips. "Fine. I'm out of that first trimester of morning sickness, thank goodness. Poor Nick, he had to take over here for me during that time because just the smell of food made me nauseated."

Wrinkling her nose, Jesse muttered, "Not good."

Stirring the bean soup with ham hock in it, Holly laughed. "I'm still getting used to walking around with this basketball in front of me. My whole sense of balance has shifted. On some days, it's okay, but on others I wobble around a bit until I find my new center."

Jesse laughed. "And your doctor said everything is fine?"

"Oh," Holly said, "Dr. Paige Alanas, is wonderful. She says I'm fine. I'm on some pregnancy vitamins, is all. I'm hoping for a home birth. She has two midwives from Missoula who will be coming down here closer to the due date."

"No Christmas baby, huh?" she teased, grinning.

Holly smiled. "No, but that's okay. Hey, how are you and Travis getting along?" Her blue eyes danced with merriment.

Heat flowed up her neck and into her cheeks. "Well...fine."

"Gossip has it that he's sweet on you." She lowered her voice. "Is that true, Jesse?"

Moving from foot to foot, she avoided Holly's gaze for a moment. "I've only known him since November first."

"Hmmmm, well, my sources tell me that you two would make a very nice couple."

She looked away. "I guess I don't feel ready for much of anything, Holly."

"Oh, because of your PTSD? You know, Nick has those awful symptoms, too." She made a flourish with her hand. "But we fell in love pretty fast. And he's the first to tell you that since we started living together that a lot of his symptoms have decreased. That's good news. I was just wondering if you two had noticed that, living in the same cabin and all."

There was no getting around Holly. Giving her a weak smile, Jesse admitted, "We've both seen a reduction in our stress levels and anxiety since we've been under one roof because of Freya and her puppies."

"That's good to hear. I think you're perfect for Travis. Do you know how sad his family background is? The guy truly deserves something *nice* to happen to him! He's so responsible, good-hearted and tries his best to make things work, but his father, Sam, is a miserable person to be around when he's in pain. I have shut-ins who are in pain all the time, and they get like that. But who can blame them? Travis really deserves someone like you. Your kind, you work hard and you do good by others." She reached out, touching Jesse's forearm. "You *do* like him, don't you?"

"Can I keep it a secret between us, Holly? I do like him, but I'm afraid."

"Afraid of what?"

"That I'm so broken by the symptoms I have. I'm not a whole person and I don't know if I'll *ever* get back to the way I was before it happened."

"Pooh! Nick has symptoms. One day, he and Travis were challenging one another on who had the most symptoms and which one has the worst ones." She grinned and patted Jesse's arm. "I married Nick because he was a decent, kind person. He was honest and up front about his issues. There was nothing there that I didn't feel I couldn't work with or compromise on."

"Has he gotten better since he met you?" she asked, hopefully. Holly's eyes gleamed.

"Yes, *much* better! Are they gone? No. But you know, when you love someone, that's a medicine that the pharmaceutical companies can't create. It's the best medicine in the world!"

"You give me hope," she murmured, giving her a grateful look.

"If you two can live under one roof now and your love for one another isn't even out in the open yet? And you *both* feel better as a result of being with each other?" She laughed and shook her head. "Let's see." She held up her hand, spreading her fingers. "I will bet you anything that by Christmas you two will be engaged!"

CHAPTER 8

November 22

THE SMELL OF the butter basted turkey made Jesse's mouth water. She was in the kitchen with Holly, placing the final touches on the sumptuous Thanksgiving meal. Nick's parents were in Hawaii for Thanksgiving and their wedding anniversary, or they would have come here, too. It was nearly four p.m., and Nick and Travis were setting the table in the open-concept dining area. Their two dogs, Snowflake and Lady, were lying obediently on their beds, watching all the action with great interest, occasionally lifting their noses to the air, sniffing with appreciation. Jesse brought over a bowl of fragrant sage dressing that Holly had already made the gravy for, as well as the mashed potatoes. She was known as the "Gravy Queen" of Hamilton and judging from a taste of it, she was more a chef than a cook in Jesse's opinion.

"You look really pretty in your pink sweater and jeans," Holly told her, a gleam in her eyes. "I'll bet Travis took notice?"

Smiling, Jesse said, "You aren't going to give up on this, are you?"

Holly handed her the bean casserole. "Nope."

"I don't see it."

"Well, you're sort of in a hurricane right now. You've just left the military and it's your first year home." She pointed her chin in the direction of the guys setting the table. "I met Nick shortly after he left the military. A lot of our issues were clustered around his symptoms."

"And yet you overcame them?"

"We love one another," Holly said, her voice softening, picking up the platter with slices of dark and light turkey meat on it. "And that's what will get you and Travis through the tough days, too." She beamed. "Well, that and a dog or two."

Following Holly across the cedar floor to the huge round, antique oak table, she placed the casserole on a trivet. Both men lifted their noses, smelling the air, emulating the dogs earlier.

"I'm starved," Nick said, winking at Holly, taking the large, bulky platter from her.

"Makes two of us," Travis joined in, standing back, pleased with their efforts.

"Come on," Holly said, "you can help us bring in the rest of the food. I want to eat it while it's still hot."

In no time, they were sitting down at the table. Holly wanted to say a prayer, so they all joined hands, bowed their heads and closed their eyes. Her prayer was short, but filled with emotion. They had already baked three turkeys in the charity kitchen below their apartment yesterday and made sure that every one of the elderly shut-ins had a wonderful turkey dinner at noon today, replete with a big slice of pumpkin pie and whipped cream. Now, it was their turn to sit down and enjoy their well-earned meal.

Jesse fought the urge to stare at Travis. He'd dressed up in a red flannel shirt with a black leather vest over it and black chinos, plus a pair of hiking boots. He'd showered and trimmed his beard earlier, too. Nick was in a pair of ivory chinos and wearing a bright red sweater. But it was Holly that had dressed up the most and Jesse felt a little under dressed for the occasion. She wore a pale peach sweater and ivory velour trousers, her bright red hair scooped up off her neck with several gold combs, looking like a model. She never wore make up, either, and Jesse liked the freckles across her nose and cheeks. The first time she'd met Holly, she thought she looked more like a fifteen-year-old teenager rather than the young, but mature woman she was.

Glancing over her shoulder, she saw Snowflake and Lady intently watching them. "Hey, Nick, do they get any turkey dinner leftovers?" Jesse teased. He'd been a WMD handler in Afghanistan and Snowflake had been his dog who found the IEDs and other bomb-making materials, protecting the soldiers. She saw him smile a little.

"Well, someone here, and I won't mention who, has spoiled my well-trained dog to expect such handouts after dinner. Lady was feral and she's never gotten over being starved most of the time before Holly spotted her in a back alley in Hamilton. What gradually got Lady to trust Holly was that she always gave her food as reward. So, yes, they will both have a special turkey dinner tonight. You can rest easy."

"Freya loves handouts, too. She gives me that pleading look and I'm mush," Jesse admitted, chuckling.

"Oh, me too!" Holly said, laughing. She glanced toward the dogs lying on their bed cushions. "Nick thinks I've totally spoiled Snowflake." She blew him a kiss across the table.

"I love you anyway," he said, giving her a warm look.

"You said Lady was starving when you found her," Travis said to Nick.

"She looks well fed now, with a nice, shining coat, and a sparkle in her eyes."

"It took us about four months after she decided she'd stay with us to increase her to the right weight. We couldn't feed her too much or anything too rich or she'd lose it. Small, simple meals, instead."

"Ahem," Holly said, raising an arched brow, "and who spoiled her? Hmmmm?"

Nick's cheeks turned pink and he gave his wife a grin. "Me. Guilty."

Everyone burst into laughter.

Jesse enjoyed the repartee between the four of them. This was like being home. She had called her parents earlier in the day and that was a wonderful treat for all of them. They asked if she might come home next Thanksgiving. What about Christmas? Jesse wasn't sure about her life yet. She didn't tell them about how drawn she was to Travis. Everything was so tentative. They seemed heartened that she had two part-time jobs, a place to live in a cozy boxcar, and a dog to keep her company. She heard the hope in their voices and that felt good to her. In fact, what uplifted them the most was that she was going to email some pictures of Freya and her puppies to them. They were dog people and her coming email gift would touch them deeply. By the time she'd ended the call, Jesse realized that she was changing for the better.

Lifting her head, she saw Travis studying her. It didn't put her on edge, rather, she felt that warm blanket surrounding her as it always did when he would trade glances with her. There was something serious there and it hung between them. How badly Jesse wished she was further along in her own healing process to be courageous enough to step into a potential relationship with Travis. But she wasn't. At least, not yet, although it was always hovering at the edges of her daily life.

"Hey," Holly said, tapping her arm, "Travis mentioned the other day that you're going to give the puppies away on December fourteenth?"

"Yes, we are. Travis and I got calls from people here in Hamilton who each wanted one."

"Wonderful! Who's getting them?"

"Katie Montgomery wants one. She lost her dog a year ago and would love to have another buddy. Alex Delgado begged Travis for one and he said okay. Who am I missing, Travis?"

"Libby Johnson whose family owns Cooper's Hardware and Joe Varner, from Fish and Game, wanted one, too. We have one pup left, a male with blue eyes. I figure someone will come forward and take him when the time's right."

"Those four pups will have good homes," Nick congratulated them.

"Katie's perfect for a new puppy in her life!" Holly said. "She was devastated when Champ was hit by a car and died."

Travis smiled. "She'll probably spoil the pup. I'm sure Alex, who runs the bakery, will spoil her puppy, too. Lucky doggers."

"You can count on them doing that," Nick chimed in, laughing. "They're both real softies."

"Worse than me, huh?" Holly teased.

"Jesse has a soft heart too," Travis noted.

"I think it's a woman thing," Nick replied. "A human touch we all desperately need on this earth. You ladies rock."

Holly patted her belly, "Well, I'm going to put all my maternal instincts into this little tyke who's coming in three more months."

"I won't ever accuse you of spoiling her or him, either," Nick teased her, reaching out, grazing Holly's cheek.

Jesse tilted her head. "You don't know if it's a boy or girl?"

"No," Holly said, spooning more gravy over her mashed potatoes, "we wanted to be surprised."

Nick squeezed her lower arm. "I think you already know."

"Yes, my woman's instincts."

"What do your instincts tell you, Holly?" Travis wondered.

"A girl."

Jesse knew she'd lost her parents in a car crash when she was twenty-two. Later, she lost her older sister to suicide. Holly was the kind of person who was so maternal, caring and giving. She was glad that they could be with her and Nick tonight on this holiday. There was something in Travis's eyes that concerned her. When they left for the evening, she would ask him what was bothering him.

"IS EVERYTHING OKAY?" she asked Travis as they let Freya out into the backyard one final time for the night. They were cleaning up the puppy space and had trained them to do their business on newspapers, which was a lot easier to roll up and toss in a garbage bag afterward.

He glanced up at her as she held open the bag and he dropped the soiled newspapers into it. "I tried to talk Sam into going to dinner with us, but he refused. Then, I tried to see if I could bring him a to-go box and he got pissed off."

"Was he in a lot of pain, though?" she wondered, hurting for him because she could see it bothered him a lot. Travis had already taken out fresh newspaper to lay down in the area that the pups utilized. He leaned over, spreading them around, the puppies feeling playful and leaping for his hands as he smoothed the paper down across the concrete surface.

"The medication I hoped would work, isn't working," he said heavily, straightening. "I try to put myself in his place: how would I feel if I had unrelieved pain day in and day out? No rest from it. No relief. It has to be a special hell."

Grimacing, she whispered, "Well? In a sense, we do know what that's like, Travis. Our pain is invisible to everyone outside of us because it's internal. And there's nothing to stop it except to drug ourselves up to our eyeballs and then we have *no* feelings at all, not even good ones."

He climbed up and over the three-foot fence. "I hadn't looked at it that way, Jesse, but you're right."

"Emotional and mental pain, to me, is just as debilitating as the physical kind. And yes, there's days when it ramps up and I'm not the best person to be around."

He flashed her a tender look. "I like being around you no matter how you're feeling. You're the complete opposite of Sam. I never know if you are suffering or not. You bury it, like I do."

"Birds of a feather," she agreed, both of them becoming somber. "Does Sam usually spend the holidays here with you?"

"He did in the past. But not this year…"

"Do you think it's because I'm here, Travis? I know how gossip flies around Hamilton."

"He's never said anything to me about you, and I see him a couple times a week. I think he had high hopes for the newest prescription to ease his pain and it let him down like all the rest have."

"He's probably feeling pretty depressed about it," Jesse agreed, feeling badly for the man.

Travis went to the basement door where Freya was standing, wagging her tail, wanting back in. He stepped aside and the dog trotted in and jumped over the fence to be with her puppies once more. Going to the sink, they both washed their hands with soap and water. Then he locked the fence door and walked with Jesse over to the stairs, gesturing for her to go up first. "I've learned everyone handles pain differently," he said, following her.

She moved into the living room, wanting to hold him because she could hear the emotion in his low voice. Travis was fighting it and his own pain he carried for his father tore at her. She reached out, taking his hand. "Come on, let's go sit down." His fingers curled around hers and he gave her a look that made every nerve in her body tingle, reminding her she was still a woman with a woman's desires.

He released her hand as they sat down. Leaning back in the corner, she came and sat near him, their knees almost touching. Folding her hands in her lap, she said, "I wish I could do something more to help Sam. And you, too. This can't be easy for you, either, Travis."

"There's some days that are worse than others, Jesse." He sighed and lifted his hand. "Like today. My mother loved the holidays and I remember how much joy she put into them a week before the holiday arrived. I used to help her in the kitchen because I always liked learning how to cook. Sam never took part, said it was women's work and then would look at me like I should be agreeing with him, but I never did."

"Sam has a dog, so that has to help him."

"It does. I don't know what he'd do without old Cyrus."

"He's not abusive to him, is he?"

"No. He loves that mutt. I think it helps him a lot. Cyrus is company for him. He dotes on him and I'm relieved he has him in his life. I can't imagine what it would be like for Sam if Cyrus wasn't around."

"Like Freya is for us," she said softly, searching his saddened gaze. This was the first time Travis was allowing her to feel the weight of the father he carried as a son.

"She's a beautiful being," he said quietly.

Reaching over, she slid her hand over the back of his. "What can I do to help you, Travis?" At that moment he seemed nearly overwhelmed by his father's chronic condition.

He turned his hand over and slid his fingers between hers. "Just this. It's enough, Jesse. Having your friendship and trust this past month has been a gift to me." He held her gaze. "You have no idea how much you help me on a daily basis. I wake up feeling better. I used to wake up dreading the coming day because Sam would want to see me, chew me out for something that wasn't my fault, and then I'd have to deal with whatever the fallout from it was. I value your trust and you've made it easy for me to open up and be honest about some things in my life that I never talk to anyone about."

She curved her fingers into his, her voice low and off key. "You have given me a haven to heal myself in. I keep wanting to tell you how much you help me every day in large and small ways, Travis. You deserve to hear that you're a good person with a good heart. You know how to help others and you put yourself second in order to help folks around town."

"Guess we're the pot calling the kettle black," he said wryly, continuing to hold her hand, never wanting to let go of it—or her.

She managed a half laugh. "I guess so. Still, if there's anything I can do to help you with your father?"

"He's a buzz saw on some days, Jesse. I don't want you around him. He'll tear you up so fast that you'll be in shock. Pain makes him angry. And he always takes it out on the person he's around. I feel protective toward you and I want to shield you from him."

"Okay…"

He sat there, staring down at their hands enclosed in one another. "If I don't admit something else to you, Jesse, I feel like I'm going to explode."

Tilting her head, she thought he was joking. "Well, don't do that. What's on your mind?"

He raised his eyes, meeting and holding hers. "You."

Her heart skipped a beat.

"What do you mean?" The words came out faintly, confused sounding.

"Ever since I met you, you've tugged at my heart. To be honest? I wasn't looking to get interested in a woman right now. I've had enough to grapple with keeping the family business afloat and then, dealing with Sam and his medical issues."

Blinking, she absorbed his low, almost growling admission. His hand tightened a little and then relaxed. Mouth dry, she searched for the right words, not wanting to hurt him. "I didn't come here looking for a relationship, Travis. I felt so shattered that even though I was drawn to you, your kindness, your taking care of all of us, I tried to ignore the need that was growing daily inside me to know you better."

Silence hung in the room for a moment.

"I know you're healing, Jesse," he began haltingly. "I know my first year was hell. I need you to know that the more I'm around you, the more we share, and how you think and see the world, means a lot to me. I look forward to my time with you." His mouth twisted. "I don't claim to have words. I'm not trying to get you into my bed. I honestly like you. I've never met a woman who appealed to me like this in every way." He opened his hand and allowed her to decide to stay or leave.

She stayed.

It was enough. Plowing forward, his words terse, spoken faster, he added, "If this is a one-way attraction, if it's just me, if it's not something good for both of us, I need you to tell me that now, Jesse. If you tell me it's all in my head, that's fine. I still want you to rent my grandparents' boxcar. I still want to pay you to work two days a week at the office. Nothing changes. I promise you that. I won't ever speak of this again. I'll work to change how I feel toward you and channel it into deepening a friendship and a mutual trust with one another through good times and bad, just like friends do for one another, instead." Taking a deep, shaky breath, he stared hard at her, trying to read what was going on behind those beautiful eyes of hers, but it was impossible.

Jesse turned toward him, still holding his hand, her knee pressed against his long, hard thigh. "It's mutual, Travis. But I'm afraid to be drawn to you in the shape I'm presently in."

Heaving an inner sigh of relief, he nodded brusquely. "I can accept that, Jesse. I know how fragile you are right now and you're working hard every day to find pieces and parts of yourself, fighting to get stronger. I've been there. I know the process."

Her smile was watery. Tears jammed into her eyes. "This is why I like you so much. You understand. I've never had a man read me as well as you do, Travis. I know you're not looking at me for sex only. I sensed it was something far deeper, more beautiful and long lasting going on between us. Until you just told me, I couldn't put into words what I felt toward you, either. I have a push-pull attraction to you. A part of me, the healthy part, is drawn to you. The rest of me is such a clutter and I'm constantly second guessing myself regarding myself...you...us..."

He reached out and with his index finger moved a stray black curl away from her temple. "We came together and I felt a strong friendship bond with you. What I'd like to do—and I want your thoughts on this—is I'd like to move along that trail with you, Jesse. That way, if you feel whole enough at some point you can be the rudder for us? I won't make a move on you. I want a woman to come to me honestly and openly. It has to be mutual, but you're in charge."

Closing her eyes for a moment, her emotions in upheaval, she whispered, "Yes...yes, I'd like that." Opening them, she saw such tenderness burning in his gaze for her, she knew he liked her far more than just as a friend. "Thank you for knowing where I'm at right now. I don't feel like I can carry an outside load like a relationship just yet."

"I know that." He released her hand, holding her warm gaze. "I like where we're at. If you want something more? All you have to do is tell me. That way, neither of us is assuming."

"I don't like assumptions. Never did."

"Makes two of us."

She sat back, feeling all the tension draining out of her. "I'm glad we talked, Travis. Thank you for having the courage to speak up. I was afraid to approach you and I know it was me, not you. I thought I'd picked up some clues from you but I talked myself out of it because my mind plays tricks on me sometimes when anxiety gets the better of me. It clouds my reality."

"I know that one, but in time, it too will start to lessen a little here and there."

"Tonight showed me so much. Nick and Holly are so happy together. I knew he had PTSD and Holly told me one time that because they allowed themselves to love one another, that it has helped his symptoms as a result. She said they talk a lot and often with one another, that it's a key to their relationship being stable and healthy. That was so good to hear because my feelings for you were there all the time, but I couldn't fit them into everything else that was going on inside me. Yet, I noticed since I've met you that my anxiety, especially, has calmed down. At first, I didn't know why, but as time went on, I was able to analyze it and figure it out. It was you, Travis. Who you are. You're good for me."

"That's nice to hear. I didn't expect this, Jesse."

Giving him a searching look, she added, "You're like an anchor for me right now. I find myself more stable since coming to Hamilton. Getting to know you and then with Freya and her puppies coming into my life, it has filled me with hope. Real hope. I thought I'd lost that, Travis, I really did. It has started surfacing slowly, now and then. And when it does, it's always when you're around. I finally figured that one out, too."

"Dogs and puppies are always good for a person's soul don't you think?"

She managed a small laugh. "Absolutely. My dog, Tag, was my best friend growing up."

"How does Freya fulfill your life?"

She liked his incisive question. "She makes me feel safe like you do." Travis cocked his head, question in his eyes. "Since my release from the military, I've felt horribly vulnerable. I used to have a sense of safety within myself, but that's gone now, too. I've lost my confidence, also. Meeting you, living in that beautiful little caboose that belonged to your grandparents, made me feel safe once again. And Freya charging that cougar, throwing herself at the rear door to get at the cat, I knew she'd protect me just as fiercely."

"More than anything, I want you to feel safe and secure." He looked around the cabin. "Does this place give that to you?"

"I don't know. The caboose does, for sure. And maybe because you live here, I feel safe in this cabin. I'm not exactly logical about this, am I?"

Shaking his head, he muttered, "Emotions are different than thoughts. Logic and emotions don't always fit together. No, it's not silly at all. This cabin was *my* safety net, my safe house, I guess you'd call it that. It made no sense to me, but that was how it felt and over the years it has been a place for me to heal since leaving the Army."

"Your emotions count more than what you have in your head. If this place gives you that sense, then you should be here," she said.

"After we give Freya's puppies away, would you like to go move back to the caboose with her?"

"I'd like that very much. I'll get to see you at least twice a week."

He rubbed his hands down his chinos. "If I invite you to dinner at the cabin would you come? Bring Freya, too?"

Her lips curved. "I'd love that, Travis. I really would."

"Then, let's make this work. After December fourteenth, we'll get you back out to your safe place. I want you to heal, Jesse. And if this is what you need I'm all for it. I'll support you any way that I can."

Tears burned in her eyes and she choked them back. "Thank you for giving me the chance I needed…"

CHAPTER 9

November 23

T HE NEXT MORNING Jesse awoke to find a foot of new snow on the ground. She pushed the heavy drapes aside and peered out the window. The cabin had stands of pines behind it, beyond the large yard and a nearby meadow. Looking up, she saw the gray sky was clearing and growing brighter. She'd awakened at six a.m. and today, she was going to be working at Katie's Koffee Bean for the afternoon. She keyed her hearing and left the window, padding barefoot across the cool cedar floor and picking up her yellow chenille bathrobe, pulling it over her green flannel granny gown that fell to her ankles.

Her heart centered on Travis and their long, searching talk with one another yesterday. She dreamt about him last night and it was filled with sweet promise. Cracking the door open, she heard him puttering around in the kitchen. Freya had come up from the basement, the door always open for her to come and go as she pleased, the clacking of her paws against the wooden floor announcing her arrival. Travis was usually up at five without fail and Freya had gotten used to being fed around six.

Smiling to herself, she gathered her toiletry articles and quietly walked across the hall to the large bathroom. She could smell bacon frying and knew Freya was VERY fond of this particular meat. As she went into the bathroom, she caught sight of Travis cooking at the gas stove. Freya was sitting alertly nearby, probably hoping for a tidbit. Her heart expanded with an explosion of silent joy. Closing the door, she turned on the shower.

Their talk still lingered within her and she felt more and more hope. There was something so special about Travis. Most men she'd experienced had never fessed up like he did. She'd always hungered for just this kind of deep, trusting talk between herself and a man. She knew he was trying to communicate better and it touched her deeply. Learning so much more about his family was an important key to understanding him and seeing how much pressure he was under with an incapacitated father. She would guess that the deeper worry in

Travis was that his father would die too soon and he'd already lost most of his family. Her heart went out to him, to all the loads he silently carried with integrity and responsibility.

After washing her hair with tangerine-scented shampoo, she noted her black strands were growing quickly. Allowing the warm streams to wash the soap off her body, her mind drifted. Her life had gone from zero to a hundred in less than a month here in Hamilton. Just thinking about it on some days scared the hell out of her. And on other days like this one, it felt so right and she was incredibly grateful for the turn in her luck after the three nightmare months before that.

Pulling on a pair of jeans, warm, thick socks, and a sweater she'd brought from home—a lavender one with a crew neck—she was ready for the day ahead. Feeling tentative, but wanting to be out in the kitchen with Travis and Freya, she drew a comb through her damp hair, the slight curls put into place. Next, she brushed her teeth and then pushed the steamy door open.

Freya perked up instantly, whirled around and clattered across the living room, greeting her at the end of the hall, tail wagging with gusto.

"Well, good morning to you, too," Jesse laughed, leaning down and petting Freya as she whirled around and around in a circle in front of her. It was her "happy dance." She loved the dog's blue eyes, seeing such love shining in them for her alone.

"Better hurry," Travis called over his shoulder, transferring the last of the bacon to a paper towel filled basket, "Freya has her eyes on the prize here. We might not get any for breakfast, Jesse."

Laughing, she walked over to the table with the prancing dog at her side. "She loves bacon, no question."

He glanced over at her, setting the iron skillet on the burner, and then turning it off. "So, do we."

We. The word was a promise filled with possibilities and she knew it more than ever as he met her gaze. Never had a man's eyes spoken so wonderfully to her. "You're right about that. What can I do to help out?"

"Coffee just got done," he said, motioning toward it on the counter.

"Mmmm, that was great timing." She poured two cups.

"I'm making scrambled eggs with venison, green peppers, potatoes and onions. Interested?"

She brought his cup over to the stove where he stood. "Very."

"You're going over to Katie's at one p.m. today, right?" he asked, taking another skillet and brushing the inside of it with some bacon grease.

She settled her hips against the counter, watching him cook. "Yes. Why?"

He looked out the window over the sink. "It snowed last night. I was wondering if, after breakfast, you'd like to go hunt up a little Christmas tree that you could put in your red caboose?"

"That sounds wonderful." She gazed toward the living room. "Aren't you going to have a tree in here, Travis?"

"Always," he promised, cracking six eggs into the skillet. "I have a favorite place where the family always put a tree up for the holidays. I thought you might like to tag along?"

"I'd love too. Can Freya come? The snow's too deep for her pups. But I bet she'd love to be outdoors for a while."

"Good idea."

SUNLIGHT SENT GOLDEN shafts down through the ragged gray cloud layer that drifted silently over them, the cold front having passed through their region last night. Travis had driven off road for about a mile and braked the truck to a stop. There was a slight knoll sprinkled heavily with blue spruce all over it, just in front of them. The trees were of varying ages and heights. Freya bounded out of the pickup, joyfully leaping like a bounding rabbit through the pristine, undisturbed snow that was up to her belly in some places. The wind had knocked off much of the snow covering the branches of the spruce. It was just below freezing and Jesse had worn her lavender knit hat, her very worn winter gloves, plus a nylon down coat that fell over her hips. She carried a small saw with sharp teeth in her right hand. Her hair had grown enough to cover her neck and it snugly protected that part from exposure.

Travis was just a step ahead of her and she skipped forward, grabbing his right gloved hand. He turned his head, surprise in his expression. But then, as she curved her fingers into his, that look turned her body into one big ache of wanting to love this man. She was having what she termed a "good day." Was it because she was outside in the crisp, cold air? The bright sun beating down upon them off and on? The natural beauty of Montana grabbing her, making her grateful to be in Hamilton? The Rocky Mountains surrounded them and were clothed in white snow. Their blue granite flanks were mostly covered below the ten-thousand-foot line with a thick, green carpeting of forest. Everything felt so alive, overflowing with hope for Jesse. She loved days like this because they were so rare. To see that burning look of longing in Travis's eyes made her lower body ache with a desire of its own. Somehow, she knew he would be a tender lover who treated his woman as an equal, not seen as something to be used and regarded as less than human. There was a gleam of satisfaction in his eyes.

Nothing needed to be said as she walked close to him, luxuriating in him being a consummate male. She hadn't thought about sex in so long—until recently, that is. Never one to act on her needs unless she was in a serious relationship, it felt good to feel the return of her old self. Jesse didn't expect it to last long. It hadn't before. She wanted to celebrate her old self that had resurfaced. Later, she would end up grieving when it submerged once more beneath the symptoms of the PTSD. Travis definitely brought out her old, healthy self, there was no question!

"Well," he said, "take a look at these trees. Grandfather and I used to come up every spring and plant at least five or six seedlings. Over the years they would grow. That's why the area has so many trees of different ages and heights."

"That's a wonderful thing to do," she said.

"See any you'd like to check out?"

Squinting against the sudden burst of bright sunlight passing across them as the clouds parted overhead, she allowed herself to be deluged with her own feelings toward Travis. Leaning her head against his upper arm for a moment, she nodded. His hand tightened around hers in response, reaction to her carefree contact. Lifting her head, she melted beneath the burning look he gave her. He was enjoying this outing as much as she was. "Maybe we should take more days outside like this?"

Nodding, she smiled. "I love being outdoors." And then she added shyly, "With the right person, of course: you." There was pleasure in his expression over her softened admittance.

"Let's make a date to do something at least once a week? Look at Freya. She's going crazy running around, just pure jubilance."

Laughing, she watched their dog go zooming in and around the smaller and larger pines, weaving in and out of them at lightning speed, snow kicked up in sparkling, diamond-like veils from beneath her hind feet. "I think it's because she knows she's going to live, not die. That her pups will go to people who will love them as much as she does and we do." Her pink tongue was hanging out the side of her mouth and she was a blur of motion, immense energy and shameless exuberance.

"This is the first time she's really gotten outside the yard to go stretch herself," Travis murmured. "I know that breed needs *a lot* of exercise. I think after the pups have left, I'll take her with me because often, I'll drive the truck to some of our fishing spots. It's outside of town and I can let her stretch her legs and do what she was bred to do."

"What?" she laughed. "Herd sheep? Don't tell me you're going to buy a flock for her?"

Joining her laughter, Travis shook his head. "I've been reading up on Border Collies. And I went online and found a photo of her with her old owner Stella. Freya has won many championships in sheep herding."

"I wonder if she's happier being with us or misses being at those shows?"

"I don't know. But judging by how she's racing around? I'll bet we could give her a home where she'd get all kinds of exercise. It might not be herding sheep, but she could go out with me on fishing guide expeditions. Some of them are overnight. She'd be a good watchdog out there for us, too. Or, when we hike a trail together. I'm sure she'd love that."

Jesse warmed to his words that she was sure had just unconsciously slipped from him: *I'll bet we could give her a good home.* Her heart ballooned fiercely with what she knew was love for Travis. No longer did she try to deny it. Today, she wasn't frightened of an unsure future because of her own shortcomings. It was the magic of this morning, the freezing temperature combined with golden slats of sunshine pouring down on the valley. And being with him in one of the most beautiful spots she could ever want to be a part of. It conspired to allow her to dream right along with Travis. Later, perhaps, she would bring what he said to his attention. It was something she wanted to explore with him.

ONCE JESSE DISCOVERED a little four-foot Scotch pine and Travis chose a six-foot tall one for the corner of his cabin, the hard part was done. After cutting them down, he dragged both of them back to his truck. Jesse helped him place them in the truck bed and tie them down so they wouldn't get blown out on the trip back to town. Later, over hot coffee in the cab, he wanted to continue their talk from last night. The engine was running and the heater on, Freya in the rear cab seat panting happily from her nonstop running around. This morning Jesse seemed almost as if she were skipping along in the snow like a happy child instead of an adult who carried untold, invisible loads that weighed down her soul. Did their opening up to one another, do it? He wasn't sure but he wanted to find out.

"About last night?"

"Yes."

"You seem lighter today, Jesse. I was wondering if our talk made you feel better?" *Or worse*, but he bit back those words. He hoped not and watched her grow contemplative over his question.

"You know how I've told you before that I have a few good days and mostly the rest are bad days?"

"Yes, and I can validate that symptom for sure. Ups and downs. I hated them, but I had to deal with them. I'm sure you're no different."

"The same," she agreed, crossing one ankle over her knee, slouching back in the comfortable seat and appreciating the beauty before her.

"I was wondering if you are having a normal 'up' day. I want to think our talk last night lifted some loads off you, not add to them?"

She rolled her head to the left, meeting his dark, searching gaze. "It was the talk, I'm sure of that, Travis. And I feel that because of it, I woke up this morning feeling happier than I can recall in a long, long time." She reached out, placing her hand on his thick, hard thigh, his Levi's damp from kneeling down in the snow to cut the trunk of the tree off. "For the first time since I got nailed with the symptoms, I felt like a giddy six-year-old this morning. I don't normally have happy emotions bubbling up through me like this. They used to before I got hit with PTSD, but not since then." His expression showed relief.

"I hope that with my being with you that you'll have more ups than downs."

"That would be lovely," she sighed, closing her eyes momentarily. "I lost my ability to dream over a year ago. From what the shrink who saw me at Bagram said, it wasn't unusual to stop dreaming. That crushed me because I used to dream every night and looked forward to it."

"Did you dream last night?" It was a bold, intimate question and Travis held his breath, watching her stare through the windshield at the picture postcard that surrounded them as she digested his question.

"It was a happy dream, Travis."

"Have you had many since your symptoms came on?"

"No. I had one the first night I slept in your grandparents' caboose in that new bed you'd bought for it." She removed her hand from his thigh and gestured toward the beauty outside. "I want to think that it's because of us, the connection we're forging with one another. You give me hope and now, after that talk last night, it just feels more solid between us. I can't exactly describe it, Travis, but it makes me feel good, more confident in myself. Most of all, I was seeing bits and pieces of my old self this morning that I thought were dead and gone." Her voice changed and grew husky. "I almost wanted to cry from the sheer joy of rediscovering those parts of me that weren't really dead, just missing in action."

"Then," he said, smiling faintly, "whatever is going on between us is good, Jesse. I feel the same way: I'm reawakening to parts of myself that I thought were gone forever, too."

"But they aren't."

"No…you're a miracle to me, Jesse. Magical. With you, I'm beginning to connect once more with the small, but important, things that make my life worth living again."

She sat there, sponging in his low, rumbling admissions. "I like how you see things, Travis. I don't know that I feel very magical…a unicorn missing her horn, I suppose…"

"Take it from me," he teased, "you're a unicorn in disguise."

Managing a slight, nervous smile she said, "On a day like today? I'm optimistic once more. Before, I always was, until that night in the village…it was destroyed."

"Or so you thought?" he probed, hearing the pain in her lowered tone.

"Yes…until now…"

"I was that way the first year, too. Over time, getting into a different rut with something I loved, which is fishing, I slowly started to feel again. Being out in nature has helped me tremendously."

"Good and bad feelings?" Jesse wondered, holding his thoughtful gaze.

"Both."

"What about your old self, Travis? Has it ever returned?"

He sighed and rested his hands on the steering wheel. "I didn't know the man inside me at all. The anxiety ripped me apart. I'd never felt like that before except out on missions. And it would always simmer down or go away when we were back behind the wire. Over time, the anxiety remained around for longer periods of time. It would simmer at first, but built up stronger the more time I spent over there outside the wire. I was at a rolling boil, the anxiety and hyper-alertness not going away. By the time I got home, I was high strung and super sensitive to everything, especially to noise. That's why I hid. I went to work, still adjusting, and glad to be going home at night to a quiet, dark cabin to be alone."

"You needed that."

"Very much so. Just," and he waved his finger in the direction of Hamilton, "like you need the red caboose right now. I really do understand where you're at in your healing process, Jesse." His mouth thinned for a moment. "The bad news is that only you can change it over time. The good news is I found that by letting a few people I trusted into my life, the anxiety began to smooth out to a degree. That was a huge gift to my quality of life."

"I have you and Freya," she noted humbly.

"Holly, Nick, Sue, Emily and Katie, too. They all adore you. There are good people surrounding you and that's what it takes: friends and family. You're close to your parents, also."

"They all help me," she acknowledged. "I guess I'm pretty lucky because you're one of the people supporting me, too."

"This is what it takes," he said somberly. "There's a lot of men and women out there who have major challenges when they get home."

"You have your father."

"I had my grandparents, too, who gave me a solid foundation growing up."

"You've said Hiram was a good person and I believe you. He doesn't sound like he was abusive to me, and you felt he was sort of like a second father to you. What was the rub between him and Sam?"

"I think I know. Sam has always been the rebellious one in our family. Everyone else was hard working, responsible and kept the strong family unit going. Sam was very different."

"Who do you take after more?"

"My mother and my grandparents. That's probably why Sam continues to this day to accuse me of being like my grandfather."

"Do you think he was jealous?"

"I don't think so."

"Was there some change in your family that might have made him this way?"

"My mother dying so young. She and Sam were deeply in love. It was what I'd term a loving marriage."

"Did Sam like being a father?"

Travis studied her for a moment. "He was uncomfortable in that role might be a better way to say it. Hiram and Inez came by it naturally, like my mother did. He had to learn how to be a father. There was never a question that he didn't love us, though. My mother quietly showed him how to be close with us, to be a guide of sorts and he took to it. When Hiram retired, he bought the red caboose and put it out in that meadow near the river. My Gram Inez loved that clearing. She had helped my grandfather decorate the interior of the place. A lot of what you see in the caboose is her creativity. Hiram was responsible for rebuilding the boxcar, which is what he worked on after he retired."

"They were really happy in the caboose."

"Both of them loved it. Gram was a very private person, very loving to all of us, but she needed a lot of peace and quiet, too. She was shy, but well loved by everyone in Hamilton. She did a lot of charity work in town for others who had less than they did."

"I wish I could have met them," she sighed, giving him a tender smile.

"They were good people, Jesse. Hard working, solid and reliable."

"But Sam was the rebellious one in the family. What were his dreams, I wonder?"

"He wanted to leave Hamilton and become a globe trotter. He liked adventures and challenges. Unlike the others in our family, he didn't see getting married or raising children as a top priority. They were way down on his scale of important things he wanted to do. He was in his late teens and into his twenties, and that's a time when a lot of people do risk taking. It wasn't wrong. Hiram never blamed him for what he chose to do, but Sam, I think, at that time, was too immature to understand what he'd like to have seen from him. It caused a lot of friction between them."

"Did Hiram lean on him to conform, then?"

He gave her a congratulatory look. "My grandfather was a very disciplined man, very organized and responsible. His top priority was that the eldest son of the next generation gets settled down, gets married and has children. Sam wanted nothing to do with that idea, so they fought all the time."

"Wow, that would be rough to live around," she agreed.

"Sam has held it against Hiram for all time and I don't know if he never forgave him," he said wearily. "Even today, he's fighting battles from back then, dragging them up and throwing them in my face on his darker, pain-filled days."

"Wasn't your fault," she muttered, her brows dipping, seeing the angst in his expression.

"No, I was a convenient whipping post, was all."

"I saw many Afghan families who were completely dysfunctional. It was always the children who suffered." She reached out and laid her hand on his arm, feeling the tension in it created by their discussion.

"Yeah, I saw a lot of that same thing while over there. Really sad."

"It's tough to deal with your father on a bad day?"

"It is. I try not to personalize it. I understand the past, how it happened and how Sam reacted to it. He was a square peg being forced to fit into the round hole of our family expectations and traditions. Getting busted up on the bull riding circuit in his early twenties didn't help matters. And today, it's running his life with his joint problems."

"I've always loved my growing up years and value them more than ever before."

"No skeletons in your family closet?" he asked, smiling thinly.

"Not that I know of. My parents are farm people and they are part of a multi-generation who came to Montana in the 1800s. I'm not much into genealogy, so I'm sure there's got to be some skeletons laying around some-where."

"My grandparents lived in a cabin in Hamilton near our shop before they moved to the red caboose. Kyle and I were lucky and grew up with them nearby."

"It sounds like you all got along?"

"Yes, we did. Kyle and I were spoiled rotten. What about your parents? What is your mom like?"

"My mom is a registered nurse and I wanted to follow in her footsteps. Grandma Susannah was a nurse. She was one of the first young women who went to school and got a job in the 1920s when it wasn't popular for a woman to be out of the kitchen or home."

"Is your mother a feminist, too?"

"Absolutely. We all believe in equality with males. We're no one's slave."

"How did your mom take you going into the military?"

"She was fine with it. My dad worried a lot, but supported me, anyway. And things went fine until that one night in-country." Jesse wrinkled her nose, not wanting to discuss it.

"Someday," he began in a low tone, holding her saddened-looking eyes, "you might look back in three or four years and have the words to give to your parents so they understand why you had to leave the military and start your healing journey."

She reached out and he closed his hand over hers. "I want that so badly. They're so confused about me. They're trying hard to understand where I'm at and the blame lies on me and not on them. I don't know how to tell them about my symptoms. We have weekly phone calls and we all feel better after getting to talk with one another."

"Are your grandparents still alive?"

"No, unfortunately. I miss them terribly. My grandfathers were in the Army and I think they'd understand if they were alive, what's happened to me."

"Usually your brothers and sisters in the service will always understand."

"It was a load off my shoulders when you offered me Wi-Fi, Travis. I got in touch with my old unit and I connected with them once again." She looked up at the cab ceiling. "It was so hard not to cry. I never realized how much they cared for me until that call."

"Military connections just don't break with time or stress," he said, nodding.

"Well, I have been calling the captain every week. Most of the other guys are in schooling here stateside. He's given me their phone numbers and I've been talking with all of them. It was scary at first, but after a while, I was so glad that I did it." She wiped her eyes as they filled with tears. "Of late, I've become so emotional."

"Because you're healing now, Jesse. Tears come when you feel in a safe place with people who are surrounding and supporting you."

"You mean I'm doing something normal?" It was supposed to come out as a joke, but her voice broke as she struggled not to let more tears form.

He released her hand and caressed the back of her hair. "It's okay to cry. It's good for us. What do you say we go home? We'll drop the trees off and then I'll take you for lunch up at Sue's Yellow Rose Diner."

She managed a wobbling smile and sat up. "That sounds like a great start to my day. Let's go…"

Putting the truck in gear, Travis slowly turned around on the fairly narrow road. The shoulders were solid and soon he was driving out of the pristine area. He could see Jesse fighting a sudden surge of emotion, talking about the team who she was assigned to. That heart-tie could never be erased or destroyed. She was uncomfortable allowing him to see her tears and he hoped that he'd handled the situation correctly. The protective male in him wanted to sweep her into his arms, hold her tight while she sobbed out all her grief from that night. True, he didn't know what had happened, but one day, he might.

Braking at the stop sign, he turned to the right, heading down the road about mile from where they'd make the turn to the red caboose. It felt right that she wanted to live there with Freya. In his imagination, he wondered if the spirits of his grandfather and grandmother were there to welcome her, to make her feel safe and loved. It was funny how a boxcar could hold so many treasured memories. But it did. Travis was glad that Jesse was in his life, living in that boxcar that still permeated with love. Giving her a glance, he saw her wiping her eyes with a tissue and then stuffing it into her pocket. Someday, he hoped, he wouldn't have to rein in what his heart wanted to do for her. What she needed right now was to be held. And he was the right person to do just that.

CHAPTER 10

"WHAT DO YOU have in your arms?" Jesse asked Travis. It was Saturday morning and Freya had led her pups up from the basement and now they were all playing around the six-foot blue spruce that he'd set up earlier in one corner of the living room. They would sniff a branch and then pounce on it. Then, two pups would chase each other around the base of the tree. Travis wisely took off all the lower branches of the tree so no bulbs would break and the pups wouldn't put tinsel in their mouths.

"Two Christmas boxes," he said. Placing them down on the floor, he picked up the smaller box of the two. "This is for your tree in the red caboose." Setting it on the coffee table, he gestured her to come and take a look at the contents. "These were Hiram and Inez's Christmas ornaments. I took some personal things from the caboose after he passed on and this box was one of them. Inez would make a new Christmas decoration each year. She was great at knitting, making quilts, crocheting and tatting." He opened the box as she approached. "There's some beautiful things in here, really old, from another time and place. I think you'll appreciate them."

Curious, she sat down on the couch, the coffee table nearby. "I'm so glad to know this. I don't have the money to go out and buy decorations and I was worried about how I was going to make that little tree look pretty."

"You can use these instead?"

She pulled out one of the flaps, pressing it down, peering into the box. "I'd love to, Travis. That is where they lived and I love the feelings inside that boxcar. I'd like to use them."

He chuckled, bringing the second, larger box up on the coffee table. "Hey, I think it's a great idea. As a kid growing up, I always liked going out to their caboose to help them trim their tree. Inez made hot chocolate with marshmallows for us." He became somber. "It was the event my brother Kyle looked forward to most in the year. Hiram and Inez always made special treats for us, like candied apples that we'd get to eat after the tree was decorated."

She moved her hand over the first shelf in the box, seeing the many crocheted and tatted items. "Those happy memories should always be saved and always come out at special times of the year. Good times should be remembered and passed on to the next generation."

Freya came over, wagging her tail, eagerly sniffing at the box. Jesse glanced up and saw the grief and memories in Travis's eyes. "Will you help me trim my tree when we're done with yours?" she asked, hope in her voice.

"Sure, I'd like to do that."

"I don't make candied apples, but I could make us a bowl of popcorn if we do this?" She looked out the window. The sky was clouding up and the forecaster was calling it a possible snow day late this evening.

"Sounds good. I'll take you up on it. Looks like the pups want to help us." He pointed toward the tree. All of them were beneath it, scampering around, yipping and giving sharp little barks, merrily chasing one another and skidding all over the polished wood floor. Freya went over, being a good mother, and watched them with parental interest.

"I can hardly wait for everyone to pick up their pup on the fourteenth of December."

"I'm going to miss all the energy and fun of having them around," Travis admitted. He opened the second, larger box. "This box has my mother's decorations. I bring them out and hang them up every year."

"What about your father? Does he have a tree, too?"

With a grimace, Travis said, "He's never been much into holidays. It doesn't seem to matter to him now. It did when we were kids, though. When I tried to talk him into a tree after I got home from the Army he told me to never bring the subject up again."

She peered into the box, seeing the same orderly neatness as Inez's box. These were people who were organized. "What happens on Christmas morning? Do you buy him a gift? Does he give anything to you?"

"No and no. After our mother died, he stopped celebrating any holidays. I can't say I blame him." He drew out the first shelf containing the electric lights to be placed first around the tree. "My mother loved all the holidays, but especially Christmas. She would go out and get a tree and we'd decorate it together. Hiram and Inez would come over and help us trim the tree. My father usually went out and visited some buddies, watched football games with them and would come home in the late evening after our grandparents had left."

Feeling sad for Travis, she nodded, not knowing what to say. The puppies suddenly zeroed in on a small, red plastic ball that could fit in their tiny mouths that he'd set on the coffee table. They loved chasing it around and Travis picked it up, rolling it away from the tree. She smiled, watching them slip, slide and scamper toward it, happily yipping in their tiny falsetto voices. Freya sat and watched, ears pricked up. Jesse was sure that the mother could tire herself out by endlessly chasing her five pups. Freya already knew the living room and kitchen area were safe for them to go scampering around in. The pups also knew where there was newspaper. They could squat and pee or do number two on it, and then gallop off to their next exciting adventure. It was a win-win for all of them.

"How about your folks? Do they enjoy Christmas?" he asked, starting to string the lights with her help.

"Oh, it's a big deal! As a matter of fact, Mom called me last week and asked if we might come home on the twenty-fourth for a visit, but I told her no and that next year, I'd plan to do something. We talked about me maybe coming to Billings for Thanksgiving, staying a few days and then coming back to Hamilton. I didn't exactly include you in on it, Travis. I wasn't sure if you'd like to do that or not."

"Sure, I would. I miss family, too, if you want the truth. My mother was the one who made the nest, made us a family, Sam didn't. And I'd like to be part of your parents' nest because I'd like to spend it with you."

"We'd have to bring Freya along."

"Of course," he said, finishing the circuit several times around the tree. "She's a real car dog from what I can tell. Given her show background and her owner driving her thousands of miles to attend shows in different states, I think she'd be fine. Are your parents okay with the dog coming along?"

"Yes, that's not a problem."

Wanting to shout for joy, Jesse said nothing, helping him open up the next box containing glittery round bulbs to be hung on the tree's limbs. Absorbing the sadness he was trying to hide, she saw the pain in his eyes. For her, the future was looking even more promising than ever before, but not for Travis. "By next Christmas I hope to not be anything like I was when I came home from the service."

He hung the glittering icicles around the tree. "You'll be in a lot better space by then, Jesse. Not cured, but you'll understand yourself and how to control the cycles when they arise, or at least divert them by putting them in a direction where you aren't hurting yourself or others."

"I sure hope you're right. I'd give anything to return to the way I was."

He came over and placed his arms around her shoulders, holding her widening eyes. "You don't see yourself, Jesse, but I do. In what little time you've been here, you've made huge, incredible changes in yourself and how you deal with this internal war that goes on within us." His voice grew tender. "If you're ever in doubt with where you're at, if you need some outside and objective feedback, see me, okay?" He removed his arms from her shoulders and went back to work at the decorations box, drawing out another level of items to be hung.

Stunned, her shoulders tingling with his contact, Jesse stared at him, thinking that what had just happened was her imagination at work. But it wasn't. Travis's touch hadn't been flirty or sexual. It was human-to-human. And how much she needed that kind of connection right now! He seemed unruffled by his affectionate stance toward her. Jesse ached for more closeness, more intimacy with him. This was a huge step that would close the gap between them. Unafraid of him reaching out to her, she'd been wanting this kind of familiarity with him for a long time. Now, it had happened. The moment he'd lightly rested his arms on her shoulders, monitoring how much weight he'd placed upon them, told her just how sensitive he was of her. That spoke volumes to Jesse. She had nothing but a bad string of experiences with men who were selfish and unaware of anything but themselves and their needs. Finding out over time that most men wanted a woman for sex, and that was it. How different Travis was from those bad experiences.

THE SMELL OF popcorn permeated the air of the caboose. The small tree looked so pretty, nearly trimmed. The box that Inez had carefully kept with all her yearly crocheted and tatted decorations were now on that tree. She'd seen Travis relax here in the boxcar, no more talk about his father. Instead, as he'd drawn out the decorations and given them to her to hang, there was a story he shared with her about each one. In an hour's time, on this cloudy winter afternoon, she'd learned more about his family than ever before. She was warmed by his trust in divulging it to her. Another sense of closeness with him layered around her like a warm blanket.

They sat together after she had placed the angel that Inez had tatted with pink and red colors, on top of the tree. Some of the colors were a bit faded, but given the angel had been made probably fifty years earlier, made Jesse appreciate it even more. They sat close to one another, the large popcorn bowl resting on his thigh, hand around it to keep it steady and available for her. Travis had gotten a satellite connection and installed a TV for her to watch a few days beforehand.

His cell phone buzzed and he grimaced. "Probably Sam," he said in way of apology, standing and pulling it out of his shirt pocket. "I'll take it outside."

It felt as if the warm, cozy energy within the boxcar evaporated in a millisecond. "Sure," Jesse said, giving him a sympathetic look. There was no happiness in his eyes as he walked toward the rear and opened the door, stepping out on the platform, and shutting it behind him. Wanting to say something that would take away that heaviness she felt around Travis, she realized this was a family dynamic and he was at the point of that particular spear. Still, Jesse wanted to do something. She ached for Travis. He was trying to be a good, responsible son but his father didn't have the ability to show love to anyone due to his pain. Getting up, she knew the day was at an end. The only time Sam called was when he wanted something. Glad that her parents had a true, loving relationship, Jesse reminded herself that there were other members who were not like Sam. Different people handled pain differently. Looking around the boxcar, she wished she could have met Hiram and Inez. They had been surrogate parents to Travis and Kyle, and she knew their stamp on them had been pure and heart driven.

The call didn't take long. She absorbed the dark look on Travis's face as he re-entered the caboose.

"Do you have to go?"

"Yes," he muttered, giving her an unhappy look. "I need to see Sam."

She lifted her hand, resting it against his upper arm. "Anything I can do?" She searched his eyes. They looked heavy with a special kind of weariness that she'd seen in caregivers who carried the load of a relative or loved one far too long.

"It's nice just knowing that you're here when I return, Jesse."

Her heart swelled with so many wonderful emotions. "I'm here for *you*." She forced herself to break contact with his arm. There was such a compulsion to throw her arms around his shoulders and hold him. Even men needed this, even if they were taught differently. "Would you like to have dinner with me at six p.m. at the caboose? I'm going to make something simple like creamed chipped beef on toast."

He perked up. "Yes, I'd like that."

"See you then…"

TRAVIS APPRECIATED THE wonderful, mouth-watering fragrances of home cooking when he returned later for dinner with Jesse. She was setting the small table opposite the kitchen sink and gas stove. Being here brought back strong, loving memories of his grandparents sitting in those exact same chairs, having a meal together. He took off his Stetson, hung it on a hook and shrugged out of his coat, hanging it up nearby. Seeing Jesse give him a warm, silent look of hello sent his heavy heart thudding in his chest. She was more and more necessary to his daily life than he had ever realized upon first meeting her.

"Smells great," he said. "Can I help?"

"No, just sit down. It's all ready. How's Sam doing?"

He waited until she'd brought over the casserole with the chipped beef white sauce and placed it on a trivet, then pulled out the chair for her. "I think he just wanted someone to talk to," he admitted, after she was seated.

"Was he in pain?"

"Yes, that's always a given." He sat down and took two pieces of golden toast from a saucer, placing them on his plate. "He sits and watches TV from the time he gets up to the time he goes to bed. And sometimes, he'll call and tell me to come over just to talk to a real, live human, I think." He managed a forced smile from one corner of his mouth. Jesse had provided a soup ladle and he put the chipped beef over his toast.

"Does he have friends here, Travis?"

"Most of the people he knows are his clients and they don't live here. I've tried to get him online to email with them, but he won't do it."

"Older people aren't very confident about the computer age," she agreed, spooning the chipped beef on her toast. "I've been thinking about something, Travis, and I'd like to run it by you."

"In regards to Sam?"

"Yes. My mother Peggy is an RN. I grew up with her telling me all kinds of true stories about patients that she cared for at the hospital where she works. The other day I was talking with my folks on the phone, and I told my mom about Sam and his joint condition. She told me that one of the osteopaths she knows, who is now retired, always used a hot tub in lieu of pain meds for his patients. Medically, it's called hydrotherapy."

Brows rising, Travis said, "A hot tub?"

"Yes, Mom said the person sits in the tub, in the hot water—usually 102 or 103 degrees Fahrenheit—for five to ten minutes. Doing this increases the blood circulation through all the joints in a person's body. Dr. Frank Morgan, the osteopath, found that his patients could go without pain meds for three to four hours or longer, between two sittings in a hot tub, one in the morning when the patient woke up and another after five p.m. When he realized that, he contacted Delos Charity, which has an office in Billings, and asked if they could donate small hot tubs for medical purposes to such patients. They did. Pretty soon, Mom said that his thirty patients with issues ranging from osteoarthritis to other joint-related injuries, were taking less than half their meds as before. And some of those who got no relief from meds, now responded just to aspirin, and it was helping relieve their pain." She shrugged. "I was wondering if Sam might be open to trying a hot tub since nothing else is working for him?"

Considering her story, he chewed slowly on the tasty fare, trying not to get his hopes up. "This is all anecdotal evidence?"

"Yes, it is. It worked, even though there's been no double-blind testing to prove it once and for all. It's better to try something like this, Travis, than have Sam hooked on opioid meds."

"That's what I've worried about. But Sam's not stupid, either. He's seen other people in the area hooked on opioid drugs and stays away from them. His doctor suggests either aspirin or an NSAID to try and help his pain."

"But none of them work."

"No."

"Who's his doctor here in Hamilton?"

"Dr. Brent Wentworth. He's an ear, nose, and throat specialist and he's only here from April to September every year."

Giving him a shocked look, Jesse muttered, "What is an ear, nose, and throat specialist doing helping your father's joint issues? He should be seeing an osteopath."

"I've tried to tell Sam that, but he knows Brent personally, so he trusts him."

"Humph!" She stabbed at her toast. "My mother would have a hissy fit over hearing this. Sam needs to be seen by an osteopath. That's all they do is deal with the skeleton of the body and that includes all the joints. What if I could get him persuaded to go to Missoula, and see a bone doc?"

"Good luck," Travis mused. "I've tried."

"But I have a true story that might get him to try it. I'd like to go over and visit him and see."

Trying to keep the alarm out of his voice, Travis said, "He's usually in a foul mood."

"What if I brought Freya along? He has Cyrus, his dog. That might create a nice combo and he might be willing to listen to what I have to say?" She gave him a long, hopeful look.

"And if he's having a bad day, Jesse, he'll take it out on you."

"I've got an ace up my sleeve, Travis. The other day when Katie and I were talking, she was telling me that Sam dearly loves pumpkin lattes. That he looks forward to the fall because that's when they're available. He used to come in once a week to her place and get one from her, but of late, he hasn't. What if I had her make one up and I drove out to his place and gave it to him? Do you think that it might soothe some of his grouchiness?"

He sighed. "I don't know. You aren't in a place where you could take his nastiness."

"I feel for you," she murmured, reaching across the small table and touching his hand momentarily. "Please. Let me try? Katie was saying that Sam loves dogs, horses and fishing. I think the latte with Freya in tow might be a great combination that could possibly sidetrack his anger and irritability? What do you think? I really want to do this for him, Travis."

"What if it works? What does a hot tub cost?"

"I have *no* idea, but listen, here's a possibility: Holly works with Delos Charities here in Hamilton. We could ask her if they would spring for the hot tub if Sam is interested?"

Rubbing his chin, he gave a slow nod, his brows drawing downward. "Maybe I should call Sam and tell him about you? Who you are?"

"No. Let me handle this. I think he'll be more receptive because I'm a stranger of sorts to him, it'll throw him off his stride a little." She grinned. "Besides, I'm a Trojan horse bringing him the gift of his favorite latte, plus Freya."

Giving her a grudging look, he muttered, "It could backfire, Jesse. He could make you a target, like he does me."

"I'm a woman. I think he's old guard and wouldn't rag on me like he does you because you're a man."

"Well…. it's worth a shot, Jesse, because I'd give *anything* to see his pain ease. It hurts me to see how it cripples him up on some days. Then he's forced to stay in that scooter chair that he hates. He is in a much better mood when his joint aches ease and he can make it around with his cane, instead. Immobility isn't his thing."

"I'm sure we'd be the same as he is if we were in his situation. I'm sorry he's taking it out on you, though. Maybe, if this hair-brained idea of mine works, he'll stop ragging on you and life will get better for everyone."

"You're a hopeful person at heart," he said heavily. Rolling his shoulders, he sat up. "Okay, go for it. Let's see how Sam reacts."

November 26

"OKAY, FREYA, YOU'RE going to have to help me out," Jesse said. She stood outside the Sam Ramsey's cabin off the highway a good quarter of a mile. It had snowed and there were tire tracks in and out of his home. It was one p.m. and she hoped he was home. Trying to quell her nerves, she held the pumpkin latte in a large paper cup in one hand and Freya's leash in the other. Ahead of her was about six inches of snow at the same height as the porch of the small, cottage-like cabin.

Girding her spiking anxiety, she walked forward. At the door, she knocked loud enough to be heard.

There was a "woof, woof, woof," on the other side of it. That had to be Cyrus. She waited patiently, unsure if Sam would answer the door. If he did, would he be in his scooter chair or stubbornly walking around with the aid of a cane? Either way, it would take a while, she supposed, for him to get to the door.

The door cracked open and Sam Ramsey stood there, cane in one hand, staring at her. "Who are you?" he demanded in a growly tone.

Giving him a slight, nervous smile, she said, "I'm Jesse Myers. I work over at Katie's Koffee Bean, Mr. Ramsey." She held out the cup toward him because he was standing, albeit stooped a little. "This is for you. I also work for your son, Travis, and he was saying one day that you loved pumpkin lattes. He asked me to bring this over to you." She gave him a hopeful look. Sam was tall, rawboned and lean but she saw Travis in his face, too. He had about a four-day old pepper-and-salt beard on his thinned features. His brows were the same colors. He stared in surprise at her and then the cup she was offering him.

"Why," he muttered, opening the door, "that was mighty nice of my son and you. Come in." He stepped aside, making a gesture for her to enter.

"Is it okay if my dog, Freya, comes in too, sir? She's a girl."

He looked over at Cyrus. "I'm sure he'd like some female company. Can you stay a bit?"

Heartened that he wasn't angry, she felt relief surge through her. Maybe Sam was having a "good" day. "Yes, sir, I can." She stepped into the home, which was toasty, lots of light within it. Watching him hobble toward the living room, she felt sorry for the man as he went to a sturdy rocker and with painful slowness, sat down. He set the redwood cane against the red brick of the fireplace that burned brightly.

Freya wagged her tail at Cyrus, who put his nose to the air to catch her scent, but he didn't move from where he sat next to Sam's rocker.

Wondering if Cyrus had joint issues like his owner, she saw Sam gesture to a nearby couch.

"Have a seat."

"Would you like me to put your latte into a glass or mug for you, Mr. Ramsey?" The kitchen, a galley type, was located on the other side of the living room.

"Why, that'd be nice. Yes, I have a large beer stein I use and it's sittin' on the counter. It has a large handle and I can hold it instead of it slipping out of my grasp."

"Freya, sit," she told the Border Collie. "I'll go get it," she said.

Instantly, Freya sat at the end of the couch, alert to Sam and Cyrus. The older dog moved to his feet and slowly came around the end of the cedar coffee table and wagged his bushy tail in greeting to Freya.

Sam chuckled. "Cyrus might be old, but he always has an interest in a la-dy."

"I think they'll get along," Jesse said. The kitchen had a lot of dirty dishes piled up in the sink, and the counter and shining cedar floor were in dire need of some cleaning and attention too. She located the ceramic German beer stein, quickly poured the contents into it and brought it out to Sam.

"Here you go, Mr. Ramsey."

He took both his hands and held it, pleasure wreathing his face. "Thank you, Miss Myers. This is right nice. Unexpected, but welcome." He took a sip and made a gruff sound, nodding his head afterward, that it tasted good.

Sitting down, Jesse petted Freya. Cyrus had come and laid down between his master and Freya. She reached out, patting his shaggy head. "You can call me Jesse, if you'd like, Mr. Ramsey."

He continued to gratefully sip the brew, looking up over the brim of it. "That's a right purty name. Are you from around here? I've never seen you in town and Travis never told me he'd hired an office assistant."

"No, sir." She gave the abbreviated story of how she'd wandered into Hamilton, minus finding the red caboose. She knew it was a sore spot for Sam and wanted this first meeting to go well, not descend into old family drama.

"So, you work with Katie, too?"

"Yes, sir, I do."

"My son, Travis, has PTSD like you."

"I've made a friend of him, Mr. Ramsey, and we've talked about our shared military challenges."

He continued to sip the coffee, making more sounds of pleasure as he did so.

"So? It was my son's idea was it to bring this out to me? Usually, I drop over to see Katie and get me a latte, but the last month, my joints have kicked up like hellfire." He pointed to the half-emptied mug. "This is a real treat."

"It was his idea to bring it to you, although it was Katie who mentioned you loved pumpkin lattes when they came into season. I think they conspired with one another." She smiled. So did he.

He squinted a moment, studying her. "Are you anything like that Holly girl?"

Raising her brows, she said, "I don't know whom you're talking about."

"Holly, the gal that runs the Delos charity here in town for the shut-ins. She just got married to Nick Conway, Sue's boy."

"Oh," she said, putting it together. "No, I just thought it would be nice to help you out. Travis said you were having a bad time because of your injuries, and we thought maybe something you loved so much, might make your day a little better. I took a chance of dropping by to see if you were home."

"Hmmm. My son put you up to it?"

Petting Freya's head, she said, "No, sir, he didn't. It just sort of happened in a conversation we had and the idea blossomed."

"Nice to see kindness in human beings. The people of Hamilton care for one another. You said your folks live in Billings?"

"Yes, sir, they do." She opened her hands. "My mother, Peggy, is an RN and she works at one of the hospitals in Billings. I grew up with her stories about people who were sick or injured, and ways that the doctors helped them." Her heart began to pound. "I remember my mother telling me about a cowboy from a ranch who had a lot of joint problems, that he'd beat up his body with the kind of work he did. He'd come to the hospital for help because he was crippled up in the knees."

Snorting, Sam drawled, "That gent coulda been me."

"Yes, sir, that's why I wanted to come and see you." Urgency came to her low tone as she held Sam's sharpened blue eyes. "Our hospital had a unit that was called hydrotherapy. It held a steel hot tub of sorts and people who had certain types of injuries, would sit in it for up to ten minutes. They put the patients in that hydrotherapy tub for five to ten minutes, to loosen up their joints. They did this day in and day out. Some of his patients with joint injuries, got better and avoided having to get around in a scooter or wheelchair and claimed a better quality of life. The doctor also gave the patients specific exercises along with getting a charity in Billings, to buy the person a small hot tub so that they could use the heat from the water to loosen up their joints and get rid of the stiffness. The effect of this was that they had many hours of relief from pain, Mr. Ramsey."

"Really?" he said, straightening, his bushy brows lifting and giving her a thoughtful look.

"Yes, sir." Reaching for her leather purse, she pulled out a sheaf of folded papers and stood, placing them on the table beside his rocking chair. "I got in touch with my mom and asked her for those exercises. Dr. Morgan, who started this program twenty years ago, is now retired, but his methodology lives on at all the hospitals in Billings. There is a Delos charity in Billings, and they took over the task of buying each patient a small hot tub that is built in Idaho and trucked to their homes."

"I'll be darned," he muttered, reaching for the papers and placing his stein on the table. "This sounds interesting. My doc never mentioned anything like this to me," he said, slowly opening the papers and studying some of the exercises.

"Is your doctor an osteopath?" Jesse asked.

"No, he's an ear, nose, and throat specialist. The only one who lives here in Hamilton part time, during the summers."

"So? You've never been to see an osteopath?"

"No." He scowled and set the papers in his lap. "Your mom is a nurse. She knows what she's talkin' about."

"Yes, sir, she does. I thought I'd pass the info along to you because Travis wants to help you, but he's at his wit's end on how to do that."

Giving a rough bark, Sam said, "That makes two of us!" He sighed and folded his hands in his lap after placing the papers on the table. "I'm afraid I've been too hard on my son. He's done his best. I get really irritable when the pain hits hard. I shouldn't be taking it out on him."

"Pain makes everyone short and irritable," Jesse whispered sympathetically, "and he realizes that, Mr. Ramsey. He'd like to see your pain alleviated just like you would."

"Have you talked to my son about all of this?"

"I did, and he was hopeful you'd be interested."

"He sent you out here instead of comin' himself?"

She heard the hurt in his gravelly tone and realized how much he relied on Travis. She swallowed hard. "He wanted to, Sam, but he felt because my mother is an RN, and with her experience with Dr. Morgan's hydrotherapy patients, that I could add information that he couldn't."

Rubbing his bristly beard, Sam muttered, "That makes good sense…"

"Travis wanted to be here, but something came up and I told him I'd come out alone." It wasn't the truth, but in her world, "white lies," which didn't hurt anyone, were okay under special circumstances. And this was one of them. Watching him, she realized just how much Travis was a part of his life and how much he relied on him. She cleared her throat. "Sam? Travis wanted your permission to contact an osteopathic doctor in Missoula. That's the closest large city and I did a check and there are three specialists there. We felt that if you were okay with me making an appointment, that you could see one of them? That he'd drive you to the appointment and be with you."

Grunting, Sam stared down at Cyrus. "Well, whad'ya think, big boy?"

Cyrus blinked his big brown eyes up at his master.

"Yeah," he mumbled, rubbing his chin, "I think that would be good. Do you think this bone doctor would suggest I get a hot tub? That story of yours sounds mighty hopeful to me."

Nodding, Jesse said, "You could talk to the doctor about it."

"You have to come along. I won't go there without you in tow. Maybe the doc would believe you because your mother's an RN and saw the hydrotherapy work on her patients?"

Surprised, Jesse gulped. She barely knew him and yet, Sam was reaching out to trust her. Sensing he was terribly lonely out here by himself, Jesse said, "Of course. I'll come along."

"Cyrus will be lonely."

"We could bring him back to Travis's place. Freya here, just had five puppies. They're down in the basement and if Cyrus got along with her, I'm sure he'd be okay with her puppies. What do you think?"

"Well, he's an old dawg like me," Sam said. "Unlike me, Cy is an easy-going kinda pooch. I'm sure he'll get along well with Freya and her pups."

Smiling, Jesse nodded. "Well, I don't want to wear out my welcome with you. I'd better get going, Mr. Ramsey." She rose and Freya got up as well, expectant and alert. "You enjoy your pumpkin latte. I'll be sure to tell Katie you loved it."

"Here," he said, leaning to one side, pulling his well-worn billfold out of his back jeans pocket, "I owe her."

"Oh, no you don't," Jesse protested, holding up her hand. "Travis bought you a year-long account at Katie's and you can have one any time you want to drive in and get it. It's already paid for. A kind of pre-Christmas gift he's giving you."

Sam leaned back, frowning and he looked away, his jaw moving.

Jesse felt an emotional energy hit her and it felt like sadness combined with love. Standing there unsurely, she waited, realizing he was fighting back tears because he wouldn't look at her. Finally, he sniffed, coughed, and wiped his eyes. Then, he looked up at her.

"That was mighty nice of my boy," he rumbled. "Tell him thank you." He patted his stein. "I feel better already. I'm gonna sit here and enjoy the rest of my pumpkin latte before it gets cold."

Wanting to go over and slide her arm around his hunched, thin shoulders beneath the dark blue cowboy shirt he wore, Jesse anchored herself. Was Sam this emotional around Travis? She'd find out soon enough. "I'll tell him," she said, her own voice slightly off key.

"Nice meetin' you, Jesse. And you can call me Sam."

"I'd like that, Sam." She raised her hand and Freya moved to her side. "We'll be in touch soon," she promised.

CHAPTER 11

December 1

DR. BOB BRANNON, osteopath, sat down with Sam Ramsey while Jesse sat with Travis. She tried to keep her hopes in check, but she could see how badly Travis wanted the doctor, who had just got done with all the tests and examining Sam, to say something hopeful. The red-haired doctor who sported a neatly clipped beard like Travis, wore black plastic-framed glasses perched on his prominent nose.

"Well," he told Sam, "I like the idea of a hot tub for you. Your joints took a lot of brutal workouts when you were riding bulls, but you already know that."

Sam nodded. "Yeah, lookin' back on it, it wasn't a smart decision. Hindsight and all."

Smiling a little, Brannon said, "I'm familiar with Dr. Morgan's work. In fact, I studied under him in regards to it. For you? I think a small hot tub would be worth a shot, Sam. I had my office staff contact Delos Charity Headquarters in Alexandria, Virginia, and they said they would provide you one."

Sam's brows flew upward. "Why…that's great. I thought if you approved the idea, I'd have to buy my own."

"Nope," Brannon said, grinning. He looked at Travis and Jesse, who were sitting up, all smiles and relief in their faces. "Delos has a charity here in Missoula. My admin nurse called and asked them and they gave me the contact number for their main headquarters. I just got off the phone with them and they are going to authorize you one via the Hamilton Delos Charity."

"That's Holly's charity," Sam said.

"Yes. They're in contact with her right now. And from the sounds of it, you'll have your hot tub ready to install in about seven days. They work fast."

Jesse could barely contain herself. "Have you found it works for some of your patients, Dr. Brannon?"

"Indeed, it does. I work quite routinely with the Missoula Delos charity. I would say half my patients that have symptoms of joint stiffness, which causes the pain, do very well taking a dip twice a day. I've been able to get them off more powerful pain medication and now, they take NSAIDS or aspirin, instead. It's a worthwhile tradeoff in my opinion to get them off opioids."

"Well," Sam muttered darkly, "opioids sure didn't work on me."

Nodding, Brannon said sympathetically, "Medically, there is a group of folks like you, Sam, who don't respond to commonly prescribed drugs. And maybe that's a good thing because we have too many people addicted to opioids. Give my office a call in three weeks and we'll set up a second appointment to see if the hydrotherapy is working for you." He wrote out a prescription and handed it to him. "Hot tub five to ten minutes, twice a day. Keep a chart on how long the pain stays away and bring it back with you when my nurse contacts you for your next appointment."

Sam took the script and turned, giving Travis and Jesse a grin. Holding it up, he said, "Well, Travis, looks like you gotta do some handyman work in that laundry room where the spa is gonna go."

"That's okay," Travis responded, smiling a little. "We'll take a closer look at it tomorrow morning and get it prepared for that hot tub that's coming your way."

Dr. Brannon stood and offered his hand to Sam. "I think you'll do well with this form of therapy, Mr. Ramsey. That and the exercise routine that my nurse will give to you on the way out. Call me any time if there are any issues."

Sam heartily shook his hand after he stood. "I will. Thanks."

"DO YOU THINK it will work?" Travis asked Jesse as they sat at the small table in the caboose. They were having a late dinner after returning Sam back to his cabin earlier. She had made macaroni and cheese with sliced brats mixed into it this morning. It had been easy to heat it up for a quick, yummy dinner.

"I do." She smiled hugely. "I'm just so happy I could burst," she confided. Travis looked younger and she realized the heavy responsibility he'd been carrying alone for so long regarding his father, was truly dissolving. "And Sam was bubbling all the way home. I loved the stories he told about his bull riding days. He was the number two rider in the nation. I didn't know that."

Nodding, Travis finished off his meal. "Yes, he was. He's proud of those days and he should be. That was when he was in his rebellious mode."

"Some people just have a different calling, Travis. I'm sorry it happened because Sam and Hiram are both good men. Your father came back after getting busted up at twenty-nine, settled down and took over the fishing guide business for the family. Eventually, he conformed to his family's ideals."

"Not willingly, but yes, he did."

"I still think he has dreams of traveling instead of being cooped up in that cabin," she said. The boxcar was warm and cozy. Outside it was growing dark. Snow was on the ground and the meadow looked beautiful beneath the darkening sky.

"I agree. He's got a lot of travel magazines around his place. And he loves the travel channels on TV, but with his present condition, he can't go hardly anywhere."

"What do you think he'll do if the hydrotherapy works?" she wondered.

"I don't know. I'm just hoping it will give him relief from his pain. Then, maybe he'll be less angry and irritable with everyone. What he does after that, is fine with me. I've taken over the business, and he's at an age where retirement should be filled with possibilities, not being stuck in a cabin because of pain."

"And he'll stop using you as his whipping post," she noted, giving him a hope-filled look. Travis grimaced, nodded and pushed away from the table. He had to get home to take care of Freya and her pups, plus feed them dinner.

"That, too." He stood and took their empty plates over to the counter, washing them off and then placing them in the dish drainer.

Her heart ached for him as she finished cleaning off the table. What he needed right now was a hug. All day, she'd wanted to do just that. When he straightened and wiped his hands off on a towel, she stepped forward. Jesse hadn't forgotten what he'd said about her having to make the first move. That's exactly what she did. Lifting her arms, she slid them around his broad shoulders. Travis wasn't expecting it and his eyes flared with surprise, but as soon as she moved, lightly resting against the front of him, they narrowed and she saw them burning with need for her.

"You've had a long haul with Sam," she whispered, moving her hands slowly across his upper back. "And you've carried a lot of load for the family. For so long, Travis, I've wanted to give back to you, take some of those loads you've been carrying off your shoulders."

"Just having you around," he said, his voice suddenly rough with emotion, "has lightened my load. I know I haven't said that to you, Jesse, but it's the truth." He slid his hands around her waist, not drawing her fully against him, waiting to see what she wanted.

His humbleness, his quiet strength, drew her even more. The scent of pine lingered tantalizingly on his dark green flannel shirt, the fragrance of leather from the black vest he wore over it, mingled with the outdoor fragrance. She felt his fingers tighten marginally as she pressed herself fully against him, more than a little aware of his growing erection against her belly. Fire simmered in her lower body and she ached to do more than this. Leaning up, her lips within an inch of his, she whispered, "I want to kiss you..." She closed her eyes, straining upward, meeting his mouth for the first time.

Her lips brushed his and his fingers dug briefly into her hips, and then he forced himself to relax beneath the soft, gliding exploration she wanted to share with him. Not all men were Neanderthals. And she knew while Travis was a man's man, he didn't push his strength or power over her in order to dominate the moment. Instead, she felt him anchor, dial back his initial cave man reaction toward her shy kiss and listen to what she needed from him, instead. There was a heat building between them, her hips resting against his, enjoying his male response to her mouth taking his, asking more participation from him. Breath coming faster, it matched his own. Inhaling the scent of him as a man, heightened her building need of him. His hands moved from her hips, gliding upward, capturing her shoulders, holding her so their mouths had maximum enjoyment with one another.

Glorying in his response, Jesse reluctantly broke the kiss. She looked up at him, her lips tingling wildly, her breasts tightening, the nipples wanting to be teased by him. "Travis...if I don't stop now..."

He managed a short rumble of agreement in his chest. "That makes two of us." He threaded his fingers through her hair, giving her a tender look. "That was a surprise, but a nice one. I liked it. Did you?"

She managed a slight sound in her throat that came out more like a satisfied cat's purr. "Very much so."

He loosened his hands on her shoulders, squeezing them gently before he released her. "If I didn't have to get home and feed the dogs, I think I'd be offering arguments for me staying the night."

She looked toward the opened door to her bedroom. "That time will come..."

December 7

SAM RAMSEY GAVE his son and Jesse a look of gratitude. They had driven over to his cabin in the late morning after he called them, telling them that the truck bearing the small hot tub had just arrived. He'd seen his son jump in and direct the two men who were bringing the light blue hot tub into the service porch area. Travis had been adamant about putting in roof ventilation equipment that would take the smell of chlorine out of the room, not allowing it to linger inside his home. He was pleased with his son's care and knowledge. Now, the tub was set up in one corner, two wooden steps put in front of it so he would have an easy time climbing in and out of it. The men filled it up with cold water, testing the pump and making sure the water circulated.

It would take twenty-four hours for it to get up to the 103F. Sam didn't want to wait that long, but he had no choice. He'd give anything to get rid of the painful stiffness in his joints. He'd tried a hot bath, but it was such a struggle to get up and down in the tub that he gave up on the idea. At least with a hot tub, it would be easy to mount two steps, swing his leg over and get into the warm, swirling water. If only the hydrotherapy would work!

"I think everything is in order," Travis told him, coming over to where he was standing. Today Sam was leaning on a cane, which meant he was far more mobile and congenial as a result. Those days when he was confined to his motorized scooter were burdensome for Sam because he was angry at being hogtied, as he referred to it. Today, he was in a good mood, hope in his expression, as the hot tub was set into the porch area.

"Looks right nice, Travis. It fits in on the service porch like it's always been there. Looks like Cy is interested in it, too." He gestured toward his dog who was sniffing and smelling around the premise of it.

Chuckling, Travis said, "He's wanting to inspect it."

"I wish you'd brought Freya with you. Cy likes her a lot. They made friends with one another the last time Jesse was out here. It occurred to me he's lonely, too."

Jesse wandered up. "We can do better than that, Sam. Why don't you see how the hot tub goes for you tomorrow morning? If your joints are feeling better, why not drive over to Travis's home and you can have dinner with us. Bring Cy with you, too. That way, he'll get to see Freya and be with her five puppies."

Sam gave her a thoughtful look. "I'd like that, Jesse. Thank you. In many ways, you remind me of the only woman I've ever loved: my wife, Sheila. She was always doing things like that for me, our family and others here in Hamilton."

"That's a nice compliment, Sam. I think women are just natural networkers and team oriented. I know Travis and I would love to have you come and share dinner with us. And if you can't drive, I'm sure Travis wouldn't mind coming to get you and Cy." She looked over at him for a response. "Would you?"

"Sure, no problem," Travis said, watching the two workmen clean up after themselves, collecting their tools and the trash. "Sam, I think that hot tub is going to help you a lot."

Sam reached out, patting him on the shoulder. "I hope you're right, Travis."

Jesse saw a lot of emotion in his eyes as his father reached out and clapped him on the shoulder. It was the first time she'd seen Sam do anything like that. Sensing that this was a major change in their relationship, she would talk to

Travis later about it.

Sam turned. "Thank you, Jesse. You're a good fit in our family and I'm glad you're here with Travis."

Swallowing her shock, she saw Sam was awkwardly trying to reach out to her. He was rusty, she thought, in expressing affection toward others, but that didn't take away from his sincerity. Smiling, she said, "Glad to be of help. Let us know how it goes tomorrow? I've got my fingers crossed for you."

"You two will be the first to know," he promised, his voice thickening.

Looking up, she saw a sheen of tears in Travis's eyes. But just as soon as she saw it, the tears were gone. What had just happened?

On the way back to the caboose, Jesse said, "What happened back there, Travis?"

"It's the first time Sam has done any kind of physical contact with me since I returned home."

"Oh…God…" she choked, sympathetic for him and for Sam. "I didn't know that."

He reached out, gripping her hand resting on her thigh. Jesse curved her fingers around his, feeling his stark vulnerability.

"Like I told you before, Sam lost a lot of himself after Mom died," he admitted gruffly. He turned off the highway and onto the snow-covered road that would lead to the caboose. "I was in total shock when he did that."

Frowning, she asked, "Did he hug you as a kid? Let you know he loved you and Kyle?"

"He did. The dad I knew growing up is the opposite of the one you see now."

Her heart hurt for him and Kyle. "Sam got choked up when he mentioned her name."

"Yes, he did love her. Fiercely." He slowed down as the red caboose came into view. "My two-cents worth, at his age and with more maturity, is that when she suddenly died, it destroyed Sam in so many ways. He's been a recluse since her death, always deep inside himself, and never outward looking, with a lot less sensitivity toward others or needing many people in his life. He used to be self-aware when she was alive, but afterward, that trait went away."

"Maybe the family dynamic is changing?"

He braked and turned off the engine as he stopped near the caboose. The day was bright, the sky so blue it would hurt a person's eyes if they weren't wearing sunglasses, which he was. Placing his hands on the steering wheel, he said, "It must be. I hope so. It would be a great and a very welcomed change." Tipping his head in her direction, he released her hand so she could gather up her purse on the seat between them. "I honestly think it's you, Jesse," he said. "I also think last week when you saw Sam for the first time it jolted loose something good and old that was buried in him. Maybe, like he said, you reminded him of my mother in some ways. Grief, I've discovered, gets buried for decades sometimes, but it will still rise in us and demand that we move through it to release it at some point in the future. My mother had black hair just like you have, and I think it might have made Sam see you differently. In a better light. I'm amazed how responsive he is toward you. He doesn't warm up fast to strangers, but he did you."

"Wow," she whispered, shaking her head. "Who knew?"

"This is just my theory," he warned her. "I've never seen him as accommodating as when you're around him. I think he likes you a lot."

"But you two don't have a woman in your life, so you're missing that energy," she said, half smiling. "It could be as simple as that. Humans are society-oriented and need one another."

"Not any woman would do," he said somberly, holding her glance. "It *is* you, Jesse. I saw that in you the first morning I met you. There's a deep caring radiating from within you, a sincerity, and I know how much it called to me. I honestly think Sam experienced the same thing. You're a nice combination of sincerity and kindness, as well as being a nurturer. My mother was very much the same way, although far more extroverted than you are. Sam is sure behaving one-hundred-and-eighty degrees different from how he usually acts around me. It feels to me as if you're a much-needed buffer zone between us."

She rested her hand on his shoulder. "I think it's something else. He told me at the first meeting how much you care for him. Has he ever called you son?"

Giving her a puzzled look, he shook his head. "No…never. Is that what he called me?"

"Yes, and I thought at the time that when he said 'son,' that it was like an emotional endearment coming from him toward you."

"My turn to say wow," he muttered, looking away for a moment and then meeting her gaze once more. "I hope he's changing, Jesse. First of all, for himself. You can't live a life in a rage all the time. I've half expected him to blow a blood vessel and stroke out from all the anger he was carrying."

"Perhaps he's growing past that? I know he relies heavily upon you and is so grateful that you are in his life. He was practically bragging about you to me. He's from a time and era where fathers never talked openly to their children or were emotional or engaged with them."

"You're right about that. Well," he sighed, giving her a warm look, "you walking into our lives has been nothing but good, Jesse. You need to know that."

Her hand tightened momentarily on his upper arm. "You're a good man," she said unsteadily, caught up in the emotions of the moment. "I like you so much, Travis, and I want what we have to keep blossoming between us."

"Just call us blooming idiots," he laughed.

Jesse laughed deeply with him. She gave him a playful punch on his arm. "Don't turn a serious moment into comedy, Ramsey. We need to be sharing with one another about Sam so we can understand what's happening, or what he's going through."

"Yeah, for sure." He took off his Stetson and scratched his hair for a moment, then settled it back on his head. "Thank you for sharing all this with me. If you hadn't, I'd never have known."

She opened the truck door and swung it open. "Well, don't faint if he calls you 'son' when he comes over to dinner. Okay?" She slid out, smiling at him. "See you tomorrow. It's my day at your office. Thanks for a wonderful day, Travis." If she didn't walk away, she was going to invite him to stay with her for the night. Of course, he had to take care of Freya and her puppies at his cabin first, who relied on him to show up. Somehow, someday soon, Jesse knew they would love one another. It was a sweetness that flowed through her as she shut the door and waved goodbye to him. The desire in his eyes made her acutely aware of how long it had been since she'd been with a man. And she wanted desperately to be with this man because he remained vulnerable to her. A month ago, Jesse would not have thought about going to bed with Travis. Now, it was hanging there like a luscious tease before her all day long. Never mind her torrid dreams that were starting to come back several times a week!

December 8

JESSE WAS WORKING in the tour guide office when the phone rang. She'd gotten there at one p.m. sharp and was filing.

"I'll get it," Travis called from the desk area where he was stacking more files that needed to be put away.

"Okay." She keyed in her hearing as he answered it.

"Hi, Sam," he greeted.

"Hey, I gotta tell you, Travis, this is a miracle! I climbed in for ten minutes at nine a.m. this morning. Got out and damned if my knees were limber, my shoulders were loose, and there was *no pain*!"

Grinning, Travis threw a thumb's up in Jesse's direction. She smiled.

"Great. It's almost two. Are you having any pain or stiffness coming back?"

"Not yet. It's amazing! When Jesse came over to tell me about it, I had my doubts. I mean, I wanted to hope, but you know nothin's worked on me before."

"I know," he murmured, frowning.

"My elbow and shoulder joints are doin' fine, too. I just am blown away, Travis."

"When is your next hot tub?"

"Doc said twice a day and I should take the second one should the stiffness start comin' back. It hasn't so far, so I'm not gonna jinx whatever is happening to me. One thing for sure? I'll be able to drive over to your place for dinner tonight without a problem! I can even walk without a cane. How about that? God, it feels good to straighten up, throw my shoulders back and walk like a normal human being once more!"

He heard his father's voice grow hoarse. Emotions welled up in him, too. His hand tightened a little on the phone. "We're eating at six, so drop by. Don't forget to bring Cyrus. I think Freya and her pups know you're coming. It should be a good night for all of us."

"Yes, I'll do that. See you tonight!"

Hanging up the phone, he relayed the conversation to Jesse, whose eyes sparkled with unabashed joy. She closed the file drawer and came over, throwing her arms around him, hugging the hell out of him.

"Oh, Travis! This is *such* great news!"

He liked the intimacy springing between them, satisfied with her hug, which she released him from moments later. "The best! I don't like to see anyone suffer when they don't have too. What are you planning for tonight's dinner?"

"I got those elk steaks out to thaw. And I had some pre-baked potatoes ready to go. You also had some frozen corn in the freezer, and I took it out for tonight's dinner. Since you have sourdough starter, I thought I might make some biscuits to go with the dinner. What do you think?"

"Sam will be over the moon. Did you know his most favorite food my mother used to make for him was her sourdough biscuits?"

"No. That's amazing."

"Did he tell you he liked those kinds of biscuits?"

"Never."

"Good thing you told me. Let's stop at the grocery store on the way home. We need some kind of dessert and I'll buy a jar of huckleberry jam, which he loves to put on his biscuits." He smiled faintly. "Kyle and I used to go with our parents into the mountains and pick huckleberries on the slopes in late summer. My mother would make jam, which has always been Sam's favorite. She would also make some of the best huckleberry pies you've ever tasted."

"Maybe next year the three of us might go huckleberry picking together? It would bring back good memories of a happy time Sam had with you."

"I'd like that," he said.

TRAVIS ABOUT DID a double-take when Sam showed up at their door right at six p.m. He had Cyrus at his side, on a leash. His father was dressed in what could be termed, his "Sunday best," clothing. Usually, Sam was a jeans and cowboy shirt kind of gent. Tonight, he showed up in a pair of black chinos, a decently pressed white cowboy shirt, a gold elk-skin vest and a black tie around his throat. Over his outfit was a Shepler coat that hung to his hips. He was even wearing his Stetson, a black one he reserved only for special occasions. Even his longish hair was washed, combed and in place. And he'd shaved! Stepping aside, he said, "Come on in, Sam."

Jesse looked up from the kitchen. "Hi Sam! Hi Cyrus. Welcome."

Travis shut the door behind him.

Sam took off his hat, placing it on a peg. "Howdy, Jesse." He smiled and said, "Watch this." He took off his heavy sheepskin coat with ease.

"No pain in your shoulders?" she guessed, beaming.

"No, ma'am, none."

Placing the coat on a peg next to his hat, Travis said, "That's incredible."

"Ain't it though? I hopped in the hot tub an hour ago before I came over here and the stiffness starting to come back went away, and just like that," he snapped his fingers, "it disappeared!"

"Come on in," Travis said, knowing that his father's hands had suffered many fractures over the years from the bull riding. For him to be able to snap his fingers blew him away. There was a miracle happening right before their eyes and he was grateful his father was not in any pain. Sam had a rolling walk, and he was walking toward the dining room table with that same easy-going gait, no longer bent over or having to use his cane—or worse, the power chair.

Cyrus walked over to the basement door, wagging his brushy black tail slowly back and forth. Travis was sure he could hear and smell Freya on the other side of it.

"I'm going to take Cyrus down to the basement while we eat," he told Sam, pulling out a chair for him. "We won't be able to eat with seven dogs up here." He heard Jesse laugh and knowingly nod.

"Sure, go ahead," Sam invited.

Jesse came over, setting the elk steaks on a platter in front of his plate. "Help yourself, Sam. Would you like something to drink with your dinner? Travis said you usually drink water."

"Yes, that'll do. Those steaks look and smell mighty good, Jesse. Did you do all the cooking?"

"No. Travis and I usually do it together."

He lifted his nose in the air, sniffing. "Don't tell me you made sourdough biscuits?"

She laughed and wiped her hands on her red apron. "Travis said you loved them and as you know, he still has his grandmother's starter."

"Oh, I didn't realize that." Sam became emotional. "The family starter?"

"Yes," she said gently, placing her hand on his shoulder, seeing sudden grief in his blue eyes. "When Travis came home, you gave it to him, and he's kept it here in his cabin ever since."

"I guess I lost track," he muttered, emotion cracking his voice.

"Well, it's stayed in the family, Sam. And tonight, we're all eating Sheila's sourdough biscuits." She squeezed his shoulder. "Travis said he'd kept the starter because it was a way of keeping his mother with him, even though she wasn't with you anymore. I think that's so sweet."

Clearing his throat, he said, "My sons are good men. I guess I didn't realize Kyle kept it until he died. I vaguely remember cleaning out his apartment in Hamilton and found the starter. I took it home. I couldn't think of getting rid of it. That would be akin to getting rid of Sheila, and I didn't want to do that."

"Of course, you didn't. Well, it's made the rounds through your family and come home. It will be nice to know Sheila is with us. It's a wonderful night to celebrate that you're pain free, Sam."

He rallied, seeing his son emerging from the basement and closing the door. "Right nice to tell me this, Jesse."

"I'm gonna get the biscuits out. Travis will bring the bowl of corn over to the table. We'll be right back." She saw the older man giving his son a loving look as he crossed the living room. Jesse hoped that the magic of the day would continue. Travis desperately needed a father, not some man who had died when his wife died, no longer available to him, as a result. It was a sad situation, but she held hope in her heart that it was changing before her eyes. Travis looked equally happy.

"Good news," he told them as he halted at the table, "Cyrus and Freya are thrilled to be together again. And he's now surrounded by five excited puppies who are just dying to play with him. He laid down and they began climbing all over him. They'll all get along just fine. We'll bring them upstairs after we eat," he promised Sam.

"Good, because I'd like to see those pups. Been a long time since I saw any."

CHAPTER 12

"OKAY," TRAVIS WARNED his father as he stood at the door to the basement, "get prepared for an onslaught."

Sam sat in the overstuffed chair opposite the couch where Jesse sat. "Bring them on," he said.

Jesse smiled, seeing the excitement in Sam's eyes. He'd eaten like a proverbial horse, giving her and Travis compliments on the food and how good it tasted. She had seen from time to time confusion in Travis's eyes. Was it because his father wasn't being angry or grouchy? Not using him as a whipping post? She'd ask him later after Sam left.

"Here they come," Travis warned with a grin, opening the door.

Freya and Cyrus were standing at the top of the stairs, the five pups squirming, wriggling and racing between their legs, all of them spilling into the living room.

Sam laughed, watching all five of the pups spotting him and changing their cannon-like trajectory, galloping toward him. He was new to their world and they wanted to check him out. He leaned down as the pups leaped up on his lower pant legs and boots, yipping, sniffing and frolicking playfully around his feet.

Travis smiled as he came and sat down next to Jesse on the couch, opposite Sam. She returned his smile and sat back, watching the antics of the pups with him. Clearly dogs loved this man. Cyrus came over to his master, laying down beside the chair, thumping his tail as the pups mauled him. Four of the pups delighted in leaping all over him, which he took in patient, elder stride. Freya sat close to Jesse, watching her happy brood tumble and play around Sam's feet and rocket around Cyrus, leaping up on his back, sliding off, yipping with glee and doing it all over again.

For the next few minutes, Jesse watched Sam come alive. He would laugh, gently pick up a pup, pet it and then set it back on the rug. She noticed the only male, who had black freckles all over the top of his muzzle and was the only one with beautiful blue eyes, hang around Sam after the others left to go romp with Cyrus.

"This is a right nice pup," Sam congratulated them, lifting him into his hands, critically studying him. He held the puppy against his chest as it snuggled into the folds between his vest and shirt.

Travis said, "He's the only one with blue eyes, like his mother, Freya."

Sam continued to hold the pup and support him. "His eyes are beautiful. Never seen a dog with blue eyes before." He grinned. "I see Cyrus really likes all those kids jumping and leaping all over him."

"It's nice to see them playing together," Jesse said. "Maybe you were right, he was lonely?"

"That could well be. Heck, I get lonely out there by myself, too. Why wouldn't Cy?"

"We're giving away the pups on December fourteenth," Travis said. "All but the blue-eyed male pup is spoken for."

Peering down at the pup, Sam said, "He's the prettiest marked of all of 'em."

"The other four are females," Jesse said.

"He's the only boy, huh?"

"Yeah, but he holds his own against his sisters," Travis chuckled.

Looking down over the arm of the chair, Sam watched the puppies playing with patient Cyrus who endured them tugging on his ears, jumping on his tail and then grabbing the hair, tugging on it and leaping on his back and rolling off it like a hair slide. "I'd like to be here when you have your puppy giveaway," he said.

"That would be fine," Travis said.

"Absolutely," Jesse said, giving Sam a warm look. "I'm sure you know all the people who have asked for one."

"Who are they?" Sam asked, placing the male pup in his lap, who instantly curled up in it, content and not wanting to move.

"Joe Varner, Libby Johnson, Alex Delgado and Katie Montgomery."

Giving them a pleased look, Sam said, "These pups will have really good homes, then. Those folks are responsible, hard-working people. I'm sure Joe will take his and train her for all the hiking and driving around he does as a fish and game agent for the state."

"This breed is very, very physically active," Travis said. "I think his pick will love being outdoors a lot of the time with him."

Nodding, Sam grinned and watched the pups. After the initial play time, they all spread out in four different directions, sniffing and moving about the living room and kitchen. "Freya is a mighty purty mother. She's had some fine lookin' pups. Are you going to spay her, Travis?"

"Jesse and I talked about that very topic last week. Even though Freya is a top show dog in the US, we don't want to show her. We'd like her to have a home with us. We talked with our vet, Emily Hardy, about it. She's going to spay Freya once the puppies are relocated."

Sam studied them for a moment, his eyes narrowing a bit. "You look like a right nice couple together, too."

Heat hit her cheeks and she gave Travis a glance.

"In the past month, we've discovered a friendship with one another," he told his father.

Jesse released her held breath. Travis seemed unruffled by Sam's unexpected remarks. Above all, she didn't want to let Sam know she was renting the red caboose. So much had gone right tonight and she didn't want it spoiled with a family squabble. Sam nodded and returned his attention to the pup who was now happy to be in his lap. Cyrus slowly got up on his old bones, sniffed the pup and then licked it a couple of times.

"I think Cyrus truly loves being around the puppies," she said.

"Yeah, I think he does, too. Maybe he's wanting to be with his own kind. Hangin' around me all the time is pretty stressful. With the pups around, he gets to enjoy playing with them."

"He's more like a doting grandfather to them," Jesse said, smiling. "Both of you are good with animals of all kinds."

"Sheila, when she was alive, had a cat, a canary, a tortoise, a dog, and me."

"She loved animals?" Jesse asked.

"Yes. We were more like a zoo. I used to kid her about it, but she enjoyed teaching Kyle and Travis about them."

"I remember," Travis said, a fond tone in his voice. "She loved anything that had life in it." He looked over at Jesse. "She always had a huge garden out back, would can, freeze and make huckleberry jam for all of us."

"I'm sorry she's gone," Jesse murmured.

"Makes all of us," Sam agreed. He reluctantly placed the male puppy on the floor. "Time for me to go home. It's been a good night, son."

Jesse saw an instant shift in Travis, feeling the huge emotional reaction to Sam calling him "son." Travis rose and walked with his father to the door. He helped him on with the sheepskin coat and handed him his Stetson. Cyrus stood by, knowing he was going to get a ride in the truck, something he loved.

Sam placed the hat on his head. "It's been a good day."

"Yes, it has."

Reaching out, Sam patted his upper arm. He lowered his voice so only Travis could hear him. "I hope you get to be more than friends with Jesse. She reminds me so much of my Sheila."

Nodding, Travis opened the door. "We'll see how it plays out, Sam.

Thanks for dropping by."

Travis watched his father make his way down to the truck. He opened the passenger-side door and then helped Cyrus up onto the seat. The dog's bones were pretty stiff, like his owner's, and he had trouble jumping anywhere at that advanced age. Sam closed the door, lifted his chin and waved his gloved hand in Travis's direction. Almost unbelieving of the changes in his father, he waved back and then closed the door.

Jesse stood nearby, an odd expression on her face as he turned toward her. "What's that look for?" he asked.

"You look shell shocked, Travis."

He laughed a little and headed to the kitchen, slipping his hand into hers. "I am. I remember when I was around five and Sam used to be like this. But after my mother died, he clammed up and went away. The man I knew then, was gone. In his place, at a much later age, was this angry male who lashed out and was always raging due to his pain."

Giving him a sympathetic look, she released his hand when he stopped at the kitchen counter. "I'm glad the old father, the good father, seems to have returned to you."

Travis brought down two mugs. "Coffee?"

"Sure, thanks."

After pouring it, they sat down at the kitchen table, their elbows almost touching.

"I guess I am really in shock," he muttered. "He called me son. He's never said that to my face since I was sixteen. After Mom died, he never called Kyle or me son."

"The past can't be changed, but I think it's his way of letting you know right now that he loves you, Travis." Reaching out, she curved her fingers over his forearm. "Sam is a proud man. I don't know if he'll ever apologize for what he's put you through, but tonight shows what hydrotherapy can do for him. He's pain free and it makes a huge difference in his life. We should understand that better than most people. We carry the pain of PTSD inside of us 24/7. We're miserable to be around, too."

"Yeah," he said heavily, giving her a knowing look. "I think that coupled with getting out, being with family, and the dogs, was like a perfect storm for Sam in the best of ways. He really enjoyed himself. I haven't seen him happy, or smiling or laughing like this since I was sixteen."

"He had a wonderful evening. I could see the happiness in his eyes from time to time."

"I haven't seen that look in so long, Jesse." Travis shook his head. "It's like he was reborn back to his old self I remember growing up. I'm reeling from it. A part of me wants to believe what I saw, but that was only one time. I guess

I'm on guard and at the same time, wanting to so badly to believe what I saw tonight. I'd like to have my 'real' father back in my life."

"Let's see if it holds?" Her fingers tightened on his arm. "If the hydrotherapy continues to give him pain-free days, it's going to probably restore who he was before this time." She removed her hand. "I was so drugged up to my eyeballs for months while still in the Army. The shrink gave me anti-depressants and later, anti-anxiety meds, and I felt out of body from it. Finally, one day, I threw them away and went cold turkey. At least I got my mind back and I could function once more. It took almost a month for my body to cleanse itself of all that crap. I suspect your father will need to detox and adjust to feeling better, too."

"Jumping into a hot tub twice a day isn't going to cause addiction, that's for sure." He gave her a weak smile.

"How are you feeling about Sam coming here for most of the day on the fourteenth?"

"Okay," he said. "Especially if he keeps improving with the hydrotherapy. We'll see if his good mood lasts or not. I hope it does for all our sakes."

December 14

JESSE HAD PUT the little collars that Travis had picked up a week earlier on each of the pups that were spoken for. Four of them had a pink collar to denote they were female. The only male sported a blue collar, but he wasn't leaving today. He would remain with Freya. She was sure the puppy would miss his siblings and Jesse felt for the rambunctious tyke. Earlier, about ten a.m., Sam had driven over. Cyrus was with him and happy to be laying near the overstuffed chair where his master was sitting and drinking coffee. Each of their friends had long ago chosen their favorite and so it became a merry-go-round of people coming and going all afternoon. The day had turned out sunny, in the forties and windy, and everyone came dressed accordingly.

She noticed that Sam truly enjoyed himself. He knew Libby, Joe, Katie and Alex. In fact, when Katie came over to get her puppy, she brought Sam his favorite, a large pumpkin latte. Jesse saw the elder tear up over her kind thoughtfulness toward him. And she'd thoughtfully brought a big Milk Bone for Cyrus, saying that coffee would stunt his growth. Everyone got a howl out of that one! Cyrus wasn't laughing. Instead, he had that Milk Bone between his paws, chowing down on it with gusto. Katie hadn't forgotten her or Travis either, bringing him an Americano and her favorite, a mocha latte.

Joe came over next and he had smoked salmon that he'd made as a thank you gift. He knew from speaking to Travis the other day, that Sam would be there. For Sam, receiving a gift of smoked salmon was pure heaven. It was like Christmas for him and Jesse felt good about that. The people of Hamilton were wonderful.

When Alex arrived, she had bags of baked goods with her. She knew Sam loved pastries and had a dozen in a box for him, wrapped in a bright red bow. For Travis, he liked the fruit-filled Danish. And for Jesse, Alex had brought a half-dozen chocolate éclairs. They wouldn't freeze well and Jesse was going to be hard pressed to eat them up soon enough. She also left enough of an assortment of cookies so that everyone could partake.

Libby Johnson had to shut down the hardware store to run over and pick up her beloved new puppy. She brought a bouquet of flowers for them in way of thanks, the bright reds of roses, green spider mums and white chrysanthemums making it a holiday atmosphere. It was a warm-hearted afternoon for everyone. Travis was happy to see the pups go to homes that would love and care for them like a member of their own family. The little blue-eyed male pup had tried to climb up Sam's leg in order to get back into his lap. Sam had leaned down, picked him up and settled him into that cozy, comfy spot he preferred. He placed a hand over him.

"Maybe I should give him a name," Sam said to Jesse.

"Why not? He needs one." She saw his expression soften as he slowly continued to pet the pup, studying him for a moment.

"He's gonna be here at the cabin with Travis. Maybe I should ask him? He might already have a name picked out for him."

Jesse hoped he wouldn't ask where she stayed. Travis was in the kitchen making another pot of coffee now that everyone had come and gotten their puppy. "Why not ask him when he's done?"

Sam turned his head, watching his son. "I will."

"Do you love his blue eyes?"

"I do. Makes him look special."

Freya came over and sat next to Jesse's leg and she smoothed her hand along the dog's broad skull.

Travis brought each of them a mug of fresh coffee and sat down near Jesse.

"So?" he asked his father, "I overheard you talking. Do you have a name for him?" He pointed to the puppy who was alert and sitting up, soaking in Sam's attention. He had cupped his hands around the pup so he wouldn't accidentally fall off his lap and tumble onto the floor.

"I'm thinking Blue would be a good name for him. It's not a fancy name, but you have to admit, his eyes are like blue Montana sapphire gems from Phillipsburg, with sunlight comin' through 'em."

"I like the name," Travis said. Glancing toward Jesse he asked, "What do you think?"

"Love the name. It's simple and easy to remember. Blue, it is."

Blue perked up his tiny, black pointed ears, studying them across the coffee table between them.

"He has a blue collar too," Travis noted, laughing at the synchronicity.

"I guess you were onto something, son, whether you knew it or not."

Jesse saw Travis's expression soften as his father called him son once again. Did Sam realize just how important that was to him? She didn't know. "I'd say this is a father-son mental telepathy going on between the two of you."

Sam gave a thoughtful nod. "I like that idea." He snuggled Blue against his chest, the puppy loving to nuzzle his head between that elk-skin vest he wore and his red and black checkered flannel shirt. "At least Freya will have company. Maybe it's not a bad thing that no one wanted Blue."

"He'll have a good home with me," Travis promised. "Like Joe, I intend to take Freya and Blue with me on some of the overnight guide trips coming up next spring. They're outdoor dogs and they need a lot of fresh air and exercise."

"You're right," Sam said. He leaned over and petted Cyrus, who was sleeping, head resting on his paws. Straightening, he said, "You know? If this hydrotherapy treatment continues, I can come back to work. Take some of the strain of demands off you."

"That would be good," Travis said. "I think you're bored being home all the time."

"Got that right. And Cy needs some exercise and likes being out in the office. He gets an awful lot of attention from our customers and he loves that."

"Any time you want to try out a few hours at the office," Travis said, "let me know? Right now, Jesse is coming over twice a week to work with me on inputting all the names of our clients into our new software database. It's going to help me schedule the trips and stay in closer touch with our clients."

"No more filing cabinets holding those one-thousand clients' names?" Sam wondered.

"We'll always keep those files as a backup. If we get hacked or the computer crashes, we'll have a physical hard copy so we can move forward."

"Good thinkin'," Sam praised. He smiled a little at Blue, who was now hiding warmly beneath his vest. "You gonna have Freya and Blue over at the office?"

"Yes. I want to acclimate them to the public. Maybe if you drop by for a while, you can bring Cy along. It will sort of be like a doggie day care center for the three of them," he chuckled.

Sam chuckled with him. "That sounds good. Starting after Christmas might be a good time."

Jesse stirred. "Sam? Do you have any plans for Christmas morning break-fast? Travis and I would love to have you and Cy come over. I'm making my world-famous French toast with peanut butter and Kahlua syrup. I can guarantee you'll love it. What do you say?"

"Sounds interesting. I never thought of those two ingredients and French toast in the same breath. I'd like that, Jesse." He looked down at sleeping Blue whose hind end and stubby tail were all that was visible from beneath his vest. "Besides, I get to see this little guy. Cy will like seeing him again, too."

"I would imagine," Jesse said drily, "that Freya will be more than happy that you and Cy have come over to get Blue's attention."

Chuckling, Travis traded a smile with her. "We've found Blue is a highly curious and stubborn little cuss. He was the last one to be weaned. Freya was going nuts because he wanted milk over kibble."

"Yeah, this pup is a little like me: bullheaded as all git out."

"Oh, you've softened a little with age," Travis teased, meeting his father's grizzled smile.

"Most likely," he agreed gruffly, a crooked grin spreading across his mouth.

"Why don't you drop over around nine a.m. Christmas morning?" Travis suggested.

"I'll do that."

Jesse watched as Sam rose with more vitality and was glad the hydrothera-py was working so well for him. Wasn't it a shame that the man had to suffer for decades and not one doctor recommended a hot tub or even taking a hot bath to ease his stiffened joints? At the door, Sam patted Travis's arm and then left. When he turned around after shutting the door, there was a new tender-ness in his face. Her heart swelled with joy that perhaps the father-son disconnect was dissolving and they were forging a new, positive relationship with one another.

"You know," Travis said, sitting down next to her, "I wouldn't have be-lieved that a hot tub could make such a change in Sam. Whatever it is, it's working."

She slipped her arm around his shoulder, nestling up against him. "I think it's wonderful. A Christmas miracle." Travis slid his arm around her waist, his hand resting against her hip as she languished beneath it. She sighed, resting her head on his shoulder, her arm going around him. "Sam seems to be trying really hard to atone for how he used to treat you from what I can tell." She looked up, meeting his slanting glance. "Is that how you see it?"

"Yes. I'm shocked by the change in him. Since I've been home, he's always been an angry, cantankerous man."

"But you said he was like this kinder version of himself when you were growing up."

Nodding, he smoothed the fabric across her hip. "Yes, he was. I guess that's why him reverting back to that time has got me spinning. I like that he's like his old self. Not that I don't like it, I do. I'm wary because I'm gun-shy about him reverting back to that angry old man."

"I think this is permanent, Travis. I'm happy for both of you. You've both had terrible losses: first, your mom and then your brother Kyle dying. I tried to put myself into your shoes. I tried to imagine my mom being gone." She smoothed her palm across his broad chest. "I relied a lot on my parents emotionally after I was released from the service. It about killed me when I left them to start wandering around western Montana, trying to figure things out and get my life back."

"I've met guys who came out of dysfunctional families and either didn't have a father or had a bad one," he said, moving his fingers through her hair. "I always loved Sam even if I couldn't understand his change of moods. He changed drastically after my mother died. By that time, he had pain all the time from his bull-riding injuries and wasn't pleasant to be around. After Kyle died, he retreated even deeper inside himself. By the time I left the military, he was a very changed man from the one I grew up with."

Sighing, she closed her eyes, contentment washing through her. Inwardly, Jesse knew that he needed this, the holding, the intimacy that always sprung strongly between them. She did, too. "My parents have been a quiet, steady beacon all my life. And, you've given me a second chance here, Travis." She gazed up at him. "My weekly phone calls with my parents and living here in Hamilton have given me the stability I was looking for." She lifted her hand, grazing his cheek, her fingertips tingling along the sandpapery length of his jaw. "Only, I never entertained the thought that a man would be so instrumental in helping me get my feet beneath me once more."

He tightened his embrace for a moment. "You've infused me with new life, Jesse, whether you know it or not. You talk about a Christmas miracle? You're that miracle to me."

Her lips twisted. "I'm hardly a miracle, Travis. I fight every day to try to appear normal when I know I'll probably never be the old Jesse. But you give me hope, so does Freya, and the friends I've made here in town."

"This little town has a special brand of magic, too," he said. Leaning over, he pressed a kiss to her brow. He allowed his lips to rest against her skin. "You'll always be my miracle. We're not perfect and never will be. I like you just the way you are, Jesse."

A small sound of pleasure hummed in her throat as he kissed her along her hairline. She pressed herself against him, letting him know she enjoyed his exploring kisses. Her scalp skittered with tiny, electric-like tingles. She leaned away, her heart starting to beat harder, her lower body feeling warm and achy with need.

"I don't want to leave you tonight," she whispered, lifting her lashes, drowning in his stormy-looking grey eyes. "I want to love you, Travis." It took every scrap of courage she had within her to ask him that. His eyes widened for a moment and then a hunter-like look came to them.

"You're sure, Jesse?"

His low, rumbling voice rolled through her. "Very sure. It's time, Travis. At least, I feel that way. Do you?" She held her breath until she saw that lopsided boyish smile pull at that beautifully shaped mouth of his. She had her answer before he spoke.

"Let's put the dogs away for the night?"

"Yes." Her voice was wispy sounding even to her. It felt as if her brain were in park and she couldn't think straight. "I'm going to grab a quick shower. I'll meet you in your bedroom."

Dipping his head, he kissed her tenderly and for a long, long time. When she came up for air, her heart was racing with wild need of this man.

"I'll see you in bed," he promised thickly.

CHAPTER 13

AS JESSE'S BACK slid against the fluffy white flannel sheet, she honed in on Travis's large, splayed hand against her shoulder. He had picked her up, naked, and carried her to the king-sized bed. Just getting to have their flesh meet finally melted her heart and heated her soul. This was the man she wanted to run to when she was scared, confused or joyously happy. He'd just come from taking a hot shower and his skin was taut and moist, the fragrance of the lime-scented soap mingling in her flaring nostrils. There was a night light near the closed door, lending just enough light that she could see the deep planes and shadows across his face. Releasing his shoulders as he positioned her on the bed, she held that hunter-like look in his eyes. Travis came alongside her, his arm curving beneath her neck, his other hand resting against her hip, and she smiled up at him.

Reaching up, she threaded her fingers through his short, damp hair, liking that he hadn't shaved, the darkness of his beard lending dramatically to his masculinity that inspired her. His erection, strong and warm, lay against her belly. Sliding his hand to the small of her back he eased her fully against him. The scent of his skin increased her hunger and she leaned up, kissing his shoulder, creating a trail along his strong neck, across his jaw, and finding that mouth of his that spiraled her into boiling heat as he captured her lips. He took her strongly, letting her know how starved he was for her. The ache between her thighs increased tenfold as he took her to heights she'd never attained before, his hand caressing her breast, sending shocking pleasure radiating through it and then tunneling downward into her clenching lower body.

Lost within the strength of him as a man, that wonderful mouth of his wreaking sweet havoc upon her, she allowed herself to become lost in the wildness building frantically between them. In an unexpected move, he rolled over on his back and then lifted her, settling her gently on top of his hard erection. Hands splayed against his dark-haired chest, eyes barely open, her fluids gliding along his length, making her groan with promise of what was to come.

Somewhere in her anesthetized brain where she could barely think coherently, Jesse understood why he'd done this. Travis knew she hadn't had sex in a long, long time, and that by choosing this position, it gave her total control of how much or little she could accept him into herself. A powerful love flowed through her as she tightened her thighs against his narrow hips, moving fluidly and slickly against him. The growl of satisfaction coming from him was like an earthquake of promises to come as his hands wrapped firmly around her hips, guiding her, bringing her down against him, triggering small explosions that promised she would quickly orgasm.

No one was more surprised than she was when she did exactly that without him ever being within her. A cry, part animal, part human, rose in her throat as the explosion tripled swiftly within her, throwing her out into a tumbling darkness that she moved into with pure, unadulterated pleasure. Eyes tightly closed, her hands digging into the taut flesh of his chest as she rode that rocket expanding hotly in outgoing undulations that increased within her, she felt him helping to prolong the gift her body had just given her. It was then, in some far corner of her mind, that she realized Travis wanted nothing but pleasure for her in every possible way. He loved her. That thought brought a second, more powerful orgasm and she screamed, hurled into the night, the Fourth of July erupting and surrounding her. For untold minutes, she was lost completely in the primal animal of her body taking its own pleasure and her being the recipient of all of it.

It was so easy to lean forward, allowing him to flow into her. She was heated and wet, her juices paved a slick ribbon deep within her body that eagerly welcomed him. The rocking motion, his hands cupping her hips, holding her in place, knowing from experience the angle and pressure she needed to orgasm a third time, catapulted her into that same boiling heat and animal gratification as before. And as she languished in the arms of that volcanic pleasure, she felt him stiffen, give out a growl and freeze as he climaxed deep within her. They swirled together, locked into one another's arms as one.

Feeling faint, she lay against him, breathing raggedly, her hands restless, curving around his head, kissing him, their mouths clinging hotly to one another. She eased her fingers through his hair, massaging his scalp, hearing him groan. His hands were exploring her and it felt as if he were mapping her body, memorizing her with his caresses and adoring her.

Travis eased upward and pulled the covers over them, the soft flannel against their damp bodies. He was feeling weak and satiated, joy pounding through his heart as he gathered Jesse up against him. They fit so well together and he closed his eyes, sleep coming quickly.

★

December 15

"ARE YOU HUNGRY?" Travis asked Jesse. They had slept together, awakened, loved one another as they showered, and then gotten dressed. It was nearly eight a.m. and Travis had fed Freya and Blue first.

"Starving," Jesse admitted, cutting up some squares of sharp cheddar cheese for the omelet that he was going to make them. Her whole body vibrated softly with the memory of last night. Waking up in Travis's arms was dream-like. She'd been a single woman so long that she'd forgotten the coziness of having a male partner to share her bed and the next morning.

Travis gave the dogs fresh water and went to the sink, washing his hands. "We slept like rocks last night."

Her lips pulled upward. "I didn't realize just how tired I was. And you know something? Ever since I had those wild, powerful orgasms, I'm not tensing up like I usually do."

He wiped his hands on a towel, dropping it on the counter, giving her a wry look. "Sex always helps people with PTSD. It somehow short circuits some of the symptoms for a while. It's a healing space for us."

"Mmmm," she replied, dropping the cubes of cheese into a bowl that held sliced tomatoes and onions. "I feel so loose and easy going this morning. Of course, having no orgasm for nearly two years also added a layer to our lovemaking last night."

"You were in ecstasy," he teased, pride in his tone. He cracked six eggs into a nearby bowl. "But so was I. It was good for both of us."

"Was it ever." She pulled the milk carton from the fridge and set it near where he was working.

He studied her for a moment. "You know this is a new chapter in our relationship?"

Becoming somber, Jesse nodded. She reached up and brought down two plates from the cupboard. "I felt ready for it...for you...us."

"What was different for you to take that step?" he wondered, adding salt, pepper and a pinch of cinnamon basil.

Shrugging, she said, "Seeing your father embrace you as his son." She saw emotion come to his eyes and he swallowed a couple of times.

"I felt like I was dying on a desert when I came home from the military, Jesse. And my father, from the day I arrived, insisted I not call him Dad, which I always had when growing up, but call him Sam, instead. I felt gutted in that moment. I literally felt like he'd invisibly took a knife and cut me open, divorced me from him and our family."

"No one's ready for something like that," she whispered, coming over, placing her hand on his shoulder. He took a whisk and beat the eggs in the bowl.

"No…I was so far away from that. After Kyle died, I'd seen him change even more. But I never knew how much until that morning he gave me my marching orders the first day home from combat."

"I don't know of any human who could suffer the loss of two of the most important people in their lives and not go through an awful time of pain and grief afterward. You were caught up in it through no fault of your own."

"I got that. It took me a year to come to grips with the reality, and I eventually realized the domino effect it had on my father. To this day, I have to bite my tongue and not call him Dad. It damn near kills me, Jesse."

"You need your dad back," she said softly, her heart twisting in grief for Travis. Standing close, her hand around his waist, she said, "And I think that Blue is going to help you get your father back. I feel the angry man filled with pain, both physical and emotional, is gone for good. I know it will take some time to prove me out, but the changes in him the last month have been tremendously hopeful."

"Why Blue?" he asked, adding the contents she'd cut up into the egg bowl.

"Did it strike you that Blue is your dad's future? Did you see how that pup just adores Sam? And that Cyrus loves him, too? I know Cy will die probably within the next year or two. He's fifteen. That's very old for such a large dog."

He stirred the mixture into a black iron skillet. "Blue does love Dad."

"Are you thinking what I'm thinking?" She smiled up at him, seeing some of the old grief he'd carried for so long, beginning to dissolve.

"Making Blue a Christmas gift to Dad?"

She patted him on the back. "Yes."

"Blue gets along with Cy. That's important."

"Cy could be like a doting grandfather to Blue, showing him the ropes of dog hood."

Smiling a little, he folded the omelet in the skillet. "You're good with words, Jesse."

"What do you think about giving Blue to him on Christmas morning?"

"I think it's a great idea. I just worry that Dad won't take him."

"I feel like he will," Jesse soothed. "Every day he's without the pain because of the hydrotherapy, he's getting more sensitive to others, more aware. And I think he's terribly lonely out there by himself. He's finding that being here with us, thinking about coming back to the office to work a couple days of the week, appeals to him."

"Well, ten days to go until Christmas," he said, cutting the omelet in half and transferring it to each plate. "Do you have a plan?" He raised an eyebrow, grinning down at her.

"I *always* have plans, Ramsey. You can't be in the military and not know the advantages of having a strategy laid out in front of you. Plus, having Plan B and C as backups if A fails. I've got this."

Chuckling, he turned off the gas stove and then handed her one of the plates. "Tell me your plan."

Over breakfast, Jesse shared her ideas with Travis. "I think we should keep inviting your dad over here for dinner. Have him bring Cy along. That way, he and Blue get to interact with one another more and more and become bosom buddies. That won't be lost on Sam. Then, I think you should talk to him about how you can use his help at the office. That you have some ideas for ads and getting more tours locked in for the coming year, and that you need his help, suggestions and ideas, too. He needs to feel he's a valuable person to your family business."

"That way, Dad feels needed," he agreed.

"That's right. And who knows? If he continues to improve, he might want to do the day tour guides to your special fishing holes. That would do him a lot of good."

"It would be the best of all worlds if he could get active again. I know he hates being hobbled. He's always been a very physical, outdoorsy man."

"I'm not going to tell him that I'm renting the caboose, Travis. I think it could distract Sam and we want him to focus on you, the business and getting Blue to become a part of his life."

Giving her a look of praise, he said, "It's a good plan, Jesse. We'll do it."

Rubbing her hands, she said, "Good!"

Finishing off his meal, he got up and brought over coffee for them. Sitting down at her elbow, he gave her a narrowed look. "We need to talk about something even more important," he told her.

"Us?" she guessed, sipping her coffee.

"Yes. Where does last night leave us, Jesse? How do you want to work this into our budding relationship? Or do you?"

"Like you said, we've opened a new chapter with one another. And I'm okay with it, Travis. For whatever reason, the last couple of weeks I've just felt more together and stronger. I'm sure you have a lot to do with that. You've been stabilizing my life since I came to Hamilton, and I'm so grateful."

"You're almost at that six-month point after leaving the service where all the confusion and mess have started to lessen. I saw a lot of my buddies, when they got out, hit that six-month point and they were like you: more clear-headed, having goals and a job that was helping to bring badly needed money into their life."

"With us, it became more than that," she murmured. "You've fed me in so many ways, especially emotionally. You've been there like a cornerstone to my new life." She reached out, slipping her fingers into his, holding his intense gaze. "I'm falling in love with you, Travis. I almost said it last night, but I was too scared to admit it. When I woke up this morning, I made a promise to myself to tell you how I felt today." She felt his fingers tighten around hers.

"This last month," he began, his voice gruff, "I knew I was falling in love with you. Only, I didn't know if it was one sided or not. It wasn't until the last two weeks that I realized you wanted me as much as I wanted you. That kiss you shared with me in the caboose did it." He gave her an uneven grin. "And if you want to continue to live out in the caboose, I'm fine with that. I just hope you know that you always have an invitation to share my cabin and bed."

"This is a new chapter, Travis. If it's okay with you, I'll stay here. I think we need to find out what we have. I'll take care of the caboose, but I won't be sleeping there." She saw relief come to his eyes.

"I'd like that, Jesse. And if there's a time you don't want to sleep with me for whatever reason, there's always the guest bedroom. I'm not going to demand anything of you. Everything has its time and place. My mother taught me as a child about the value of patience." He gave her a tender look. "I want nothing more from you than what you freely want to share with me."

December 24

THE FIRE SNAPPED and crackled, lending to a cozy Christmas Eve. Jesse sat with Travis, finishing their pumpkin bread topped off with a dollop of whipped cream. At their feet was Freya and Blue. The pup had been completely weaned off her milk and was now putting on some muscle mass and weight from his twice-a-day feedings. Freya was regaining lost weight, too, from feeding five pups for six weeks. Her black fur was thick for the freezing Montana winter. Her white blaze on her face and the white ruff down the front of her chest gleamed with good health.

"It's tough not giving them a bit of the pumpkin bread," Travis mumbled, trying to ignore the pleading look in Blue's huge, sparkling eyes so full of life in their depths.

Laughing softly, Jesse nodded. "I think Blue picked up that begging look from his mom. Look at her!" She pointed her fork in Freya's direction.

Grinning, he said, "She's a pro at this. She must have gotten her owner to feed her tidbits because she's way too good at it."

"I've got two small Milk Bones stashed away in my pocket," she told him, meeting his amused gaze. "It's enough to reward them but not enough to make them gain weight or start eating human food."

Travis set his empty dessert plate on the coffee table. "That was good," he said. Leaning back, he slid his arm around Jesse's shoulders. "I keep thinking I'm in some kind of dream," he confided, catching her glance as she popped the last piece of the bread into her mouth. "These past ten days have been nonstop heaven. Has it been for you?"

She nodded and set her plate on top of his, feeding the dogs their Milk Bone treat. Then, snuggled back beneath his arm, resting her head on his shoulder, holding his warmth-filled gaze. "Ever since we made love, I've had fewer and less intense symptoms. That amazes me."

He sobered. "It doesn't happen like that for most."

"Maybe because we're getting deep, uninterrupted sleep after we've loved one another?"

"I'm sleeping a lot better," he admitted, moving his fingers lightly across her forearm covered with a dark green knit sweater. It had been a Christmas gift from Katie for Jesse, who knitted it when she had time. He'd tried to get her to buy some more winter clothes, but she'd resisted, wanting instead to save her money.

She sighed and kissed his jaw. "And even your dad is continuing to improve. Dr. Brannon gave him a rave examination yesterday. Sam is glowing from his progress. Who could *ever* think that hydrotherapy would have that powerful and positive of an effect on his joints?"

"It's a miracle, no question." His voice lowered. "And you're *my* miracle, Jesse. You need to know how much more hope I have. I wake up every morning grateful for you in my bed and in my arms. I've never laughed as much as I have as when you walked into my life."

She made a mewing sound of comfort and wrapped her arms around his shoulders, giving him a long hug topped off with a long kiss. Easing back, her lips tingling and wanting to love this man right now, Jesse stilled her desire for the moment. Their talks had been long and deep. It was refreshing to hear what was on his mind, what he thought and how she made him feel. All of their intimacy on every level the last ten days had done nothing but deepen her love for Travis.

"I'll be back in a minute. Freya and I have been practicing something that involves you."

She sat up, curious. "You and Freya?"

Easing to his feet, he gestured for the dog to follow him. "Yes. We'll be back in a minute. Stay where you are?"

She smiled and curled her legs beneath her. "I won't move," she promised, watching Freya bound after Travis. Blue gave a yip, scrambling to catch up to his leggy mother. Leaning back, she enjoyed the Christmas tree in the corner. There was a newfound sense of peace overcoming her life and she welcomed it. Never had she thought that she'd come to Hamilton and fall in love with a dog and her puppies, and then the man who welcomed all of them into his home and life.

She heard a yip and saw Blue burst out of the hallway, galloping toward her. Next came Freya. Jesse laughed and sat up. The dog had a twine handle attached to a small red sack that had silver tinsel swinging around the middle of it. Travis was last, his smile widening as he urged Freya toward her.

Freya came and sat down in front of her, thumping her tail, her blue eyes alight with mischief and merriment.

"Go ahead," Travis urged, "take the sack from her."

Gently, she eased the red twine handle from Freya's mouth. She cocked her head, tail thumping madly.

"Wow, did you train her to do this?" Jesse held the sack in her lap as Travis sat down next to her. He leaned forward, roughing up Freya's fur, lavishly praising her.

"I did. She's so smart that it didn't take long. But the problem was Blue," he chuckled. "The pup thought it was a play toy in his mother's mouth and would leap and grab it, pulling it apart."

Petting Freya and then Blue, who was wagging his stubby tail, she said, "And how long did the training go on?"

"Oh, about two weeks."

She smiled and looked down into the sack. It was filled with red and green paper. "Pretty neat trick," she congratulated him. "I thought everyone opened their presents on Christmas morning?"

"Nah, I always believed Christmas gifts should be handed out all year long." He motioned toward the sack. "Go ahead, dig around in it. See what you find."

Excited, she pulled out the crepe paper, finding a small silver box within it. "What is this?" she demanded, looking at it, giving him a wary look.

"Something hopeful," he said, his voice low, his gaze locking with hers. "Go ahead, open it, Jesse."

"Okay," she said, easing her fingernail beneath the gold latch and opening it. Her lips parted. There, on a gray velvet cushion was a ring with red and green stones in a silver setting. "What is this?" she asked, breathless, her eyes widening, her voice growing hoarse. She saw a bashful look cross his expression.

"It's called a friendship ring, Jesse. I know we've only had two months together, but I wanted to get you something special, from my heart to yours. The jeweler in Missoula said that a lot of couples who were living together often used a friendship ring as a sign that they're going together. I thought...I mean, I hope, that you'll take it in the spirit it was meant from me to you." He took the case from her and eased the ring out of it, taking her right hand and slipping it on her finger. "It fits," he murmured, relieved. Holding her hand, he said, "The red stone is pyrope garnet. The green one is tourmaline. The setting is platinum." Nervously, he held her hand. "Do you like it, Jesse?"

"It's lovely," she choked, moving the round, faceted stones, watching the light refract through them. "So beautiful." She reached out, caressing his jaw. "Thank you. This is perfect."

"So? You're okay with it?"

"I am. I know two months isn't a long time but I feel comfortable being with you, living here and doing my daily work on myself."

"You really like it? The colors of the gemstones?"

She knew enough about gemstones because her father was a rock hound. The quality of the translucent blood-red garnet was of the highest quality. She wasn't going to ask how much he spent, but knew it was enough. "I really like it, Travis. Thank you. This is so unexpected. Such an incredible surprise."

"I didn't want to give it to you in front of my dad. He's old fashioned, a Baby Boomer, and he thinks men and women shouldn't be living together without being married first."

"I understand. My parents are uncomfortable about it, too."

"Are you? We've never talked about this before."

"I'm fine with it. What do you think your dad will say when he sees it on my hand?"

"That it's a friendship ring, which is the truth. That we are good friends and it's a Christmas gift for you."

"Do you think he knows we're living together?"

Snorting, Travis said, "Hamilton is a small town and gossip is faster than a lightning bolt across the sky. I'm pretty sure he knows. I'm hoping he won't say anything about it. So far, he hasn't. And so far, no one has told him that you've rented out the caboose." He crossed his fingers.

"I think he's okay with us being together," Jesse said, giving him a tender look. "I feel he's trying hard to fit in, not stand out and be rebellious like he was in his younger life."

"He asked me the other day what my intentions toward you were," he admitted. "We were working on an ad for the business, to draw in new clients, when he asked me that out of the blue."

Blue whined, hearing his named called, sitting between their feet, panting and wagging his tiny tail.

Laughing, Jesse picked him up and plopped him onto Travis's lap. He really did like being with the men of the Ramsey family. "Uh oh, then I'm sure the gossip's reached him."

Grimacing, he said, "Right. I told him that we were drawn to one another in every way."

"What did he say?"

"Nothing."

"How do you interpret that?" she wondered.

"My dad isn't one to mince words when he's got something on his mind." We went back to work and it wasn't brought up again. I did tell him that I had bought you a special gift for Christmas that would let the world know we were serious about one another."

She held up her hand with the ring on it. "That's good. At least when he sees it, he'll understand."

"That's what I'm hoping. I always live in fear he'll start blowing up again and getting angry at me or you."

"But he hasn't."

"No, but I had three years of it, Jesse, and I'm gun shy. I want so damned badly to believe that the hydrotherapy is the reason why. That and not suffering in pain all the time. I'm afraid he'll slip back into that dark area."

Reaching out, she touched his shoulder. "I want to kiss you." She leaned upward, cognizant of Blue between them.

Whispering her name, he slid his hand around her neck, guiding her mouth to his. Blue whined and started getting excited, leaping up on his chest. He probably thought that they were playing with one another. Taking her mouth, he slid his lips along hers, feeling her softness and quiet strength. That small sound in the back of her throat told him she was enjoying the kiss as much as he was.

Breaking away from him, Jesse smiled and said, "Blue wants to play…"

With a chuckle, Travis roughed up the pup's furry head. "I want to play too. Maybe later?" He gave her a teasing look that she returned, the silent promise mirrored in her eyes.

"We have to get some sleep tonight," she told him, setting Blue down on the floor. He scampered off to where his mother was laying and chewing on the rubber ball that she loved chasing when outdoors.

Travis stood and slid his arm around her waist. "We'll get some sleep."

"Sure. I wonder just how much that means?" she asked, giving him a wicked look.

CHAPTER 14

JESSE TRIED TO contain her surprise when Sam showed up with a huge grocery bag containing Christmas gifts. He hadn't exchanged gifts with anyone since Travis had left the military and come home. She hugged him after he came inside and Travis took the sack, placing it near the tree. Christmas music was in the background, the tree glowing with lights in the corner, the fireplace filling the space with warmth. Outside, it was snowing once again, the white flakes twirling and dancing in the gunmetal-colored sky, as if celebrating the morning with them. As he took off his heavy sheepskin coat and hung it up, she admired the bright red flannel shirt he wore beneath his elk-skin vest. It was obvious that he'd taken pains to clean up for the first Christmas he'd spent with Travis in over a decade. Jesse knew how much it meant to Travis, and invited Sam to sit down at the dining room table. Even Cyrus seemed in a jaunty mood as he laid near the fire, warming himself, his coat scattered with snowflakes that had melted and turned to droplets of water.

"You can take those gifts out and put them under the tree," he told Travis. "When are we opening them?" he asked Jesse.

"Right after breakfast," she promised.

"Where's Blue and Freya?"

"Oh, we're feeding them down in the basement right now. We'll let them up when we get ready to open packages."

Sam nodded, taking the red linen napkin and unfolding it. "Sounds reasonable. Blue is a terror, but he sure makes Cy and I be less bored with his antics."

Jesse laughed and made her way to the kitchen, preparing her special French toast recipe.

Travis joined her and in no time, they had their fragrant breakfast on the table. Sam was pleased and chose a bunch of crisp bacon as a side. He fed Cy a piece or two in the process, much to the dog's delight.

"Well, looks like there's lots of gifts under that tree of yours, son."

Travis sat at Sam's left elbow, Jesse on the right. "It's nice to see us all here," he said. "That's the best gift of all, for me."

Chewing on the French toast, Sam said, "Did you get that green envelope out of the sack?"

"I did." Travis pointed in the direction of the tree. "Yes, right there. It's perched on a bough."

"Oh," he said, peering at it, "that's good…good…"

"Did you trim your hair, Sam?" Jesse wondered. Usually it was long and combed, but today, it seemed shorter to her.

"Yes, I came into town and our only barber, Henry, trimmed me up." He grinned a little. "I guess I'm getting tired of looking like a Phillipsburg sapphire miner."

Jesse was familiar with the sapphire mining in the Rocky Mountains around Phillipsburg, Montana. Travis had told her that a lot of rock hound tourists would come up in the summer months and try their hand at finding gems in the sandy soil in the forest. "Well, you look very dapper," she said, enjoying the peanut butter and Kahlua tastes of her French toast. His cheeks turned ruddy. Sam had been through a lot, too. They all had. Life wasn't easy on anyone, yet here he was trying, she felt, to patch up his relationship with Travis. She knew how much it meant to this man she loved with all her heart and soul. Both he and Sam had been caught in a terrible double loss, and each man had to gut through the grief in their own time and way. Only Sam's grief was compounded by earlier injuries.

"Thanks," Sam said, puffing out his chest a bit. "I was thinkin' that for my age, I didn't look half as bad as I'd felt before the hydrotherapy treatment came along. I think I look twenty years younger. Don't you think?"

Brightening, Travis said, "Definitely." His eyes twinkled. "You've always had kind things to say about Sassy Jones, the gal who owns the Montgomery Furniture store in town."

"Really?" Jesse asked, perking up, giving Sam a merry look.

"Oh, now," he mumbled, clearly uncomfortable, "Sass and I go back a long way. To childhood. We were born and raised here in Hamilton," he told Jesse. "And in grade school, I had a crush on her and we were an item of sorts, if you could even call it that. Later, she married Stan Jones, another childhood friend of mine. They had a good marriage, had three kids who are now grown and gone. Stan died five years ago, leavin' Sass a widow. I felt badly for her because she's a good person."

"I've yet to meet her."

"She's usually over at Sue's diner at lunch," Travis said. "I'll make sure we go over there soon and you can meet her."

"She's a real lady, but has an earthy sense of humor that I have always ap-preciated. As kids, we were always laughing. She made me real happy," Sam confided to Jesse.

"Hmmm," Travis said, "maybe that spark between you two never died?"

Jesse gave Sam a warm look. "Just because of your age? The heart never stops loving."

"Well, now," Sam sputtered, "don't either of you get any ideas!"

"But you have a nice past with one another," Jesse pointed out gently. Sam's cheeks were a burning red right now. Travis was grinning like a coon who had just stole a cob of corn to eat.

Sam scowled. "The past is the past."

"Right," Jesse said, reaching over and patting his arm, teasing in her tone.

Travis traded a wicked look with her but said nothing more. His father was clearly uncomfortable about bringing Sassy up in their conversation. She was his age. Was there a romance there to be stoked to life, perhaps? That would sure get the town talking, he thought, smiling over at Jesse. There was a gleam in her eyes and she knew there was a lot more to this story than he could tell her right now.

After breakfast, they all sat in the living room while Travis brought the wrapped gifts over to Sam, Jesse and himself. There were three from Katie Montgomery, and even one for Freya and Cyrus. Sam was surprised but pleased, setting the wrapped gift on Cy's paws, who was smelling it appreciatively. Sam also received two gifts from them. After settling all the presents near each of them, Travis said, "How about we let Blue and Freya up?" He headed for the cellar door.

"Yes," Sam crowed. "I miss seeing Blue!" He leaned over, patting Cyrus on the head. "And so does Cy."

Jesse smiled and said nothing, watching Travis open the door.

Out shot Blue. He was wearing a knitted blue and red Christmas collar that had been made by Katie.

Sam chuckled and leaned down as the pup licked Cyrus hello on the muzzle and then turned his attention to his favorite human being.

"Why look at this," he said, pointing to the blue and red knit collar around Blue's neck. "That's right purty."

Travis sat down next to her. "Katie made a Christmas collar for all three dogs. We opened Blue's earlier because we wanted to give you the pup as a gift."

Sam's face fell as Blue settled immediately on his lap, eagerly licking his fingers. "What?" he gasped. "You're gonna give me Blue?"

Jesse saw the sudden tears of gratefulness in Sam's eyes. "We sure are, Sam. We talked about this and decided Blue is yours to keep."

Travis blinked a couple of times, touched that his father had tears in his eyes. He'd never seen him like this. "Sam, that little pup chose you from the beginning. He's yours if you'd like to keep him?"

"Why, sure I'd like to keep him!" Sam gave Cyrus a warm look. "He likes him, too, you know."

"We saw that," Travis agreed, reaching out, squeezing Jesse's hand. "Then it's settled. You'll take Blue home with you. He's your dog and Cy's new buddy."

"And Travis bought you a bag of kibble for him, too. He'll put it in your truck when you're ready to leave."

Sam's face softened as Blue leaped up, his little paws on Sam's vest, wagging his stubby tail. He gave Jesse a watery smile. "This is just the best Christmas gift I've had since my Sheila and my son Kyle died." He gave her and Travis a grateful look. "Thank you…both of you…this is just the best gift I could have gotten except for one more."

"One more?" Travis asked, confused.

"You'll see," Sam told him enigmatically, ruffling up the fur on Blue's back as he cupped his hand beneath his rear and allowed him to play inside the vest, which was a favorite game of his. "But now? Why don't you each open your gifts I got for you?"

Travis nodded, and handed Jesse her large box. "I think we will," he replied, tearing into the paper.

Jesse smiled and did the same, paper flying in all directions. Opening her box, she smiled. "Oh, Sam! This is perfect!" She held up the sweater jacket, a bright red with white Christmassy designs. "I really needed this. I was putting off buying one for myself."

Pleased, Sam said, "Can't have you cold, Jesse. I'm glad you like it."

She stood up, pulling it on and zipping it up the front. "Fits perfectly!"

"Thank Travis. He gave me your size so I wouldn't get it wrong."

Jesse winked at Travis and he grinned. "What's in your box?" she asked, pointing to it.

"Dunno…just a minute." He pulled the top off, revealing a dark green knit sweater with white designs and snowflakes all over it.

"Oh, I like that!" Jesse said, pulling it out. "Come on, put it on, Travis. I want to see you in it."

Sam chuckled, pleased and watching his son pull it over his head. "You look really good in it," he told him.

Pulling it down and into place, Travis said, "Well, I got us some fun gifts." He handed one to Jesse and then to Sam, across the coffee table. "This is to celebrate our family getting together after a long time."

Jesse heard the thickening emotion in Travis's voice as he sat down. She opened hers and crowed with laughter, pulling out a Santa Clause hat. "Oh, this is perfect, Travis!" She pulled it on her hair, smiling.

Sam chuckled and held his up. "I like this idea, Travis." He set Blue down in his lap and pulled on his hat, putting it at a jaunty angle.

"You look great!" Jesse said. Glancing toward Travis, she saw him pull his on. Okay, so this was something fun, but she understood the deeper meaning of it, of a family torn apart decades earlier. The look in Travis's eyes touched her heart as he smiled over at his father. Truly, it was the right gift to symbolically restart the holiday between him and Sam once more.

"Open your gifts, Sam," she pleaded.

"Oh, okay," he said, picking up the small one. "This one is from you, Jesse."

"Yep," she said, hardly able to wait to see his reaction. The Ramsey family wasn't rich in anyone's world. Travis and Sam had kept the business going and so much of the money was sunk back into it. She'd saved all her money since coming to Hamilton and had bought these two men something she hoped would keep on giving to them.

Sam opened the gift and there was a red envelope inside it. He frowned and then opened it up. Reading it, he lifted his head and gave her grateful look. "You've paid for Blue's veterinary expenses for the first year of his life. That's," he choked, looking down at Blue who was watching him intently, "a nice gift, Jesse. Thank you."

"Emily sells a yearly insurance plan for dogs and cats. I thought it would be nice to take that burden off you, Sam. Most of the costs are in the first year of the dog's life."

He nodded. "Thank you," he said, letting Blue sniff the envelope. "Jesse is gonna make sure you're a healthy little guy."

Sam set it aside and then brought Travis's gift up, setting it on the side of the armchair. "You shouldn't be getting me anything, son. You already paid for the rebuilding of my porch so that hot tub would fit. That was enough."

Shrugging, Travis said quietly, "This is something you've been wanting ever since I was a kid. It's about time you got one given to you."

The gift was the same size as Jesse's. "Another envelope?"

"Door number two," Travis teased, giving him an excited look.

Opening it, Sam gasped, "No!" He jerked a look over to Travis. "Are you serious?"

"Sure am," he said. "That's a gift certificate to pick out the fly fishing rod of your choice. I know which one you've always talked about buying, but we never had the money for it. Now, you do."

Jesse heard the pride in Travis's voice as his father continued to look stunned and in disbelief as he read and reread the gift certificate. She knew from discussing fly fishing rods with Travis before, that their clients were all rich and could afford the best rods in the world when they went fly fishing. The rods they brought with them could easily cost five to ten thousand dollars apiece. Sam had wished for a handmade bamboo fly rod his whole life and could never afford such an extravagance. He had a favorite maker and Travis had given his father a thirty-five-hundred-dollar gift certificate to visit the rod maker in Missoula.

"I can't believe this," Sam whispered.

"You're no longer in pain," Travis said. "You can go out and do the fly fishing you did all your life until the pain stopped you. Now, you can take out day fishermen and bring your own rod along that's just as good or better than theirs."

Sam set the certificate aside. "I just never thought I'd ever have something like this." His lower lip quivered. "Thank you, son. I don't know how you did this. We live on such a thin line between being in the red and black."

"I'd been putting money away for a long time before I left the military, Sam. I had it in the credit union and had the money wired from our local bank to the rod maker, so a gift certificate could be created for you."

Jesse got up and went around the coffee table, giving Sam a gentle hug. "Merry Christmas, Sam. We're both so happy you're going to order a hand-made rod and by spring of next year you'll be out catching trout for all of us. We do expect some fab trout dinners with you."

Sam hugged her in return. "You're somethin' else, Jesse. Thank you."

She turned to the couch, pointing at her gift to Travis. "Open mine?"

Travis took the huge silver wrapped box and pulled off the bright red ribbon. When he opened the box, his expression changed to surprise.

"A sheepskin coat!" he rasped, giving her a shocked look. Pulling it out, he saw it was a Shepler, one of the best made, and very necessary for long, cold Montana winters.

"Do you like it? Sam was telling me you wore out your old one last year, and that it was really pathetic looking, Travis. This one will last you a good decade like the other one did."

He reached over, curving his hand around her neck, giving her a swift, deep kiss. "Thank you. I like gifts that keep on giving. Every time I wear it, I'll think that it's your arms around me."

Sam cleared his throat. "Well, what did you get, Jesse?" he inquired, raising a white eyebrow.

"Something wonderful," she told the elder. Getting up, she held out her right hand. "It's a friendship ring, Sam."

He picked up her hand. "Mighty purty, but can't match you. What does a friendship ring mean?"

She smiled. "That we're serious about one another, that we want to be to-gether to see where our relationship is going to grow."

"Humph. Like a pre-engagement ring?" he asked, looking up into her smil-ing eyes.

"Yes," Travis said. "That's a better way of putting it. We're committed to one another, Sam. That's the bottom line."

"Good," he congratulated them. He released her hand. "If I were you, son? I wouldn't let this filly range too far away from you."

"No, I'm not going to," Travis said, smiling as Jesse came and sat down next to him, her hand resting on his thigh.

"Well, this is just good news all around," Sam said, nodding and petting Blue who had his head tucked inside his vest, asleep. "You gonna open up my gift to you?"

Travis leaned down, scooping it off the coffee table. "Last but not least," he promised, sitting up and opening the green envelope.

Jesse saw his face become suddenly emotional as he opened the letter inside it. Tears came to his eyes and he didn't try to hide them as he looked up at Sam who was staring intently at him. "This," he rasped, "is..." but he couldn't finish, swallowing hard.

Sam got up, set Blue on the rug and came around the coffee table. "Come here, son," he said, holding out his hand toward him.

Travis handed her the scrawled note as he stood up.

Swiftly looking at it, Jesse saw Sam grab his son and hold him in a long, tight embrace. The note said, *"Dear son, I love you. Please call me Dad from now on? I don't deserve it, but I want a second chance to be a real father to you once again. I'm sorry for all the hurt and pain I've caused you. Love, your dad."*

A lump formed in her throat as she saw the two men cling mutely to one another. So much loss and pain had separated them for so many, many years. Tears filmed her vision and the warmth of them trailed down her cheeks as she held the scrawled words on that piece of lined paper. Every hand-scrawled word meant the world to Travis. Sam had the courage, the love, to ask his only son to come back and be loved by him once again. It was more a story of a prodigal father returning home than the Bible's story about the prodigal son returning back to his family. She sniffed and saw that both men were unashamedly crying. There were decades of grief and hurt in those hot tears they released, and she sat there realizing the thaw in the winter of their relationship had truly begun.

The Christmas music conspired to make the best gift that Travis had ever received that much more special for him and his father.

"Okay," Sam said, his voice low and wobbly, "we have to start this Christmas tradition in our family and with one another." He clapped Travis on the back as he eased away, wiping the tears on his face. "I was wrong to ask you to call me Sam. It was me, son, not you. I-I just couldn't take any more pain. I'd had too much, and I didn't have the strength to extend anything to you at the time."

"I understand," Travis said hoarsely. "We both got dealt a double blow..."

He patted his son's drooping shoulder. "But it was my burden to carry, not yours. I threw off my responsibility to you, which wasn't right or fair. The past couple of weeks, with the pain going away, I began to realize what had happened, and how I was reactin' to it. I realized what I'd done to you, and I'm here to apologize for it and tell you it's never gonna happen again."

Travis pulled a white handkerchief from his back pocket, blowing his nose. "I never blamed you…Dad…"

"I figured you were far ahead of me on what happened and why I sank so low afterward. Sheila was the love of my life. No one can ever replace her. That totaled me and took me to a dark place. When Kyle died in that auto accident, I felt as if the world had shattered forever around me. I just didn't have the guts or strength to fight through it. I was consumed by it and I took it out on you." He gripped Travis's shoulder. "I'm so damned sorry, son. I'd do anything to make things right between us from now on. If," he said brokenly, "you'll give me a second chance to behave like the father you deserved all along…"

Travis gripped Sam's hand in his. "There's nothing to forgive, Dad. I love you. I never stopped loving you. I understood what had happened to you." He glanced down at Jesse who watched them with compassion. "If I lost Jesse, I'm sure I'd go to just as dark a place as when Mom suddenly died and we lost her. I'm not here to judge you. And yes, I want that second chance with you, Dad. I love you…"

"I LOVE THIS picture your dad took of us with Freya," Jesse said, holding up a printed copy to Travis. They had just said goodbye to Sam, seeing Cyrus off with Blue in the pickup. She couldn't decide which of the three were happier with the addition of the little puppy. Blue would change the dynamic at Sam's cabin, but in a good way.

Travis dried his hands after putting the dishes into the dishwasher. Outside, the snow continued to fall in lazy, dancing flakes across the sky. He looked at the photo and smiled. "Freya looks so happy."

Sliding her arm around his waist and drawing him against her, she whispered, "So do we."

He looked up and slid his arm around her shoulders. "This Christmas is so special. Dad and I haven't celebrated one since I was home and I know before that, he refused invites from his friends here in Hamilton, as well."

Sighing, she leaned her head against his shoulder, contentment filling her. "Grief eventually comes to a place where you can get on with your life from what I can see," she said. "I think Sam reached that plateau within himself."

"He gave us thoughtful gifts, too."

"Yes, he did. I think he's trying to atone for his behavior toward you, Travis. Don't you?"

"Yes, I do." He laid the photo on the counter and turned, resting his hips against the counter and enfolding Jesse against the front of him.

"I think Sam's trying very hard, and he's been brutally honest toward you and what he's done to make your life as miserable as his."

"It's the past now," he murmured against her hair, kissing the gleaming strands. "There's nowhere but up from here, Jesse, for all of us, including you."

"Hamilton has been good for me," she agreed. "Especially you, the red caboose and Freya, plus her pups."

He eased her away from him enough to meet her softened gaze. "That boxcar started off a whole new chapter of life for you. If you hadn't had the courage to come and hunt me down as the owner of it, none of this would have happened. You're so much stronger than you realize, sweetheart." He kissed her wrinkled brow, feeling it smooth beneath his mouth. He settled his hands around her hips, Jesse content to be melded against him. "Do you agree?"

Nodding, Jesse rested her hands against his chest, feeling the softness of the green and white sweater he wore. "I do. I think we've all been good for one another in many different ways. This has truly been a boxcar Christmas. In some wistful way, I feel the spirit of Hiram and Inez with us tonight, too. Maybe now, Sam will start to soften toward his own parents and bury the past, realizing that you can't kill love and that it will return to you."

"It takes a village," he agreed, using his index finger to push a few strands away from her face. "I don't know about you, but this winter is going to be a huge change in our lives in good ways. My dad loved the idea of having his own rod made. He's entertained that dream all his life. I remember him talking about it when I was a kid…about owning an expensive bamboo fly rod, which was the ultimate for him."

She reached up and kissed the tip of his nose. "I feel your greatest gift is having Sam ask you to call him Dad once again."

Travis breathed in deeply and released it. "I didn't expect that. It was such a shock. It shook me to my soul, and I couldn't stop crying."

"Your dad knew how important a gift it would be…to give you back your father once more. He needed that cry. Tears are always good and they're an emotional release valve for everyone."

"Some of the greatest gifts can't be bought," he agreed, his voice low with feeling.

"And we gave Blue to him. That was something that couldn't be bought either. By coming out here with Cyrus, Blue worked his way into Sam's heart. Someday, when Cy passes, Blue will be a great comfort to him."

"If Dad continues to improve, I know he'll want to take day clients out like he did before. And Cy is too old and crippled up to go with him, but he'll have Blue, instead."

"It's a gift that will keep giving for a long, long time."

Freya came up, her blue eyes shining with happiness, wedging herself between their legs as they separated to allow her entrance. Travis had put the knitted red and green collar on her and she looked perfect with it around her neck.

"I think she'll miss her puppies for a while," Travis murmured, petting her head.

"I'm sure she'll see all of them from time to time. Especially Blue, because Freya will be with you at the office."

He nodded and cupped her face, kissing her gently. As he drew away, he whispered, "I love you, Jesse. The gifts from this Christmas are just beginning for all of us."

"For all of us…"

"Love isn't something that can be bought or sold," he said, releasing her.

Freya moved on to the water dish.

Jesse stood with him at the edge of the kitchen, looking into the glow of the tree along with the fire crackling. Outside, it was snowing more heavily now, the dark green of Douglas fir covered with the white stuff. It was a perfect Christmas morning. Her heart swelled with joy because she knew that spring of next year would bring new changes. It would be a good time to marry Travis. Who knew? Maybe if Sam continued to be more like his old self, he might get interested in Sassy Jones, his grade school sweetheart! Her own life had taken difficult twists and turns. Having family meant everything to her and she wanted to call her mom and dad, to tell them the wonderful news about her new relationship with Travis. They would be happy for her. Relieved, too, that she was finally starting to knit her life back together again, one pearl at a time. It was a quaint analogy, but that was how Jesse felt. Every day had triumphs and setbacks. That's how healing went. Finding love had not been on her radar and she realized just how important it was to her journey as well. Yes, this Christmas that started out with a boxcar in a meadow, had led her forward to the most important chapter in her life—with Travis and courageous Freya, along with the good people of Hamilton and especially the love of her parents buttressing her efforts to climb out of the darkness and into the light once more. Travis gave her a space to heal, always there, never a shadow in her life, but someone who filled her daily with support and hope. She would love him forever.

END

Don't miss Lindsay McKenna's next book,
Sanctuary
Available from Blue Turtle Publishing!

Turn the page for a sneak peek of *Sanctuary*.

Excerpt from

Sanctuary

TEREN WAITED PATIENTLY outside the customs area at the Khartoum airport. She had her cell phone in hand, scrolling through messages from her two office assistants. Her mouth tugged at the corners as she looked up at the double doors, expecting Nolan Steele to come through them at any moment.

His color photo flashed on her screen. He had an oval face and large, hawkish marine-blue eyes that reminded her of the ocean's depths. His mouth was something else—sensual, yet firm. He was almost painfully good-looking—far too handsome for his own good! He probably had an ego the size of Jupiter. She hoped not, because the moment the email from Wyatt Lockwood had appeared on her laptop, her whole body reacted to the stranger's photograph. Those eyes...so full of secrets and, Teren sensed, pain. It didn't appear on his unlined thirty-year-old face, but it was there.

She was just a year younger than him. She thought back to when she'd been an idealistic eighteen-year-old, filled with hope and the belief that the world was essentially a good place. She found out differently later that year and after her own traumatic experience, Teren had quickly revised her views about men. From that time on, they had been creatures she couldn't understand or relate to. She'd become gun-shy around them, and now, over a decade later, she still felt that way.

But as she studied Nolan's face, Teren felt her heart slowly begin to open, like petals on a lotus. Not wanting to feel like this, fighting it, she clicked her phone's screen off but left the phone on, because he had her phone number in case they missed each other here at the busy, crowded airport.

A potpourri of spicy scents filled the air. Men wore either light-colored silk business suits or the traditional *jalabiya*, a loose-fitting garment, collarless, ankle-length, and long-sleeved. Some wore caps, others turbans. Because it was August, a season of dry, blistering heat, the *jalabiyas* were either white, cream, or tan, made of cotton-linen or silk, to deflect the burning rays of the sun outside this air-conditioned facility.

She nervously smoothed her *tob*, a head-to-toe gown of white cotton topped by a white silk *hijab*, the traditional scarf Muslim women wore over their heads when in public. She wasn't Muslim, but Teren tried to fit in, not stand out. Knowing how dangerous it was to be a white, American woman in this third-world country, she didn't want to draw attention to herself any more than necessary.

Normally, she wouldn't have been here waiting for someone at the airport. She liked the red clay walls that surrounded Kitra, the sense of safety that was always there because Captain Ayman Taban ran his security force like the military man he'd been for twenty years.

So, where was this Steele guy, and was that even his real name or a cover one? After talking with Wyatt by sat phone, she knew he was going to be her personal bodyguard, and that he was ex-military, but Wyatt hadn't said anything more than that. Tapping her slippered foot, Teren began to feel restless. She didn't like being out in such a huge, bustling area with so many men and so few women. She knew she'd stand out because of her lighter skin.

In Khartoum, she dressed conservatively, the *niqab*, over her brow and nose, only a slit for her eyes, trying to hide her skin color. Here at the airport, her face was fully visible, the scarf draped around her head, neck, and shoulders. Steele had to be able to identify her once he came through the doors of customs. Sudan wasn't a safe place in many areas and it was especially dangerous to a woman who stood alone without a male escort in tow. Too many terrorists were lurking around, and it always made her tense. Her nervousness this afternoon was heightened because she felt inexplicably drawn to Nolan Steele.

Teren wasn't prepared when she spotted him at the exit doors of customs, along with several other Sudanese businessmen dressed in their robes. He was moderately built, wearing a tan T-shirt beneath loose-fitting khaki jacket and trousers. Their eyes briefly locked upon one another, and Teren's heart began to accelerate. He was here! Why did it feel like a homecoming instead of a first meeting? Her lips moved and then tightened, and instead, she lifted her hand.

He gave her a bare nod, his eyes narrowing, and every nerve in her body reacted to that swift, intense perusal he gave her.

And then, just as quickly, he lifted his chin, his gaze sweeping around the noisy, busy airport. She had the distinct impression he was actually a lordly leopard in disguise, calmly surveying his kingdom, not a stranger coming to a strange country. He walked like a hunter, light on his feet, avoiding any living animal in the immediate vicinity.

She watched in amazement as he threaded his way through the crowd. He moved like water flowing around rocks, disturbing nothing, gaining no one's attention. Teren's respect for him as a security contractor rocketed.

His shoulders were broad, squared with pride, his hand on a single bag that appeared to hold a laptop. His right hand was free. And as his gaze swept to her once again and briefly halted, Teren felt in that one, scorching moment, he had memorized her from head to toe.

It wasn't sexual. It wasn't lust. It was something indefinable, but just the power of it stirred up the heat simmering in her lower body. Once he was clear of the bustling crowd, his gaze locked on hers once more, and Teren felt as if she were being surrounded by such intense protectiveness, it stole her breath away.

Protection! It had been so long since she'd felt safe. *So long...*and he seemed to be invisibly embracing her, the sense of safety he radiated even stronger the closer he drew to her.

For once in her life, Teren found herself speechless. Their gazes clung to one another, and something passed between them that made her throat tighten. She fought back old, wounded emotions as she absorbed the look in his eyes, feeling his quiet authority and power. Now she lifted her chin and realized that, on some level, she didn't want him to step away from her. It was the craziest, most out-of-this-world sensation she'd ever felt!

Almost dizzied by his palpable masculinity as he drew to a halt about four feet away from her, she stared up at Steele—gawked was more like it. Teren suddenly felt like an innocent eighteen-year-old who held all the hopes of the world in her heart.

Steele was a stranger. Ex-military. Black ops. So different from the world she lived in that what he was bringing with him was alien to her culture. Then his eyes warmed as he smiled down on her, and she felt heat sheeting through her, arousing her dormant body, ripping away all her fear, the sense of danger that always hovered around her. She felt a fire sparking to full life deep within her body, as if on some unknown plane of existence, she was meeting him after a long absence.

"Ms. Lambert?"

His voice was low and quiet. The vibration, though subtle, tingled through every cell within her. Teren barely nodded. "Yes." The word came out smoky and soft, so unlike her. Nolan Steele brought out her female quality with just his mere presence.

Looking deeper into his eyes, Teren didn't see arousal or lust. What she saw, however, was even more powerful: gentle understanding and yes, compassion burned in his eyes, aimed directly at her. How could that be?

She felt tongue-tied, scrambling inwardly to snap out of that magical cocoon he'd just woven around her. The feeling left Teren unsure of herself—normally, she exuded a quiet confidence wherever she went. Whatever magic he possessed made her feel excruciatingly female, and she gratefully absorbed it.

Steele gave her a wry smile, his eyes crinkling, the lines in the corners deepening. "Are you all right? You look a little dazed."

Teren felt heat burnishing her cheeks. She *never* blushed, but she was now. She managed an apologetic, "I'm sorry...long day." Well, that wasn't a lie, just not the whole truth. "The heat, too." She lifted her hand gracefully toward the automatic doors.

"Understandable," he agreed with a nod. Holding out his hand, he said, "Nolan Steele. It's nice to meet you, Ms. Lambert."

His large hand engulfed her thin, narrow one, and the touch of his callused palm sliding against hers sent wild electric sensations up her lower arm. His fingers were long, strong, yet gentle, as he lightly squeezed her hand in return. Teren felt his latent strength, reminding her once more of that proud leopard who, while in repose, looked tame and nonthreatening—but he wasn't. Skin against skin she sensed much more and couldn't hold off images that had nothing to do with a simple "hello."

Unsteadily, Teren pulled her hand free, her skin vibrating with his energy. "Do you have luggage?" she asked, trying to restore the impression of competence she'd brought with her.

"Yes." He broke contact with her flawless gray eyes, which brought to mind the color of the sky just before dawn. "I've been here before, and baggage is that way." He pointed in the direction of the highly-polished hall that led to the right.

She blinked, her mind slowly returning online. "You have? I mean, you've been in Sudan before?" The way his lips parted in a grin, part boyish, part secretive, told her that Nolan wasn't wearing his game face. He was being genuine.

Wyatt had warned her that she probably wouldn't be able to read him or know what he was thinking or feeling. But that wasn't true, at least not here and now. It was as if they were both standing before each other, exposing themselves boldly and fearlessly. She could almost feel his essence, and it swept her away in a glorious cloud of heat, light, and promise.

"Yes, ma'am. In fact, I've been here too many times," he assured her. Nolan knew better than to cup her elbow and guide her down the massive, gleaming hallway leading to the escalator down to baggage. This was a conservative country, and a strange man could not touch a woman. Only family could touch family, and even then, it mattered which person in the family it was. Earlier, when they shook hands, any passerby would automatically think they were related and from the same family. They would think nothing of the greeting. Nolan gestured and said, "This way."

The Books of Delos

Title: ***Last Chance*** (Prologue)
Publish Date: July 15, 2015
Learn more at: delos.lindsaymckenna.com/last-chance

Title: ***Nowhere to Hide***
Publish Date: October 13, 2015
Learn more at: delos.lindsaymckenna.com/nowhere-to-hide

Title: ***Tangled Pursuit***
Publish Date: November 11, 2015
Learn more at: delos.lindsaymckenna.com/tangled-pursuit

Title: ***Forged in Fire***
Publish Date: December 3, 2015
Learn more at: delos.lindsaymckenna.com/forged-in-fire

Title: ***Broken Dreams***
Publish Date: January 2, 2016
Learn more at: delos.lindsaymckenna.com/broken-dreams

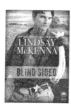

Title: ***Blind Sided***
Publish Date: June 5, 2016
Learn more at: delos.lindsaymckenna.com/blind-sided

Title: ***Secret Dream***
Publish Date: July 25, 2016
Learn more at: delos.lindsaymckenna.com/secret-dream

Title: ***Hold On***
Publish Date: August 3, 2016
Learn more at: delos.lindsaymckenna.com/hold-on

Title: ***Hold Me***
Publish Date: August 11, 2016
Learn more at: delos.lindsaymckenna.com/hold-me

Title: ***Unbound Pursuit***
Publish Date: September 29, 2016
Learn more at: delos.lindsaymckenna.com/unbound-pursuit

Title: ***Secrets***
Publish Date: November 21, 2016
Learn more at: delos.lindsaymckenna.com/secrets

Title: ***Snowflake's Gift***
Publish Date: February 4, 2017
Learn more at: delos.lindsaymckenna.com/snowflakes-gift

Title: ***Never Enough***
Publish Date: March 1, 2017
Learn more at: delos.lindsaymckenna.com/never-enough

Title: ***Dream of Me***
Publish Date: May 23, 2017
Learn more at: delos.lindsaymckenna.com/dream-of-me

Title: ***Trapped***
Publish Date: July 17, 2017
Learn more at: delos.lindsaymckenna.com/trapped

Title: ***Taking A Chance***
Publish Date: August 1, 2017
Learn more at: delos.lindsaymckenna.com/taking-a-chance

Title: ***The Hidden Heart***
Publish Date: September 14, 2017
Learn more at: delos.lindsaymckenna.com/the-hidden-heart

Everything Delos!

Newsletter

Please visit my newsletter website at newsletter.lindsaymckenna.com. The newsletter will have exclusive information about my books, publishing schedule, giveaways, exclusive cover peeks, and more.

Delos Series Website

Be sure to drop by my website dedicated to the Delos Series at delos.lindsaymckenna.com. There will be new articles on characters, my publishing schedule, and information about each book written by Lindsay.

Made in the USA
Coppell, TX
29 September 2020